The North Bay

Reto Koller

The North Bay

Thriller

© 2025 Reto Koller

Publisher: BoD · Books on Demand GmbH,
Überseering 33, 22297 Hamburg, bod@bod.de
Printer: Libri Plureos GmbH, Friedensallee 273,
22763 Hamburg
ISBN: 978-3-8192-0763-1

Chapter 1

Tåkevik, 80 kilometers outside of Tromsø, Norway, 1988

With growing dread, she watched as the heavy oak door swung open before her, revealing a pitch-dark night. Snowflakes whirled against her face, and the wind tugged at her thin pajamas, making her realise that this venture would not end well.

She stepped out into the night, feeling the cold wrap around her body like a wet cloth. Within seconds, she was shivering from head to toe. Everything appeared to her through a misty veil—blurry, unclear, terrifying. And yet, she could hear him; his wheezing breaths blending with the sounds of the wind. She could feel his presence, the force emanating from him, his skin against hers. She was more disgusted by him than by spiders. She hated his stench, the sounds he made as he breathed, the greasy hair, the scars. She hated the way he looked at her; a gaze that was both caring and creepy.

She tried to turn around, wanting to plead with him to finally let her go, but he didn't even acknowledge her. Gently, yet firmly, he nudged her forward. He kept urging her on, away from the house, although where they were going, she could only guess. She couldn't scream—he had taped her mouth shut. He gripped her hands tightly behind her back.

She stumbled through the deep snow, hearing the distant roar of the waves, which grew louder the further they walked. She realised he was leading her to the water, where it was even colder, where there was no escape.

Suddenly, the pressure of his hold eased, and her hands were almost free. In a swift move, she yanked her arms forward, surprising herself by breaking free. She wanted to run back to the house, but only managed a single step before he grabbed her by the forearm again. She twisted like an eel, kicking his shins, but only managed to hurt herself in the process.

"Come on, keep going," he muttered calmly, giving her a push.

The roar of the waves grew louder, the pain in her arms intensified. Desperately, she searched the surroundings for anyone else, but it was too dark to see beyond twenty metres.

Suddenly, even the snow vanished from under her feet. There was no path anymore, no bushes—just darkness, wind, and the sound of the sea. The fog lifted, revealing a thin crescent moon. Below, she could see the gleaming white foam on the waves.

A faint sobbing reached her ears, and she turned around. To her surprise, she saw tears in his eyes, his sad gaze haunting like a shadow. He murmured something unintelligible, but the words were carried away by the wind. Gently, he removed the tape from her mouth, and she screamed into the night as loudly as she could. She heard her own echo, bouncing off the surrounding cliffs, and hoped someone back at the house would respond.

Instead of stopping her from screaming, he now looked at her with a fatherly gaze, kissed her forehead, and in the next moment, she felt a gentle push, followed by a wave of nausea. The moonlight faded, and the shining white crests on the waves disappeared like plankton at dawn.

Chapter 2

Tromsø, 2016

My name is Sondre Iversen. I am forty-five years old.

Funny—just a year ago, I would have sworn that I wouldn't live to see my forty-sixth birthday. As it stands, however, it seems I'll be able to celebrate it after all. When I look at myself in the mirror today, I find a few gray hairs among the brown, and I'm certain they weren't there a year ago. The hairline has also receded a bit, but at least I don't have to comb my longer hair forward to cover it up.

Since I can no longer work as a police officer, I've grown a beard. My once chiseled six-pack has been replaced by a soft layer of fat, and although my biceps are still toned, they have lost some firmness. Yet, I don't worry too much. I've resolved to exercise more, though so far, that has been defeated by my lack of willpower. I also find myself out of breath more quickly than when I was on duty, which makes sense. My son always tells me it's because of the smoking.

Perhaps he's right, and I really should quit. At least I've managed to cut down from a pack a day to just four cigarettes, with the goal of quitting entirely by the end of the year.

I have lived in Tromsø since I was a year old. I attended all my schooling here, held boring summer jobs as a teenager, eventually became a police officer, and, after four years, left that job with a heavy heart to train as a teacher. A skiing accident in the Lyngen Alps almost rendered my left hand useless. I had to go through numerous therapies, and even now, I can't use my left hand fully. I was no longer suitable for police work; I could no longer restrain suspects, much less handcuff them, though such actions were rarely needed in our area. The personnel department offered me a desk job, but I would have preferred scraping bird droppings off park benches than to sit at a desk eight hours a day. So, I had to look for something else. I had always been interested in teaching, even before I joined the police, so I decided to follow in my father's footsteps. He had been a teacher for years and fulfilled it with passion. He's now enjoying retirement, unfortunately without my mother, who died a decade ago from a heart attack.

I can say that I enjoy teaching. Regular hours, no night shifts, no drunken people puking in my car. But I can't deny that I miss the uncertainty at the beginning of each shift, the tension before starting work, the adrenaline rush during assignments. That's all missing in teaching a bunch of pimply teenagers. The daily routine is more or less predictable, with little variation and no intense adrenaline rushes. Deep down, I feel something is missing. A void that needs filling. In the summer of 1999, I married Marit, who is now my ex-wife.

Why did we divorce? I wish I didn't have to ask myself that question, and even more, I wish that my deceased son didn't play a role in it. Raik died of leukemia at the age of five. Such a loss is almost unbearable for any couple. Either you drift apart, like ice floes in the North Sea, or you find a way to face such a fate together. For us, unfortunately, it was the former. At the time of Raik's death, I could never have imagined that this tragedy could ever drive Marit and me apart. From the start, we had been two peas in a pod, doing everything together, always considerate of each other, arguing little and loving each other all the more. For me, nothing in my life was more important than Marit's happiness. Every day, I asked myself the same question: How can I make her happy today? I wanted to be the best husband. Marit enjoyed the attention, and she gave it back to me in the form of unconditional love. But even fairy tales have a last page. And ours did not end with the words: And so they lived happily ever after.

Our fairy tale ended differently; the little prince died at the beginning of the story, and the palace of the king and queen began to crumble, as if made only of shale. Grief consumed us, sapping all our energy and zest for life. Marit had no desire to talk with me about our son's death. She shut herself behind an impenetrable curtain of self-pity and sorrow. Our older son, Jørn, noticed the change, seeking his mother's comfort all the more in its absence.

To watch your own child deteriorate, then face their death with heartbreaking clarity is perhaps the worst thing parents can endure. We often hear from other families who have faced similar fates and about their attempts to cope. In those moments, you feel for them, think of them, but what it means to lose your own blood only becomes clear when you have looked into the abyss of death yourself.

Some days I don't even want to get out of bed, don't want to brush my teeth, make coffee, or drive to work. You lie on a mattress that feels far too hard, staring at the ceiling, asking yourself over and over how your own life is supposed to continue. On days like these, I often get in the car and drive to a beach on Håkøya, where I can sit for hours looking out at the strait and the shadowy mountains behind Tromsøya. Only there, in that solitary spot, do I feel like my dark thoughts are carried away by the current, allowing me to breathe freely for a few hours.

Despite all the grief and the rift that had formed between Marit and me, that was not the sole reason for our separation. What finally broke the camel's back was another incident.

One rainy evening in August, I went to the study. I still had exams to grade, so I sat down at the computer. As the screensaver photos disappeared, I noticed an open email addressed to my wife. I was about to close it, but the salutation made me pause. I leaned closer to the screen and began reading:

Hey beautiful
Once again, that was an exciting evening. You are incredible,
Marit. My wife would never agree to do such things with me. I'm
already looking forward to the next time.
Fredrik!

Fredrik?

Where did I know that name from?

Ah, yes—her colleague at the hospital.

I read the message a second time, ignoring the tight knot forming in my stomach. A wave of nausea and coldness washed over me, and my hands began to shake.

What was this? Was it a joke?

It had to be a joke—Marit would never do something like this to me. Marit went out to dinner with her friend Selma last night. Or at least that's what she had told me.

I stared at the screen, unable to think clearly. I heard our son Jørn in the living room, shouting at a video game on the TV. I heard the steady ticking of the clock on the desk, the rain tapping against the window, and the pounding of my own heartbeat, like drumbeats on a Roman galley. What should I do? Confront her? Call Selma and ask where they had dinner last night?

Marit came down the stairs and stopped in front of the study. Something in my expression made her pause. She looked at me. "What's wrong?"

At first, I couldn't say anything. I wanted to break down right there, but that wouldn't have made anything better.

"Can you explain this message?" I nodded toward the screen.

Marit's face froze. Her cheeks flushed a deep red. "W-what message?" she stammered, taking a hesitant step forward.

"This one," I pointed to the email.

Marit looked at the screen and swallowed hard. "Are you going through my emails?" she said indignantly.

"No, the message was open when I sat down at the computer. So, what's this about?"

Marit remained silent, her eyes fixed on the lines. Tears welled up in her eyes. I felt a lump in my stomach. I feared I would throw up my lunch.

Marit backed away from the computer, going to the window, crying quietly. I didn't know whether to feel angry or sad.

"I'm sorry. You weren't supposed to find out."

Great! That was supposed to explain everything? "Could you be a bit more specific?"

Marit lowered her head and buried her face in her hands. "I'm so sorry," she said, sobbing.

"What are you sorry for?" I asked, my voice half-choked.

"What else, Sondre? You read it yourself." She let out a sob.

"Yes, I read it. But I don't understand it."

Marit shook her head, taking a deep breath. "I'm unhappy. I have been for a long time. But you didn't seem to notice. Either you're blind, or you just chose to overlook it. For months, I've hardly been able to talk to you. So many times, I wanted to tell you, but I just couldn't—I couldn't hurt you."

I felt as if I were falling into a bottomless pit. My mind was racing, replaying countless past situations. I searched for clues, for events that could confirm her statement. But I couldn't think clearly; I could barely breathe.

Sobbing, she continued: "You're so focused on me, and yet you miss my signals. I don't understand it."

My initial confusion turned into anger. "I don't know what you mean, Marit!" I said, louder than I intended.

She turned around. "How many times have I rejected you in bed? How many times have I declined to go for a walk with you? How many evenings have we sat in the living room without saying a word to each other? Did you really not notice?"

I still remember that moment in the study, when Marit revealed the truth to me, as clearly as if it had just happened. Her words hit me like a hammer blow. I suddenly noticed the sad expression that had followed her like a shadow for some time—a sadness I had simply failed to see due to the comfortable numbness of routine. The joy in her laughter and the affection she once showed me now seemed to belong to another era in our relationship. Her gaze looked as dry and devoid of warmth as if it was a desert.

Realising this was, however, too late. There was no going back for us. The traces of our shared life had been erased, covered by a winter storm, and forever buried.

The following weeks and months were pure hell. I stumbled through life as if lost in the whiteout of an arctic tundra.

For our oldest son, Jørn, it was a particularly difficult situation. How do you explain to your child that from now on, they won't sit down with both parents for meals, that family vacations are a thing of the past, and that Christmas movies won't be watched together anymore? Jørn was seventeen years old. He was no longer a little boy, but that didn't make the feelings of loss he tried unsuccessfully to hide any easier. Custody was divided fairly, yet an emotional distance grew between Jørn and me that was more devastating than a long separation. Before the divorce, we had often spent time outdoors together, skiing, climbing mountains, fishing. But after the divorce, Jørn lost interest in those shared activities. Whether he had simply lost the desire or didn't want to experience them with me anymore, I didn't know. He wouldn't talk about it, even when I asked him directly. He had grown reticent, withdrawn, introspective, and I didn't want to push him. I knew how hard this must have been for him. It was almost unbearable for me, and I was many years older. How must a seventeen-year-old boy have felt?

Three weeks after Marit's confession, I left our home in Kvaløysletta and moved into a small apartment downtown. It wasn't much. A bedroom, a kitchen, a bathroom, and a cramped living room. But for the time being, it had to suffice.

I can still picture myself on the first evening, sitting amidst moving boxes and a few sparse pieces of furniture. Everything that had happened over the last few months and years had come crashing down on me like a house of cards. Like a small child, I began to cry uncontrollably. My mind reeled with thoughts and images of the past months and years. I summoned the good memories with Marit, trying to understand when and where I might have gone wrong and where I should have reacted differently. I wanted to turn back time. I wanted to hold Marit in my arms, to comfort her, to help her forget her frustration, even if only for a short while.

But that was impossible—it was just wishful thinking!

Realization was so crushing, that I didn't know how I was supposed to go on living. I had lost everything!

One of the moving boxes had "Kitchen" written on it in large letters. I stared at the box for a while before I finally opened it. Inside, I found two large butcher's knives, and I pulled one out. The blade gleamed in the light from the window lamp. I ran my finger along the edge and brought it down to the underside of my wrist. What had my friend, a surgeon, once told me? Most people who try to cut their arteries do it wrong. They cut across the wrist, when really, the cut should be made vertically so the wound doesn't close too quickly.

I started sweating, yet I felt an inner coldness. My hands began to tremble, and my heart was pounding against my chest. Images of Raik filled my mind. I saw him smile at me, hold my hand, snuggle against me, lie pale in a hospital bed, barely able to keep his eyes open from exhaustion.

As if an invisible hand gently pulled my fingers away from the knife, I let it fall and collapsed onto the floor, sobbing.

Chapter 3

A few months later, I was wandering through the snow-covered streets of the city, accompanied by dark thoughts, without purpose or intention. I glanced into several shop windows without truly seeing the displays. When I reached the small park in front of the cathedral, I stopped at a bench and gazed toward the mountains in the south east. The clouds had cleared, revealing an orange sun in the sky whose rays made the surrounding mountain peaks glow. A biting cold swept through the streets, but the warm light from above felt like a natural heater. On the rooftops, seagulls screeched in competition, and from the fjord came the deep horn of an arriving Hurtigruten ship.

I turned away and kept walking. A few hours earlier, I'd had a phone call with my son. Jørn had been in a bad mood, as he so often was lately. I had the feeling that he was usually in better spirits when he was with his mother than with me, but perhaps I was imagining things. My work, too, was becoming increasingly unsatisfying. Over the past few months, working with the current principal had become extremely challenging. His ideas and directives, which went against all reason, had already driven two colleagues to resign.

Did the principal care?

Of course not. He stuck to his strategy, even sitting in on lessons to later criticise them in a condescending manner, despite not having taught a class in years. At first, I let his reprimands roll off me. But over time, I could no longer accept his rebukes and began desperately searching for a solution. I often imagined standing in front of him and telling him to his face what a lousy principal he was. But every time he actually stood before me, with his greasy red hair and oversized glasses, the lenses as dirty as barn windows, my courage failed me, and I shrank like a grape left too long in the sun.

A month ago, however, after a sleepless night, I finally mustered the courage. I wrote my resignation letter at the breakfast table and slapped it on his desk with enough satisfaction for three people. The look on his face made up for everything I had endured in recent months. With my head held high, I left his office and felt better than I had in a long time—for a few hours, anyway.

It soon dawned on me that an even harder time lay ahead as I now had to look for a new job. But I wasn't sure I even wanted to continue teaching.

In the pedestrian street, I stopped in front of a bookstore and looked at the books on display. The store's owner, an old, eccentric-looking man named Yorick, rarely updated his window displays—or so I thought. But today, I noticed a selection of modern paperbacks, notebooks, children's books, and colouring books. The dusty classics I usually saw were nowhere to be found. I often wondered how his shop managed to survive in the age of e-books. Surely he couldn't make a living off people like me who still enjoyed holding a real book in their hands.

Movement behind the glass startled me. A man, perhaps in his mid-forties, grabbed a book and replaced it with a nearly identical copy. Before disappearing into the darkness of his shop, he nodded at me. I nodded back and continued on my way.

Chapter 4

The next day, it was Friday, and I had to be in my classroom in an hour. I sat at the kitchen table, nibbling on a piece of toast and leafing through the newspaper without much interest. When I got to the job listings and was about to flip the page, I noticed an ad that, unlike all the others, was visually more appealing. It wasn't very large and contained only a few sentences, but above the text was an illustration of a house—or rather, a castle—with turrets and bay windows. Below the drawing, written in ornate script, were the words *"Fog Castle"*:

We are seeking a teacher for Mathematics, Geography, and English to start immediately or as agreed upon.
Our boarding school is a prestigious institution with a history spanning several decades. We emphasise discipline and excellence in education. Our teaching staff are a well-coordinated team looking forward to welcoming a new colleague.
The boarding school is somewhat remote, located in Tåkevik. Teachers are provided with modern, furnished accommodation.

Have we piqued your interest? Send us your application today. If you have questions, you can also reach us by phone at 489 39 691. Ask for Sigrid.

I read the ad a second time, put the newspaper aside, and stared at my coffee mug. The boarding school was looking for a teacher who taught exactly the subjects I currently taught. Was that a coincidence?

I knew of *Fog Castle* from my time as a police officer and from photos in the newspaper. Although I hadn't been involved in the investigation back then, I seemed to recall that the incidents had been suicides. I also vaguely remembered an article about the castle-like building.

Three hours later, while standing by the coffee machine in the teachers' lounge, Ines joined me. She was close to retirement and clearly counting down the days. Her mood improved with each passing day, and she was constantly joking, wishing everyone a good day, and smiling from the first period to the last. I was happy for her. She was one of the school's pillars, and she had achieved a lot over the years, which had surely added a few wrinkles to her face. I noticed her glasses hanging around her neck. They were the same pair she'd worn in photos from twenty years ago.

"Well, Sondre, how's it going?" she asked in her usual cheerful voice.

"Can't complain," I lied.

"Are the students behaving?"

"So far, yes."

From my curt replies, Ines probably gathered that I wasn't in the mood for small talk and began preparing her coffee. I wondered if she might know more about the boarding school, so I brought it up.

Ines paused and looked at me with narrowed eyes. "*Fog Castle*? Sure, I know it. Well, 'know' is a bit of an exaggeration. I've never been there—it's private property, as far as I know. Why do you ask?"

I shrugged. "Oh, just curious. I read something about it in the newspaper."

She placed her cup in the coffee machine and pressed the start button. "In the newspaper? Then it couldn't have been anything good!"

"Nothing good? Why do you think that?" I asked, even though I already knew what she meant.

"Because there are some strange stories surrounding that boarding school. Haven't you heard any of them?"

I didn't mention that I'd only heard about the investigations back when I was with the police, so I shook my head.

"Well, I don't know much either. People say there have been occasional suicides there. It's not exactly angels that go to school there."

"I've heard that, yes."

"Has there been another suicide?" she asked.

"N-no idea. I read something online about the school yesterday. Could have been an older article—I didn't check. Anyway, it wasn't about suicides." I was surprised at how easily the lie rolled off my tongue, and I felt guilty.

"Ah, I see. Well, you should check it out for yourself. But be careful—I don't know if they have wolves or something." She chuckled, grabbed her cup, and left the teachers' lounge.

I was left alone with my thoughts, sipping on my coffee. The illustration of *Fog Castle* lingered in my mind, and I felt an urge to see the place up close. However, I figured this could only happen if I submitted an application and was invited for an interview.

The recess bell ended my coffee break, and I returned to my class.

Chapter 5

After class, I didn't go straight home. Instead, I strolled down to the harbour to get some fresh air. Swarms of tourists in heavy clothing and even heavier boots were trudging through the streets. Some looked as though they were about to embark on a North Pole expedition. The souvenir shops were packed, and the cafés were bursting at the seams. Much to my dismay, even my favourite café on Stortorget was filled to the brim. I spotted Svea, busy serving customers behind the counter.

My phone rang. It was Jørn, and as usual, the greeting was brief.

"How are you?" I asked, hoping this time I might gain some insight into his mood.

"I need 2,500 kroner for a new bike."

So much for my hope.

"Don't you already have a bike?" I asked, puzzled.

"I can't get through the snow with it. I need one with wider tires and better gears."

From experience, I knew that getting through Tromsø's snowy streets with a regular bike was nearly impossible. "But those cost way more than 2,500 kroner, don't they?"

"Mom's paying the rest. But she said you should contribute too."

Of course, I thought. As if I wasn't already paying enough every month. "Do you have one in mind?"

"Eirik has a brand-new one. He got two for his birthday—one from his uncle and one from his godfather."

I knew Eirik's family. They were loaded. "2,500 is quite a bit, don't you think?" All I got in response was a long sigh.

I could have said no and explained to my son that I had already given him money for new sneakers last month, even though his old ones were barely a year old. I could have told him that you can't always get everything you want. But I knew exactly what would happen—a reproachful call from my ex-wife, and Jørn would distance himself from me even more. "Fine," I said instead. "When are you coming over?"

"Tomorrow evening."

"Alright. I'll be waiting."

After he hung up, I stared at the screen, feeling like I could cry. The emotional distance that confronted me during every meeting and every phone call with Jørn hurt me to my core.

Sullenly, I looked out over the fjord. A wooden sailboat, the *Hermes 2*, was leaving the harbor, chugging northward, accompanied by screeching seagulls. I watched the

Fjellheisen cable car on the opposite mountain as it transported tourists to the viewing platform. It was late afternoon, and the sun cast its last, barely warming rays over the fjord, bathing the entire city in golden light.

I recalled the job ad and replayed the text in my mind. On the one hand, the idea of teaching in such an extraordinary place fascinated me. On the other hand, I was unsure whether a workplace so far outside the city would suit me.

Suppose I applied for the position, got it, and moved to that godforsaken bay, even if only during the week. What would I find there? How would I feel in the evenings, alone in the apartment? Without restaurants, bars, or shops nearby?

And yet, I couldn't deny the familiar urge for something new, something exciting, something that would distract me. It gnawed at me; it dominated my thoughts.

A seagull landed screeching at my feet, grabbed the remains of a hamburger bun, and flew off with a strong flap of its wings. I watched as it circled around the harbor boats before disappearing over the rooftops to the south. Maybe I should follow the seagull's example—venture into new territory.

I went home, sat at my computer, and began drafting an application.

Chapter 6

During lunch break the next day, I tried to learn more about *Fog Castle* and retreated to the computer room.

I typed "*Fog Castle* " into the search engine and waited for the results. There weren't many hits. Upon closer inspection, I found that only the first two entries were related to the boarding school. The first link directed me to the school's homepage, while the second led to a website documenting paranormal locations in Norway.

I frowned. Paranormal locations? *Fog Castle*? Admittedly, the name of the school did have a ghostly ring to it.

I decided to start with the school's homepage. On the front page, the school's crest was prominently displayed. With its lions heads and spears, it resembled a medieval military flag. Below the crest was a photograph of the boarding school building, shrouded in fog. Still, one could make out a bay and steep mountain slopes on either side. The massive house resembled a castle from England's era of knights, looking somewhat out of place on Norwegian soil.

The facade was made of stacked rectangular stones, their colours alternating between dark green, gray, and black. The window frames were painted white, though they appeared weathered and yellowed in places. The house had five towers with cone-shaped roofs, each topped with a pennant bearing the school's crest.

All that was missing were arrow slits and a moat!

The windows on the side facing the camera served as navigation buttons, each representing a different topic. I moved the mouse across the interface and clicked through photos of the classrooms, dining hall, and dormitories. The students didn't have private rooms; they shared with a roommate. The classrooms resembled cozy living rooms more than places where academic subject were taught.

The website revealed little about the school's history. It was built in the 1980s by a wealthy Englishman and converted into a boarding school in 1987. Another detail, that the school was not open to everyone, I already knew. It only admitted young people who had either gone astray or were struggling with psychological issues.

I wondered whether such students wouldn't require specially trained teachers.

Next, I clicked on the second search result. With a hint of scepticism, I navigated through various reports on supposed haunted houses until I finally came across one about *Fog Castle*. The group that had researched and published their findings on this website claimed they had once been chased off the property. The group members were convinced they had been driven away by a ghost.

I shook my head, turned off the computer, and looked out the window. The information I'd gathered about *Fog Castle* didn't help me much in making a decision. I had hoped to find an old newspaper article, but perhaps those had never been uploaded to the internet.

One thing was clear—*Fog Castle* knew how to maintain an air of mystery. This alone stirred a sense of excitement within me that I hadn't felt in a long time.

In my mind, I imagined teaching in such an exclusive classroom. Compared to my current workplace, it seemed surreal. However, teaching delinquent youth would undoubtedly be anything but easy.

"Everything alright, Sondre?"

I startled. Arvid, a fellow teacher, stood in the doorway, frowning at me.

"Yes, everything's fine, Arvid, thanks. I'm just a bit tired. Didn't sleep well."

"I know the feeling." He glanced at the clock. "Come on, two more hours, then you can go home." He smiled encouragingly and disappeared down the hallway.

I rubbed my face, stood up, and returned to my classroom.

Chapter 7

Night had fallen over the ancient walls of *Fog Castle*, and an oppressive silence enveloped the building. Now and then, a faint cough could be heard through the closed doors of the dormitories, and somewhere, a toilet was flushed.

However, not all of *Fog Castle*'s residents were granted the luxury of sleep. For one amongst them, night was never a time for rest—it never had been. The night belonged to him, and to him alone. In the darkness, he felt strong, confident, dominant, and untouchable. He reveled in the late hours, prowling the cellars of the house, restless yet determined. Occasionally, he muttered something incomprehensible to himself, his thick lips producing clicking sounds, and he snorted like a wild animal. For years, he had followed the same ritual, night after night, regardless of winter storms or the midnight sun. His walk to the cliffs by the water was like a lifeblood to him; only there could he find his peace, his memories, and his pain.

At the edge of the cliff, he inhaled the cool, salty air and felt renewed energy coursing through him. The bay lay quiet under a massive starry sky, and he saw the slender crescent moon just beginning to rise in the south. He closed his eyes. The milky, clouded surroundings disappeared, and he found himself back in his childhood room. He had pulled his blanket up to his nose and smiled in his sleep, lost in his dreams, while the purring of his cat Raya barely registered in his subconscious. Comic books were strewn across the bedspread, some open, others crumpled. He knew them all by heart. Occasionally, his mother would buy him a new one, but since they rarely left the bay, he mostly made do with his old, worn copies. He remembered the dream that had haunted him that night—a dream of fire and raging waves, of ships smashing against the jagged coast. He heard the dreadful sounds of death and despair and, every time, opened his eyes in that moment to escape the memories, even though it nearly broke his heart.

He felt the emptiness inside him, the fear, and the sensation that no food could ever satisfy his gnawing hunger, no water in the world could quench his thirst. He missed—he mourned—he lamented. He sensed that the time had come. His desire would not tolerate any further delay.

He opened his eyes, bid farewell to the moon, the dark water, and the endless horizon, then turned and vanished into the walls of *Fog Castle*.

Chapter 8

After a restless night in which I had to get up four times to use the bathroom, I sat at the breakfast table, annoyed, staring at my phone for almost fifteen minutes. Next to it lay the newspaper clipping with the job advertisement from the boarding school. The application was written and ready to send, but the printer had yet to spit out the papers. I hadn't taken that one decisive step. Too many uncertainties, too many doubts still haunted my mind. A new beginning was always an opportunity to forget the old, to make peace with the past. At the same time, it also brought doubts and fears that couldn't simply be ignored. Over and over, I asked myself whether I should just stay in my current job, preserve the routine of everyday life, and enjoy the security that had, at least temporarily, made life easier. Was I emotionally ready to leave my safe environment just to experience something new? Would this supposedly new experience feel just as dull after a few months as my current situation?

While I pondered solutions, it occurred to me that a phone call with the responsible person on-site might alleviate some of the uncertainty. Perhaps they would even allow me to visit the school.

Sighing, I dialed the number provided in the ad and waited with a pounding heart for someone to answer on the other end.

"Fog Castle, Sigrid?" The tone of the voice suggested that the person was in a hurry and had no time for foolish questions. I considered hanging up right away. "Y-yes, hello, this is Sondre," I stammered instead.

"How can I help you?"

"Sorry to bother you so early. I'm calling about the advertised position..."

"Yes?"

"I'm currently teaching at a secondary school in Tromsø and am interested in the job."

"I'm glad to hear that. We look forward to receiving your application."

She wanted to get rid of me.

"Yes, um... before I do that, I wanted to ask if I could visit the boarding school beforehand?" I held my breath as silence lingered on the other end.

"Yes, we can arrange that," Sigrid finally replied. "When would you have time?"

Surprised by her quick agreement, I stammered as I mentally sifted through my calendar. My classes for the day ended just before noon. "I could drive out this afternoon if that's not too short notice?"

"No, that works for me. Let's say two o'clock?"

"Perfect."

"Do you know how to find us?"

"I think so, yes. Past Tromvik, over the mountain pass to the bay."

"Exactly. At the pass, there's a gate. Next to it, you'll find a phone. Pick up the receiver and wait until someone answers. The gate can be opened from here."

"Got it. Thank you very much."

"One more thing," she added quickly. "What subjects do you currently teach?"

"Exactly the ones you're looking for," I replied enthusiastically.

"Thank you. See you later, then," she responded curtly. The line went dead. I stared at the display, my hand trembling. Whether from anticipation, nervousness, or a lack of caffeine, I couldn't tell. Perhaps it was a bit of everything.

I set the phone aside and went to the window. Unbidden, my thoughts turned to Jørn. He had stopped by last night to pick up the money for his new bike. He had intended to leave right away, but I managed to convince him to stay for a soda.

"Take a seat," I said, fetching his drink. When I returned to the living room, he was texting on his phone. I placed the glass on the table, sat on the sofa, and waited for him to put the phone away. After half a minute of silence, I asked, "Who are you texting?"

"Eirik!" he replied.

"How's he doing?"

"Good."

I waited a few more seconds. "Could you text him later?"

Sighing, he shoved the phone into his pocket and gave me a look of mild annoyance.

"Did you take the bus here?" I asked.

"No. Fredrik drove me."

I clenched my teeth. "Do you want me to drive you home later?"

"No, it's fine. I'm meeting some friends at Nerstranda."

"Alright," I said with a shrug. "When are you getting the new bike?"

"The day after tomorrow."

"Will you come by so I can see it?"

He shrugged briefly. "I don't know when I'll have time again."

At that moment, his phone vibrated, and he pulled it out again.

It was frustrating. Having a normal conversation with him was nearly impossible these days. I consoled myself with the thought that it was just a phase, one every teenager goes through.

I had brought up several other topics during Jørn's visit, but his answers were brief, and our meeting ended after barely twenty minutes.

Annoyed, I glanced at the clock above the oven. I had to hurry—class was starting in fifteen minutes, and I wasn't even dressed yet.

Chapter 9

Mikkel Hansen strolled leisurely through the hallways of *Fog Castle*. In his left hand, he carried a worn-out toolbox. Along the way, he encountered numerous students. Some were chatting animatedly, while others moved through the corridors with their heads down, shutting out the world around them. None greeted him, none even acknowledged his presence, as if he were invisible. In the past, students had shown respect for his appearance, which reminded them of a Nordic warrior. But now, having aged, his demeanor seemed to have lost its former lustre and authority.

He stopped in front of a door on the second floor, set his toolbox on the ground, and inspected the door. A student had vented their anger on it. The lock had been ripped out of the door, and the frame was splintered. The damage was too severe for his tools to fix. A new frame would be needed.

Back in his small attic apartment, he placed the toolbox in a corner, ambled over to the window, and gazed out at the sea. The wind had picked up, and the sea was churning.

He could hear the waves crashing against the cliffs farther north. The seagulls screeched as if there were no tomorrow. He both loved and hated the bay. He longed for nothing more than to leave this place forever, but he hadn't managed to do so yet. The bay clung to him, refusing to let him go. It had become his home, whether he wanted it to or not.

His gaze fell on a locket hanging on a chain around the window latch. Gently, he ran his finger over the photo on the front of the locket. A smile formed on his lips, and his eyes filled with tears.

"Papa?"

"Papa?" It was his daughter's voice—distant—but unmistakably hers.

"I'm here, little one," Mikkel whispered.

The bay faded, the sound of the waves receded, and the seagulls fell silent. He saw only the glow in his daughter's eyes, her inner excitement in eager anticipation of the next day. For the first time, she would be allowed to accompany him fishing, which was as exhilarating to her as the first day of school. She had gone to bed fully dressed and had struggled to fall asleep.

Mikkel smiled at the thought.

At four in the morning, he finally woke her, and she was instantly wide awake. The entire way to the boat, she talked nonstop. She carried her own fishing gear as proudly as a knight carried their lance. He could see her face as the first fish bit and she struggled to muster enough strength to haul her catch into the boat. He heard her squeal with delight when the wriggling fish finally landed at her feet, and he saw the joy in her eyes when he told her she could take her catch home for lunch.

He closed his eyes. The images disappeared, and his daughter's voice fell silent, as it had so many times before.

Chapter 10

I left my classroom shortly before noon, got into my old Nissan, and started the engine. With a nervous churning in my stomach, I set off, merging into the traffic heading toward the tunnel that would take me under the city and out to the other side of the island. Visibility in the tunnel was hazy, caused by the roughened road surface worn down by the studded tires that most cars used here for added safety.

As I exited the tunnel, I saw the mountains on Kvaløya in the distance and further west, those of Ersfjord. The white peaks glowed orange in the February sun, looking like the perfect subject for a beautiful painting. To the north, however, the sky was growing darker.

I passed the airport, crossed the Sandnessund Bridge, and drove on Kvaløya toward Kaldfjord. The upcoming meeting at *Fog Castle* made me nervous. This unease likely wasn't caused by the conversation with Sigrid herself. Rather, it was the fact that I was actively looking for another job, turning my life upside down—at possibly the worst time to do so.

Maybe I was exaggerating it, blowing everything out of proportion, dramatising unnecessarily.

Fifty minutes later, I reached Tromvik. The weather had changed by then. Dark clouds hung over the village, and it had started to snow. Visibility worsened by the minute, and I searched for the turnoff to Tåkevik. To my right, I caught a glimpse of the sea and a small harbor, both gradually being veiled by a curtain of snow. There were barely any people outside. A woman exited a grocery store and loaded two shopping bags onto her kicksled. Two boys played in a garden with colourful snow shovels. Other than that, the place seemed deserted. I slowed down, convinced I had missed the signpost. Cursing, I stopped the car. While rummaging through the glove compartment for a map, a sudden knock on the side window startled me.

I jumped. An older man with a cigarette dangling from the corner of his mouth stood there, smiling kindly at me. I rolled down the window and greeted him.

"Lost your way?" he asked with a grin.

"I'm looking for the turnoff to Tåkevik," I replied.

The man gave me a look as if I had said something inappropriate.

"What are you going there for?"

Slightly unsettled by his bluntness, I responded, "I have an appointment at the boarding school."

"An appointment? Well, well!" He took a drag on his cigarette, exhaling the bluish smoke slowly as he looked up at the mountain beside us and raised his eyebrows. "Pretty lousy weather for a drive over the mountain."

"I know. But I can't reschedule."

The man stared at me for a moment, scrutinizing me. "The road should be cleared, but be careful. The descent on the other side is steep. It's easy to skid."

"I'll be careful, thank you."

He nodded. "Drive back four hundred metres. After the green house on the right, the road leads straight into the mountains."

I thanked him, turned the car around, and drove back to the edge of the village. About five hundred metres later, the green house came into view, and just behind it, I spotted the signpost to Tåkevik. I turned onto the road and followed it into the mountains. The first two kilometres were relatively easy to navigate, but after that, the road became steeper and more winding. Without studded tires, I would have had to turn back. To my right, I saw a few reindeer searching for food. The wind picked up, blowing snow across the road. After about twenty minutes, a red barrier appeared ahead of me, and I stopped. I found the gray telephone box, picked up the receiver, and waited. It rang almost ten times before a tinny voice answered.

"Fog Castle, Sigrid."

"Good afternoon, Sigrid. It's Sondre here," I announced my arrival.

"I'll open the gate," came the brief response.

I hung up, got back into the car, and drove past the now-open barrier downhill. I felt as though I were entering another world. Fog enveloped me, reducing visibility to just a few meters. The road descended steeply. On either side, colored markers indicated the path; without them, I would have completely lost my way. After about five minutes, the weather suddenly cleared, the fog lifted, and I saw the serpentine road ahead of me, ending at a large parking lot. Beyond it, Fog Castle loomed like a rock rising from the snow — a truly strange sight, an English castle nestled in a Norwegian bay.

I could see a narrow strip of beach below, squeezed between towering cliffs. My pulse quickened with each meter I drove. More and more details of the imposing building became visible until, finally, the entire house presented itself in all its glory before me. The photos on the internet had not been exaggerated. I felt as though I was approaching an abandoned haunted castle.

Alfred Hitchcock would have been delighted by its appearance!

I parked my car next to several other vehicles and stepped out. Up close, the building appeared slightly more inviting. It had four stories, and light shone from most of the windows. At each corner of the rectangular structure, small turrets reached toward a leaden sky. Some of the windows had black streaks running downwards, making it look as though the building was crying.

I didn't want to imagine how eerie this place must be at night!

Leaving my car behind, I followed a footpath leading to the entrance. The closer I got, the more it felt as though the house might swallow me whole at any moment. The windows above the entrance looked like the eyes of a beast, and the steeply rising facade gave the impression of an overhanging.

At that moment, I noticed a shadow behind one of the windows and saw a young woman with red hair. I tried to smile and nodded at her. She nodded back.

I stopped in front of the entrance and studied the intricate carvings on the dark door. Grotesque faces glared at me with diabolical expressions. Horses with flaming manes reared up, their mouths agape.

I felt like I was in the movie *The Haunting*, arriving at a ghostly mansion, unsure whether I should actually enter.

In the center of the door hung an iron ring, adorned with a lion's head at its base. I searched in vain for a doorbell. So, I lifted the heavy iron ring and let it fall against the iron plate fixed to the door. The resounding clang made me jump. I wondered if anyone in this enormous building would even hear such a sound. I had barely finished the thought when the rhythmic staccato of high heels echoed toward me. The door was suddenly yanked open, and I found myself face-to-face with a woman of about sixty, perhaps seventy years old. Her gray hair was tied into a flawless bun at the back of her head, so tight it looked as though it might hurt. Her lips were thin lines on her otherwise round face. Her skin was pale and smooth, like candle wax, and her black eyes stood out like coal buttons on a snowman. Her gaze was eerie, almost intimidating.

To complement the sternness of her face, she wore a white blouse beneath a gray blazer, from the pocket of which peeked a pen. Around her neck hung a necklace with a crucifix. If I had had her as a teacher in school, I might have cried out of fear as a child.

"Sondre Iversen, I presume?" she said in a tone that could freeze the Sahara.

I nodded.

"Come in." She stepped aside, allowing me to enter.

The entrance hall was immensely impressive. The floor consisted of a series of sand-coloured stone tiles interspersed with burgundy mosaic tiles. Tall indoor plants stood in the corners, landscape paintings adorned the walls, and wall-mounted lights provided warm illumination at regular intervals. The hall was at least four metres high and seemed much larger from the inside than one would expect from the outside. The smell, a mixture of old wood and musty cellar, reminded me of my grandfather's house.

Opposite the entrance, a wide stone staircase led to a mezzanine, branching off to the right onto the next floor. A burgundy carpet lined the center of the staircase, running from the first step to the last.

I felt as though I had stepped into the castle from *Beauty and the Beast*!

"Follow me, Mr. Iversen," she instructed.

I found it extremely odd that Sigrid addressed me by my last name. In Norway, everyone was on a first-name basis, except with the king.

I followed her brisk steps, noting how her stiff gait suited her demeanor perfectly. A corridor extended from the entrance to the left and disappeared into the unknown. We passed several closed doors, but I couldn't read the plaques due to our pace. Sigrid suddenly turned, and I found myself in a bright office with thick Persian rugs covering the floor. On one wall, I noticed a wide fireplace with charred logs inside. Above the fireplace hung the school's crest, beneath which two crossed sabres were displayed. Paintings adorned the walls, and various artifacts were scattered in the corners, their purposes unclear at first glance. I counted at least four crucifixes mounted on different walls.

Sigrid took a seat behind the desk and motioned for me to sit in a chair. On the right side of her mahogany desk, I noticed a framed photo of a girl with long, dark hair, jet-black eyes, and a round face. The desk was meticulously organized. Everything was aligned, even the pens pointing in the same direction.

"So, Mr. Iversen," Sigrid began formally, "you're interested in our institution?"

"That's correct," I replied.

"Are you familiar with our boarding school?"

"To be honest, not very well. I only know what I could gather from your website." I deliberately omitted mentioning my previous work with the police.

"There's no need to worry about that," Sigrid said quickly, allowing me to relax a bit. "We voluntarily avoid advertising and publicity. Our boarding school is not a typical school—at least, not when it comes to the students."

"Young people with issues! Did I get that right?"

"Precisely. Our students have taken a wrong turn in life. The school's founder, John Birch, established this institution in 1987. He had experience with delinquent and psychologically troubled youth, as he had a son who got involved with the wrong crowd and ended up in trouble. Birch used that experience to build this boarding school. In our country, we are known primarily by schools and psychiatric services. These institutions are the ones that support our work. The parents of these young people often don't know how to deal with their children anymore. They are desperate and at their wit's end. Many of these young people would end up in prison sooner or later if we didn't offer them a second chance here. We are, so to speak, their last hope. And we can proudly say that we are successful with nearly all the young adults who come to us."

"Do you employ psychologists here as well?"

"Of course!" Sigrid replied. "We have one, to be exact."

"And the teachers? Don't they need experience with psychological conditions?"

Sigrid shook her head. "Not necessarily. They are primarily responsible for teaching the curriculum. Naturally, all our teachers receive an introduction to the subject. They attend workshops and discussions with our psychologist and sometimes participate in sessions with the students. But it's not a prerequisite to have prior experience in this area."

I nodded, swallowing the nervous lump forming in my throat.

"Mr. Iversen, you will understand that we cannot conduct a formal interview here and now. We first require an official application. The decision is not mine to make; that responsibility lies with Jori, our head teacher."

"Of course. It wasn't my intention to bypass the official process," I said with a nervous laugh. "It's just that I'm at a point in my life where I need a change. A new challenge, a role that pushes me. And since this position is not exactly an everyday job, I wanted to get a preliminary impression. I hope this doesn't come across as too forward."

Sigrid scrutinised me for a moment, her penetrating gaze making me feel as if she could see right through me. I held her stare, resisting the urge to look away out of embarrassment.

"Very well," she said finally. "If you're genuinely interested in the position, we can address a few points now. Perhaps this will give you a clearer picture of us." She reached for a notepad, retrieved a navy-blue fountain pen from a drawer, and slid a pair of reading glasses onto her nose. Looking over the glasses as though reading from an invisible script, she outlined the daily routine for teachers at the boarding school, the general structure, and the current staff, using an organisational chart. By my count, there were eight teachers, one psychologist, a cook with an assistant, Sigrid, and the director, John Birch.

During a brief pause, I inquired about the staff accommodation. "The job ad mentioned apartments?"

"That's correct. Some of our teachers come from far away, and the road is often impassable in winter. That's why we offer housing to our staff."

"That's very impressive."

"Would you need a room if we were to hire you?"

I wanted to say, *Yes, but only if it's free!* "I have an apartment in Tromsø. Financially, I can't afford to maintain a second one."

She raised her eyebrows. "So, is that a yes or a no?"

A bit thrown off by her bluntness, I replied, "Essentially, yes! But as I mentioned, I couldn't afford a second residence."

"You wouldn't have to. The apartment would be provided free of charge. But you don't have to decide that now. First, we need to make a decision." Her ensuing diabolical laugh gave me the feeling I had just sold my soul to the devil.

"If you feel convinced by our institution, we'd be happy to receive your application." She removed her glasses and folded her hands on the desk, looking at me.

"I'll gladly think it over," I replied.

Sigrid smiled faintly. "I'll now call for Jori so you can have a brief conversation with him. As I mentioned on the phone, he reviews the applications and makes the final decision."

She picked up the telephone, dialed a number, and issued a curt command to Jori. Less than five minutes later, there was a knock at the door, and a lanky man of about fifty entered, wearing a goofy grin. He sat in a chair and crossed his legs. He sported a three-day beard, protruding ears, and a toothpick that bobbed up and down between his lips. He had a bald spot, and the top of his forehead shone like freshly polished floorboards. His clothes reminded me of a parrot: yellow trousers, a green-and-brown sweater, and a blue wool scarf.

"Good day, Jori," said Sigrid. "May I introduce Sondre Iversen? He's interested in the open teaching position. He hasn't submitted an official application yet, but perhaps you could explain the teaching methods we use here. I'll wait in the lounge."

She rose from her chair and clicked away on her heels.

Jori and I were left alone, looking at each other awkwardly.

"So, where are you working currently?" he asked.

Over the next fifteen minutes, I answered several questions about my teaching career. I also explained that I was seeking a change and found the boarding school intriguing. Jori listened attentively, nodding occasionally and asking short follow-up questions. Finally, he slapped both hands on his thighs and said, "Very interesting. I can relate to your situation. It's not always easy with superiors. I had the same problem at my first school. As I mentioned earlier, teaching here isn't drastically different from your current work. However, you'll need more patience, resilience, and determination. The students can really test your limits, and you have to be aware of that. But if you're willing to face the challenge, the work here is incredibly rewarding."

He flashed his goofy grin again and stuck the toothpick back between his teeth. I thanked him for the insights and promised to submit my application in the coming days.

"Wonderful!" he said, standing up. "Let's go back to Sigrid. Perhaps she'll show you around the building."

We left the office, crossed a long corridor and the entrance hall, and approached a standing table near a window, where Sigrid was reading a magazine.

"We're done, Sigrid," Jori announced.

"Thank you, Jori," she said, closing the magazine and turning to me. "I'll now show you some of the key areas." Addressing Jori, she added, "You can return to your class. I'll see you later."

Jori shook my hand and disappeared up the staircase to the upper floors.

Sigrid gestured toward the stairs. "We're going up as well. If you'll follow me..."

She led the way, and I tried to keep up with her pace. Her way of walking reminded me of a penguin. She didn't waddle from side to side, but her upright, stiff gait bore a striking resemblance to the flightless Antarctic birds.

"On the ground floor, we have the dining hall, the administrative offices, the psychologist's meeting room, and the infirmary," Sigrid explained as we ascended the stairs. "The classrooms are located on the first floor. The second floor houses the students, and the third floor contains the apartments for the teachers, the psychologist, and the cook."

So far, we hadn't encountered a single student. I assumed they were all in their classrooms, which made the building feel eerily deserted.

We reached the first floor. Sigrid turned to me. "Here you'll find all the classrooms. At the moment, only one is unoccupied. Let me show it to you."

We passed three closed doors, each bearing the nameplates of the respective teachers. The fourth door stood open, revealing an empty room. As we stepped inside, I was momentarily breathless. The classrooms were even more stunning in person than they appeared in the online photos. I felt like I had stepped into a classroom at Hogwarts. The teacher's desk resembled the one in Sigrid's office—it, too, seemed to be made of mahogany, giving the impression of an industrial magnate's office. A luxurious leather chair with armrests and the school's crest embroidered on it served as the teacher's seat.

The students' desks were no less impressive. Although not made of mahogany, they were clearly crafted from high-quality wood. The room was adorned with plants, pictures from various climate zones around the world, multiple chalkboards, and a ceiling-mounted projector. Thick curtains hung by the windows, tied back on either side with cords.

Compared to this classroom, mine felt like a prison cell. "Quite impressive," was the best I could manage to say.

Sigrid smiled smugly. "Our boarding school is well-funded."

I simply nodded.

"Let me show you one of the staff apartments now."

We returned to the staircase and ascended two more floors. The third-floor corridor was significantly different from the first. A red carpet, identical to the one on the staircase, stretched through the centre of the hallway. Wall sconces, designed to resemble antique torch holders, were spaced every three metres. Windows were only present by the staircases and at either end of the hallway.

Sigrid opened the third door on the left and stepped inside. Stale air greeted us as she turned on the ceiling light. The apartment had everything one might need to live comfortably. Behind the door was a small kitchen; a cozy-looking sofa sat by the window, accompanied by a coffee table with a fruit bowl on it. Across from the sofa hung a flat-screen TV with an attached DVD player. Next to the TV, a door led to the bedroom.

"When the building was renovated, they combined two rooms to create these apartments. A bathroom was integrated into the bedroom by adding a wall," Sigrid explained.

After inspecting the bedroom, I returned to the main room and looked out the window. The view was breathtaking. The fog had lifted, and the bay lay before me, bathed in amber February light. The small waves on the water sparkled and shimmered, almost dizzyingly. The snow-covered mountains on either side of the bay glowed in the sunlight, making me squint.

As a Northerner, I was used to such sights. What was new, however, was this house—this enormous estate that seemed so surreal it felt like stepping into the Middle Ages. If I hadn't known I was in Norway, I would have sworn I was somewhere in England.

"Are you ready?" Sigrid asked suddenly.

Startled, I replied, "Of course, my apologies. I was just captivated by the view. It's truly stunning."

"It certainly is." She held the door open for me. "Come, let's head back downstairs."

You can't have a normal conversation with this woman, I thought to myself.

She led me back to the entrance hall, where she stopped near the main door. "I hope I've given you a good first impression of our institution," she said, her hands folded in front of her, her expression stern.

"You certainly have. Thank you for allowing me to visit on such short notice."

She gave a curt nod. "Mr. Iversen, before you leave, one question: Why should *Fog Castle* hire you as a teacher?"

The question came as unexpectedly as a hot summer day in Tromsø. I felt heat rising in my face and scrambled for a suitable answer. "Well, I, uh…" I swallowed and simultaneously felt Sigrid's penetrating gaze, saw the blackness in her eyes, and felt as though my life depended on this one response. "Let me put it this way: I'm almost fifty years old, and I've reached a point in my life where I need to catch the next turn. I've experienced a lot—good and bad, boring and exciting. I've had—well, I *had*—a family. My second-born son died before he could properly go ice fishing with me. My relationship with my ex-wife died the day we laid our son to rest. Since then, I've been living in a world that feels so foreign and dark that, most mornings, I can't tell if I've slept or stayed awake all night. Working with students keeps me afloat; it gives me energy, though it also sometimes drains me. One thing I know for sure: I need a new challenge. What I've seen of your boarding school both fascinates and frightens me. The house exerts a pull that's hard to ignore. I can see myself living here, working here—I can see myself giving these students a second chance, an opportunity to take control of their lives again." I had to clear my throat because my voice was on the verge of breaking. "And that's exactly what I need now: a second chance."

Sigrid stared at me unblinkingly, her gaze unwavering. I felt my mouth go dry, my throat parched like after a mountain run. I didn't know what had come over me, only that I had likely just ruined everything.

"I understand. Thank you for your visit. Have a safe journey home." She turned and disappeared into one of the dark hallways.

As I stepped outside and the cold air hit my face, I felt as though I had stepped out of a movie and back into reality. The tension fell away, but my head felt as though I was suffering from a fever. I scooped up a handful of snow and dabbed it on my cheeks. My gaze fell on my car, and although I wanted to leave, I felt I wasn't ready for the drive back just yet.

I made my way through the snow, eventually reaching the west side of the building, where I stopped at the corner of the house. Pulling a cigarette from my jacket pocket, I shook one loose and lit it. I inhaled deeply, savouring the smoke, and looked out over the bay and the snow-free beach. There wasn't a soul in sight. I wondered whether this remote location might take an even greater toll on my already fragile psyche. Loneliness was an undeniable factor out here. Sure, you weren't alone in the large building, but you were in an unfamiliar environment, surrounded by new people and new problems, with friends feeling two days away.

And yet, the thought of working in such a curious place sparked a fire within me that I had thought long extinguished. A tiny ember that needed only a gust of wind to reignite fully. Whether this flicker of flame would be enough to throw myself into such an adventure was something that would occupy my thoughts in the hours and days to come, likely robbing me of one or two nights of sleep.

Sighing, I took one last look at the bay, tucked the cold cigarette butt into my pocket, and returned to my car.

Chapter 11

I drove back toward Tromsø along the coastal road. It was windy, and the waters of the Kaldfjord were choppy. The last rays of sunlight were already being swallowed by the mountains, and the land glowed in the orange-red light of evening.

I replayed my conversation with Sigrid and had to admit that the woman had left me a little unsettled. Her stiffness, formal manner of speaking, and the curt words she used made her come across in a peculiar light. But it wasn't just Sigrid. It was the entire institution that sent a shiver down my spine. The house seemed to me like it was full of secrets that were better left undiscovered.

I glanced at my phone and saw that Jørn had called. I tapped his name, and the call connected. He answered after a few seconds.

"You called?" I asked.

"I wanted to ask you something about our vacation."

I waited for the question, but none came. So I pressed on. "What about the vacation?"

"Well, Fredrik wants to take me on a dog sledding tour near Hammerfest…"

"Okay!" I replied, already feeling a knot forming in my stomach.

"It would be for eight days."

"And what do you want to ask?" I was getting a bit impatient. When it came to Fredrik and my son, my patience was paper-thin.

"It's during the time you and I were planning to go to the cabin."

I knew it! That bastard was trying to drive a wedge between me and Jørn. That was just like him, that arrogant, self-important jerk. I could kick his ass right here and now until it turned as blue as a Smurf's.

"Dad, are you still there?"

"Yes, I'm still here," I said, more annoyed than I intended. "Does it have to be during our vacation together?"

A long sigh was the only response. "But it's a chance that won't come again," Jørn countered. "And the cabin isn't going anywhere!"

"No, it's not. But I was really looking forward to us finally spending some time together again. And not just for a few hours." The line went quiet. "You love going to the cabin," I said, almost desperately.

"Yes, that's true. But going on a husky tour sounds really exciting."

Well, what could I say? Of course, he was fascinated. A husky tour sounded much more impressive than sitting on a frozen lake all day, waiting for a fish to bite. At least for a boy Jørn's age. But I had already set my mind on spending this time with him, and the thought of Fredrik taking my son away—even if only for a vacation—pulled the rug out from under me. I was boiling inside. I wanted to tell Jørn off, to make him understand that he was my son and that he *should* spend the vacation with me!

But I couldn't do that. He would have been rightfully angry, distanced himself from me even more, and, with his mother's help, likely written off any future vacations with me altogether. "Alright," I said instead. "Do what you think is best. If the husky tour appeals to you more, then you should enjoy it."

"Thanks, Dad! Talk soon."

"Talk soon." He had already hung up. I slammed my fist on the steering wheel. This was infuriating! I had been looking forward to this trip for weeks. Now it was ruined. Should I go to the cabin alone?

Great idea!

From early morning to late evening, I could philosophise about my current life and drown myself in the icy water alongside the worm on the hook.

The loud honking of an oncoming car brought me back to reality. I had drifted out of my lane and crossed the centerline, which was barely visible under the snow. I jerked the steering wheel back, returning to my side just in time to see the other driver give me the middle finger. My heart pounded in my chest, and my knees were trembling.

This couldn't go on!

At that moment, a glimmer of hope surfaced within me—a kind of defiance, a breaking free from invisible chains. It was time to embark on a new journey, to move to a different life, a new environment—away from ex-wives, their new partners, and a job that brought no fulfillment. To hell with my doubts, my hesitations, and my fears.

I reached the Sandnessund Bridge and crossed it at a snail's pace. A truck from the Netherlands, struggling with the local road conditions, crawled up the small incline to the middle of the bridge in first gear.

Ten minutes later, I entered my apartment, printed my application, placed it in an envelope, and dropped it into the mailbox around the corner. Then I returned to the apartment, sat by the window, and lit a cigarette. For a brief moment, I felt contentment, calm, and at the same time, a tension—a sense of uncertainty that didn't bother me. I leaned back in my chair, closed my eyes, and enjoyed the evening sea breeze drifting through the streets into my apartment.

Chapter 12

Night had fallen over *Fog Castle*. The students and staff lay in their beds, asleep. At least, most of them. Four of the house's inhabitants, however, found no rest. Kjell, the sixty-one-year-old psychiatrist, couldn't sleep and was reading an Agatha Christie mystery. He did this almost every night until he finally drifted into the land of dreams, the open book resting on his chest and his glasses askew on his face.

Agna, the fifty-six-year-old kitchen assistant, lay in her bed staring at the screen of a tablet. When she couldn't sleep, she watched cheap TV dramas, shedding tears over the romances of the series' protagonists. Subconsciously, she registered the sound of a door closing. But she was so engrossed in the story that she didn't notice the footsteps passing her door, nor the shadowy figure creeping along the walls of the staircase, moving downward.

On the ground floor, the figure paused, listening for any sounds. Hearing nothing suspicious, it continued to a door marked *Cellar*. Quietly, it unlocked the door with a key and slipped through. Flashlight in hand, the figure descended the stone steps into the basement and followed a hallway that ended at an iron-bound door. Passing through, it pulled a woolen scarf tighter around its neck and stepped outside.

With quick strides, the figure approached a person standing like a statue on a rocky outcrop, gazing out over the bay. In the milky moonlight, the figure recognised the man's face, and her spirits lifted. Her heart warmed, and she felt a surge of pride as she looked at her son, so tall and strong, so complete and perfect. He was her everything, and like any mother, she would walk through the fires of hell for him.

What she couldn't see—or perhaps chose to overlook— was his imperfection, his vice, his addiction, and his desire, which she could not satisfy for him. This flaw was her fault. She was responsible. No one could blame him. Even though he was no longer a child, she still saw in him the little boy who needed her help and care. She had to keep protecting him, shielding him from the dangerous outside world. He couldn't live without his mother, and she was determined to do everything in her power to see him happy until the day she died.

Sighing, she rested her head on his shoulder, and he wrapped his arm around her. They stood there silently for nearly half an hour, lost in memories. Wisps of milky clouds drifted across the sky, and somewhere far out at sea, a buoy's bell tolled faintly.

She could no longer remember how many times they had stood together here, deep in thought, haunted by fear and regret, with no idea what the future might hold—whether joy or ruin. Each time, she was reminded of how closely linked those two feelings were and how quickly everything could come to an end. She knew that their story, their life, couldn't go on like this forever. But it didn't matter; she would endure it, if only to be strong for him, her son, her everything.

A green curtain of northern lights appeared between the clouds. The tide was rising, and the sound of waves echoed through the bay.

The woman cast one last look at her son, kissed his cheek, and returned to *Fog Castle*.

Chapter 13

Mikkel Hansen relished the peace that the night always brought with it. The house was asleep. But he himself could not sleep—not for a long time now. Sleep had been for the days when his heart and bones were young and craved nothing but rest after an exhausting day. Today, his life was much quieter, much more leisurely, and so his body no longer grew as tired as it once had.

He reached the entrance hall and exited the building through the grand front door. An icy wind blew against him, but he barely noticed it. The snow reflected the ivory-colored moonlight, casting the entire bay in a muted blue glow. The surrounding mountain peaks looked like they had been painted on, their steep, snow-free rock faces resembling the hungry mouths of beasts.

But tonight, the mystical view left him cold. He was here for something else.

Under the brim of his hat, he followed the steps of a figure emerging from the shadow of *Fog Castle*. Taking long, purposeful strides, the figure moved toward a nearby cliff, seemingly unaware it was being followed.

At the very edge of the anvil-shaped cliff, the figure stopped, and Mikkel could see its body begin to tremble slightly. A faint, low whimpering came from the figure. Mikkel felt an old anger rising within him—a rage he had tried unsuccessfully to suppress for many years. But this anger was accompanied by an equally potent sorrow, and he needed that sorrow. It was like an invisible tether to his past, and he was afraid that forgetting this anger and sorrow would sever that connection.

The man's whimpering turned into sobbing, then into loud, sniffing cries. Mikkel swallowed his grief, leaving only raw hatred. He wanted to hurt him, to show him what it meant to feel true sorrow. He wanted to push the man off the cliff to his death, to watch his body smash against the rocks below, and to see his blood carried away forever by the dark waves.

But, as with all his previous attempts, he couldn't do it tonight either. He simply lacked the strength. What held him back most, however, was the thought of what his beloved daughter would think of him if she could see him. He couldn't do that to her, and it wouldn't bring her back.

Her face appeared before his eyes—her sweet, smiling face. But tonight, her cheeks were flushed, her gaze weary. She had a high fever. He had held her hand as she tossed and turned in her sleep. He stayed by her bedside even as she awoke the next morning, her nightgown soaked from the night sweats. He helped her sit up, fed her chicken soup, dabbed her hot forehead with a damp cloth, and brought her favorite teddy bear to cuddle. She looked into his eyes, a tired smile on her lips, and he kissed her hair.

Mikkel stood on the cliff for another hour until the man at the edge suddenly turned and disappeared into the shadow of the house. Mikkel himself turned back toward the ocean and let himself be consumed by the sounds of the bay.

Chapter 14

On the morning of February 11th, I got into my car and headed toward Tåkevik. In the trunk, I had packed a bag containing everything I would need to survive for a week at *Fog Castle*.

As I drove, I felt more nervous than I had in a long time. The past few days had been exhausting, even though leaving my previous school had been a relatively light burden to bear. Preparing for my upcoming classes, however, had taken a lot of time—I wanted to make a good first impression. After my figurative mental collapse in front of Sigrid, I had been convinced I had dug my own grave. But nine days after my visit to *Fog Castle*, Sigrid had called to offer me the position. She said Jori had been impressed with my demeanor and application materials, and therefore, so was she.

After that short conversation, it had taken several cigarettes and a few glasses of wine to come to terms with the idea of a new workplace and a new apartment, even though I would be keeping my current one. I had chosen a new path—one as uncertain as the weather in northern Norway.

An hour and a half later, I parked my Nissan on *Fog Castle* grounds and walked toward the front door. A few students lounged on a bench near the entrance, scrutinising me with wary looks. I offered a greeting in their direction, but only received unintelligible murmurs in response.

As I reached for the door handle, it opened on its own, and there stood Sigrid, her smile practiced and stiff.

"I've been expecting you. Welcome to *Fog Castle*," she said formally, stepping aside to let me in.

I entered the building, surprised by the buzz of activity inside. Students darted past me, teachers strode purposefully among them, disappearing either up the staircase or into one of the many ground-floor rooms. The noise level was significantly higher than during my previous visit.

Once again, Sigrid set off at a pace that made it seem like she was about to miss a train. She led me to her office, where she spent the next hour explaining many details about the school's operations and the timetable. I noticed I had fewer lessons to teach than at my previous job, despite earning a higher salary. She told me that the boarding school typically had about seventy students, though currently only around fifty-five were in attendance. She explained that the number of students fluctuated from year to year—sometimes there were more, sometimes fewer. Sigrid also spoke about Kjell, the school psychologist. It was entirely normal, she said, for some students to miss classes regularly to attend therapy sessions. In such cases, they were required to present a written exemption.

After this initial orientation, Sigrid leaned back in her chair, placed her hands on the armrests, and said, "Well, that's enough for now. Do you have any questions?"

When nothing came to mind, I shook my head.

"Excellent. I'll take you to your apartment now."

We climbed the stairs to the third floor, and I noticed that every student we passed greeted Sigrid with almost reverential respect. They seemed like subjects paying homage to their queen.

When we reached my future apartment, Sigrid unlocked the door and handed me the keys. "Here we are. If you need anything or have questions, I'll be in my office until six o'clock. Otherwise, you can contact Jori."

"I will. Thank you."

She gave a curt nod and walked away with brisk steps.

I watched her retreat down the hallway until she disappeared around the corner. Shaking my head, I entered my new apartment and set my travel bag on the floor. On the living room table was a bowl of fruit, and on the sideboard, I found a woven basket filled with pasta, tomato sauce, potatoes, and other daily necessities.

It felt almost like a hotel! All that was missing was a mint on the pillow.

I placed the keys on the sideboard and began unpacking my bag. A feeling crept over me, like the moment before an exam—an inner nervousness that clenched my stomach like a cold hand. With the closing of the apartment door, a new chapter had begun. There was no turning back now. I was here, in a new environment, at a new school—and I had only the faintest idea of what to expect.

After successfully battling my rising panic and settling into my apartment, I decided to explore the house a bit more thoroughly. I left my apartment and stepped into the deserted hallway. At the far end of the corridor, I noticed a window and headed toward it. It faced northwest and offered a breathtaking view of the bay. For a while, I watched the waves playing along the beach, the wild flight maneuvers of the seagulls, and, far out, a buoy bobbing in the water. A somewhat stocky woman stood not far from the building, smoking and talking on a phone. Judging by her clothing, she had to be Mathilde, the cook. My gaze drifted back to the sea, and I felt my eyes grow unfocused as the image blurred.

I thought about my empty apartment downtown, about Jørn, about my old school, and about my previous work with the police. Unbidden, Raik's face intruded upon my thoughts. I heard his voice, smelled his skin—so vividly that I believed he was standing just inches away from me. Everything in that moment felt so real, so tangible, that it nearly tore me apart inside. I missed his soft voice greeting me when I came home from work and he ran toward me. I missed the teddy bear he always carried with him, which now lay in Marit's bedroom. I missed his big brown eyes following every word as I read him a story. I missed everything about Raik. And the worst part was knowing that none of it would ever come back to me.

My vision blurred further, the sea and cliffs fading into a haze of memories.

"Hello!"

I jumped. A young woman with long black hair and a moon-shaped face stood beside me. A piercing adorned her left nostril, and below her right ear, I noticed a tattoo, though I couldn't make out what it depicted.

"I'm sorry, I didn't mean to scare you," she said apologetically.

I took a deep breath and forced a sheepish smile. "It's okay, no problem. I was just lost in thought."

She nodded and studied me curiously. "Are you okay?"

"Yes, I'm fine, thank you. I was just thinking about something that made me feel very sad…"

She nodded again. "You're the new teacher, right?"

I confirmed this and told her my name. She introduced herself as Tiril and then looked out the window. "Beautiful place, isn't it?" she said, nodding toward the bay.

"Gorgeous!" I replied. "But pretty isolated for a school."

"It is. But for most people here, that's probably for the best. You can't get into much trouble here, not like in the city," she said, winking.

"True. There aren't many opportunities for mischief here."

"Did you just arrive today?" she asked.

"That's right. I just moved into my apartment and thought I'd take a look around."

"Want me to show you around the house?"

"That would be wonderful."

"Well then, come on." She turned, and I followed her. "Has Sigrid already shown you anything?" she asked.

"When I came for the interview, she gave me a brief overview. But I'm sure there's plenty I haven't seen yet. What's especially interesting?"

Tiril glanced at me with a conspiratorial look. "She probably didn't show you the attic, did she?"

"No, she left that out."

"I figured. Come with me!"

I followed Tiril up the stairs, and once again, I noticed the sullen faces of the students we passed. So far, I hadn't seen many cheerful people here, except for the student in front of me. I asked her if she was supposed to be in class.

"Not for another hour," she replied.

We reached the fourth floor. The air smelled of dusty attic and old clothes. I noticed three doors: two on the left and one on the right.

Tiril pointed to a door on our left. "I don't know what's behind that one. It's always locked. Even when I first started poking around here two years ago, it was sealed."

I raised my eyebrows. "Maybe it's a secret room?"

"Who knows? It could also be this castle's torture chamber!" She smiled mischievously and moved to the next door. With a loud creak, it swung open, and a wide beam of light spilled into the hallway. Tiril stepped across the threshold, and I followed her. The air in the room was stale. Against the wall stood two bookshelves, each holding only a single book. There was a table with a chair and an old typewriter, covered in cobwebs, lying on the floor. Dust coated every surface in thick layers, and I felt a tickle in my nose. But what impressed me most was the enormous oval window facing west, stretching from floor to ceiling.

"What a strange room," I said. "Who used to live here?"

"No idea," Tiril replied with a shrug. "Maybe an old writer whose ghost now haunts the house." She had that mischievous smile again.

"Are you even allowed to be in here?" I asked, inspecting one of the books. When she didn't immediately respond, I turned to see her hesitant expression, as if she were deciding whether to lie or tell the truth.

"Well, it's not exactly forbidden," she said finally. "The boarding school administration says we have no business up here, but since there's hardly anything of interest in these rooms, no one really cares."

I nodded, placed the book back, and walked over to the window. "This would make a great office."

"You could always ask Sigrid."

I laughed. "I think I'll wait a few days before doing that."

She joined me by the window. "Are you from Tromsø?"

"Yes, born and bred. What about you?"

"Finnsnes."

"Beautiful area."

"Yeah," she said, lost in thought. "But not much happens there."

"Maybe not at your age. But when you're as old as I am, you might appreciate the peace more than the buzz of a party."

"Maybe. But I've got time before then. And unfortunately, this place isn't much more exciting than where I'm from."

"How much longer do you have to stay here?"

"If all goes well, one more year."

"Any plans after that?"

"I'll probably go to university—if I make it."

"What do you want to study?"

"Social sciences."

"Good choice."

"We'll see." She smiled. "Come on, let's keep going."

She led me across the hallway to another door, opening it into darkness. Tiril flipped a light switch, and, at two-meter intervals, ceiling lights flickered on, revealing, to my surprise, a chapel. It had four wooden pews, a small altar, and a wooden crucifix on the wall above it. The side walls were decorated with paintings, but I couldn't make out what they depicted.

I looked at Tiril in surprise. "You have a chapel here?"

"The original owner of the house had it built," she explained.

"Is it open to everyone?"

"Of course. But most of the time, it looks just like this—empty. As far as I know, Sigrid spends the most time here. She's very religious."

I raised my eyebrows but refrained from commenting.

"Are you religious?" Tiril asked.

I shook my head. "No, I'm not."

"Why not?"

I shrugged. "Religion never played a big role in my family, except with my grandmother. I didn't grow up with much exposure to it, and looking back, I don't think I missed out on much."

"Why do you think that?"

"It's just how I feel. Religion is for those who want it, who need the belief in a higher power, who explains things through the Bible and faith in God. For me, facts, evidence, and natural laws matter more. Faith doesn't have a place in that."

Tiril regarded me silently for a while before responding. "I'm sure plenty of people would disagree with you."

"They're free to. Everyone should believe whatever they want."

She smiled and nodded, closed the door to the chapel, and led me back downstairs. As we reached the first landing, I caught movement out of the corner of my eye. I turned back and froze. A tall man with a hat and gray hair stood motionless at the top of the staircase, staring at me. I missed the next step and stumbled, managing to grab the railing at the last second.

Tiril turned around, puzzled. "Are you okay?"

"Yes, sorry. I tripped."

"Already having an accident on your first day?"

"Let's hope not." I shook my head and looked back up. But the man was gone. "Hey, we were alone up there earlier, weren't we?"

She looked at me, confused. "Yes. Why?"

"I just saw a man standing up there."

"Up there?" She pointed to the fourth floor.

"Yes. Where we just were."

"Are you sure?"

"I'm certain."

"What did he look like?"

"Tall, broad-shouldered, gray hair, wearing a hat."

Tiril seemed to think for a moment. "I don't know who that could have been. Sander has gray hair, but I've never seen him wearing a hat."

I glanced back again, but the attic hallway was empty. Was this building already causing me to hallucinate?

"You probably imagined it. The lighting up there is bad; it was probably just one of our shadows."

"Maybe," I replied, unconvinced.

"Have you seen the classrooms yet?" she asked, steering the conversation away from the mysterious figure.

"Sigrid showed them to me during my first visit."

"Well, then I guess that's the end of my tour." She smiled at me.

"What about the towers?" I asked curiously.

"One of them, the one facing the bay, is part of Sigrid's apartment. The one on the south side houses Director Birch's office, but he's rarely here. I'm not allowed to show you the towers; they're off-limits. They drill that into us on day one. But you might have to visit the Director's office someday, which usually means you've done something wrong." She winked at me.

"Have you had to go there yet?" I asked, winking back.

"Of course, like almost everyone here." She shrugged. "Most of us aren't exactly model students, as you can imagine. But usually, we're sent to Sigrid instead of him. The Director is barely ever here."

"Have you met him?"

"Sure. But only twice."

"And what's he like?"

She shrugged again. "No idea. I've never spoken to him. I only saw him outside the house once and another time when he went into Sigrid's office. I don't think he's very involved with the boarding school. Sigrid and Jori handle almost everything."

"I see."

"Is there anything else I can help you with?" she asked, tilting her head.

"No, I'm good. Thanks for the tour. It was very interesting."

"You're welcome. Have a great first day. And don't let it get to you."

"I won't, don't worry."

She smiled and disappeared down the stairs, and I returned to my apartment.

Chapter 15

A few hours later, in the basement of the boarding school, a heavyset man sat on his bed, staring at a photo in his hand. Lovingly, he stroked the features of a young girl with long dark hair and coal-black eyes. Alternating between pressing the photo to his heart and staring at it intently, he repeated this ritual for over half an hour. Waves of memories washed over him. He felt the heat under the blanket, his body drenched in sweat. His pyjamas clung to his skin, and the sheets were soaked. The walls of his basement room seemed to dissolve, the musty smell replaced by the scent of smoke.

He heard the loud crackling of wood and noticed the flickering light outside his old bedroom door. He saw himself crawling out of bed, sneaking toward the door. He opened it. Acrid smoke filled his lungs, making him cough and gag, his eyes watering. He saw the hallway of his parents' house, the thick carpets, the floral wallpaper, and the door to his sister's room, shrouded in a thick haze of smoke.

On his knees, he approached the door, hesitating to open it, fearing what lay behind. Yet he forced himself to press the handle, squeezing his eyes shut, clenching his fists, holding his breath. Then he dragged himself back to the present. The smoke had dissipated, the glow of the fire had faded, and his sister's room was gone.

He set the photo aside and resolutely left his basement room. At the end of a long corridor, he climbed a stone staircase, unlocked a door at the top, and stepped into the silent entrance hall of *Fog Castle*.

Silence greeted him.

He closed the door behind him and made his way to the second floor, where the students' bedrooms were located. As he climbed the stairs, his emotions spiraled out of control—nervousness, impatience, fear, and curiosity swirled within him. He couldn't understand these feelings anymore; they were unfamiliar despite experiencing them countless times before. They unsettled him, paralyzed him, and yet heightened his senses like nothing else. A relentless longing and grief drove him forward, giving him strength for what he was about to do.

On the second floor, he crept from door to door until he stopped at Room 212. Gently, he pressed down the door handle, and the door swung open slowly. Darkness greeted him, but the dim light from the hallway allowed him to make out two beds. From his pocket, he retrieved a small vial and a cloth. With trembling hands, he uncorked the vial, poured its contents onto the cloth, and approached the bed on the right. His heartbeat quickened, his breath came in gasps. With his massive hands, he pressed the cloth against the girl's face. Sweat dripped from his face onto her forehead. She woke up and stared at him with wide-open eyes. He pressed the cloth harder against her nose, and in the next moment, the girl fell unconscious. He repeated the process with her roommate, who also lost consciousness within seconds.

After stowing the cloth and vial, he lifted one of the girls from her bed and left the room with her in his arms. As he reached the staircase, he heard a dull thud beside him. Startled, he jumped to the side and realised the vial had fallen to the ground. Groaning, he knelt down, picked it up, and tucked it back into his pocket. Glancing around nervously, he continued, passing the first floor and heading to the intermediate landing. Just before the entrance hall, he thought he heard a noise behind him. Alarmed, he turned, almost bumping the girl's head against the banister. Gently, he cradled her head to his chest, scanned the hall, and crept to the basement door. With one hand, he opened it and slipped through. After locking the door behind him, a sense of relief and anticipation washed over him. The tension drained away, his pulse calmed, the heat waves subsided, and he felt better than he had in a long time.

In his chambers, he placed the girl on a bed and rested her head on a soft pillow. Protruding from the wall behind the bed were two iron brackets, each fitted with a chain ending in padded leather cuffs. He gently placed her hands into the cuffs and fastened them with leather straps. Then he struck a match and lit the wick of a half-burned candle. The girl didn't stir, so he sat down beside her on the bed. For a while, he simply looked at her, admiring her long lashes, her button nose, her rosy cheeks, and her dark hair. A nearly forgotten joy spread through him, a comforting warmth rising to his head. With his thick fingers, he lightly touched her cheeks, as delicately as brushing dew from a blade of grass. He closed his eyes, savoring the moment he had long awaited, the moment he had yearned for. And now it was here. Tracing the contours of her face in a trance, he breathed in the floral scent of her hair and ran his finger over her lips, soft as butter.

He wasn't lonely anymore! She was here now—the princess!

With a deep breath, he opened his eyes, let her hair slip through his fingers, and inhaled its scent again, as if it were an aphrodisiac. He took her hand and noticed how cold it was. At the foot of the bed lay a blanket. He picked it up and spread it over her sleeping body. Then he bent down, kissed her forehead, and climbed into his own bed with a satisfied smile. With his eyes closed, he listened to her steady breathing, and gradually, he drifted into a deep, memory-laden sleep.

Later that same night, the door to the basement chamber creaked open, and the face of a woman appeared in the dim light. She entered the room and approached the sleeping girl. For a moment, she just stared at her, torn between despair and relief.

When will this finally end? she wondered.

But she already knew the answer. She had known for a long time. The end would only come with her own end. She would never find peace until death claimed her or everything came to light. The past years weighed heavily on her body; she was exhausted and drained. The story felt like a curse—a curse that was also, paradoxically, a blessing. At times, she caught herself wishing for a quick end to it all, for the anxious days to cease, for peace and normality to take their place. Yet each time, she felt ashamed for even thinking such thoughts. This was her life's task, her burden to bear. She had been chosen for it, and she would face her fate, come what may.

Sighing, she placed a hand on his shoulder until he blinked awake and stared at her.

"Are you sure this time?" she asked.

"What, Mama? What?" he croaked.

"I asked if you're sure this time."

"Yes, Mama, I'm sure. Just look at her! Isn't she the loveliest thing?"

She turned her head.

Yes, she was indeed lovely—beautiful, graceful, gentle, and far too delicate for her son. As if sensing that she was the subject of discussion, the girl began to stir. She moaned softly, writhing under the blanket, trying to pull her arms close to her body, kicking with her legs, and finally opening her eyes. She blinked several times, her gaze dazed and confused as she scanned the room until her eyes locked onto hers.

"W-what's going on?" she stammered, her voice thick. "Where am I?" She tried to get up, but the chains pulled her back down onto the bed.

"Calm down, girl. You'll only hurt yourself," the woman said.

"Let me go!" The girl began to scream, and the woman saw her son clutching his ears with a frightened look.

"Let me go!" The girl's voice reached a fever pitch, and her son buried himself under the blanket.

The woman approached the girl, grabbed a roll of duct tape, tore off a piece, and pressed it over her mouth. The girl squirmed like an eel, shaking her head. The woman seized her chin, gripping it firmly between her thumb and forefinger, and glared at her menacingly.

"SHUT — YOUR — MOUTH!" she hissed and pushed her back onto the bed.

She wiped a strand of spit from her face and turned to her   son.

"Stay where you are!" she ordered.

The woman left the room, retrieved an old rope from the adjacent basement storage, and returned to the two of them.

The girl stared into the cold eyes of the woman, unable to move even a finger. The gaze hypnotised her, filling her with panic. Her bladder emptied, soaking her pajama bottoms in seconds. Helplessly, she watched as the woman bound her legs together, rendering her immobile. Then the woman approached the man's bed, caressing his bloated cheek with her palm, which seemed like a doll's hand against his swollen face. He lifted his head, nuzzling into her hand. She kissed his forehead and left the room without sparing her another glance.

The moment the door closed behind her, the man threw off the blanket, crawled out of bed, and approached the young girl. Instinctively, she tried to recoil, only to be held back by the chains. She wanted to scream, but the duct tape silenced her. As he stepped closer into the candlelight, she recoiled in horror at the contours of his face. Again, she tried to move away from him, but it was futile. With a faint smile, he reached out and tore the tape from her mouth. "HELP! HELP!" she screamed.

The man recoiled, startled, and stared at her indecisively for a moment before grabbing a pair of scissors and moving toward her head. "What are you going to do with that? Leave me alone...! HELP!" she cried. She tried to kick at him, but the rope prevented any defense.

The man placed one hand on her head and pressed her into the pillow with the other.

"Shhh... shhh! Nothing will happen to you," he whispered.

She felt the immense pressure of his hands, as if her head were caught in a vice. Powerlessly, she watched as he brought the scissors to her hair, cutting off a lock and twirling it between his fingers. Closing his eyes, he sniffed the strands, letting out a short grunt while rocking his head back and forth. After a while, he placed the scissors in a drawer and carefully stored the lock of hair in a wooden box on the nightstand. Then he returned to his bed, lay down, and pulled the blanket over his shoulders. Within minutes, he was asleep.

Paralyzed, she had watched the entire process, and now, as he left her alone, she realised she was trembling all over, as if she had been lying naked in the cold for hours. The blanket had slipped off her legs, and it took what felt like an eternity to pull it back over her body. Exhausted, she sank onto the pillow, sobbing as she stared up at the stone ceiling. With every passing minute, she prayed to wake up from this nightmare. But the minutes dragged on endlessly, accompanied by the deep snoring and occasional grunting of her captor. Disgusted, she looked at his greasy hair and the hairy feet sticking out from under the blanket.

A thousand questions raced through her mind: *Why was there a man living in the basement of the boarding school? Was she even still in the school? Or was this the basement of another building? Why was she here? What did she have to do with all this? Was she really his mother?*

She considered screaming for help again. The walls of the room looked so massive that no sound would likely escape. Besides, she didn't want to wake the monster.

Despair overwhelmed her, and she began to cry.

Chapter 16

My first night at *Fog Castle* wasn't exactly filled with deep, restful sleep. I tossed and turned, feeling alternately cold and hot, and after a while, I started worrying that I might be coming down with the flu.

The clock read just past midnight, and I felt as if I had been in bed for at least ten hours. Frustrated, I threw back the blanket and went to the window. The night was dark—darker than I was used to in the city. The moon was hidden behind clouds, and I couldn't even see the sea. I opened a windowpane, inhaled the cold sea air, and thought about sleepless nights with the children. Those nights were so far behind me that I had forgotten how they felt. I tried to figure out where the time had gone—where all the years had passed by, leaving me with only memories. The daily routine and work had made time fly by, and if you didn't consciously live every day, you suddenly found yourself years later, the elapsed time feeling like a dream you desperately tried to recall.

At that moment, I heard a dull thud and wasn't sure where the noise had come from. It had sounded as if it were out in the hallway. I went into the living room and listened, holding my breath, but aside from the hum of the refrigerator, I heard nothing. I quietly opened the apartment door, stuck my head through the gap, and looked down the hallway. The wall lights were dimmed, making the lighting poor, but I couldn't see anyone. As I moved to close the door, another noise reached my ears. This time, it sounded like shuffling footsteps.

I stepped into the hallway, my heart pounding, and listened. A faint, almost imperceptible snuffling sound echoed through the halls. It seemed to be moving away from me, but then it grew louder, accompanied by a rasping noise. Like a blade slicing through my spine, a shiver ran down my back. Barefoot, I crept toward the staircase and peered over the railing. A faint whistling sound, like someone breathing through a blocked nose, drifted upward. I descended a few steps to the next landing but still saw no one, even though the strange noise continued. I went down to the second floor, scanning the hallway in both directions, but it too was empty. The sound grew fainter, as if it were retreating. A peculiar smell lingered in the air, stale and reminiscent of rancid grease. I moved forward and eventually reached the deserted entrance hall. There, I stopped and looked around. The light was dim here as well, and shadows lurked everywhere. The entire scene reminded me of a horror movie in which I played the lead role.

After taking another careful look around, I had to admit to myself that I was starting to let my imagination get the better of me. After all, I was in a house full of people, one or two of whom, like me, probably had trouble sleeping and wandered the halls as a result.

I was about to turn back when a figure emerged from one of the shadows. A jolt of adrenaline shot through my body, and I froze. The figure stepped into the light, revealing a slightly stout, heavyset woman in a gray nightgown. Her fuzzy slippers made a shuffling sound on the floor. Her hair was tied in a messy bun at the back of her head, and dark circles framed her eyes, making her look like she hadn't slept in a week.

"Can't sleep?" she asked as she dipped a teabag into a mug.

"You could say that," I replied. "And you?"

"Pfft!" she scoffed. "I could sleep, but I had to prepare something for tomorrow's lunch. I'm the cook here. Name's Mathilde! And you are?"

"Sondre. I'm new here."

"Ahh! I've heard about you. First night?"

"Indeed!"

"Well, I hope for your sake that not every night is sleepless. Otherwise, you'll have rings under your eyes like mine in no time."

I wasn't sure how to respond, so I simply gave her a polite smile.

"I'm heading back to my room," she muttered, taking a sip from her mug. "You should do the same before the ghosts come out."

"The ghosts?" I asked.

"Every castle has its hauntings. But if you get scared, room 304—that's mine." She winked at me before disappearing up the stairs to the upper floors.

Surprised by her straightforwardness, I stood there for a few seconds, wondering if she had meant what I thought she had.

Shaking my head, I left the entrance hall and headed back upstairs. When I reached the second floor, I noticed movement at the edge of my vision. A female figure stood outside one of the students' rooms, staring at me.

"No one's sleeping tonight, it seems!" I said to her.

The figure stepped into the light and approached me. As she drew closer, I recognised her as the young woman who had watched me from one of the upper windows during my first visit. She wore black pajamas and slippers embroidered with skulls. She looked like she had just rolled out of bed; her hair resembled a bird's nest struck by lightning.

"Hello!" I whispered.

She returned my greeting with a slight nod. Two ring piercings adorned her lips, another was in her right nostril, and she had one in each ear. Her face had a soft, vulnerable look that made the piercings seem out of place.

"Shouldn't you be asleep?" Her voice didn't match her appearance, much like the piercings—it was raspy and hoarse, although that might have been due to the late hour.

"I could ask you the same thing," I replied. "You've been watching me for the second time now."

"Touché!" She cleared her throat. "You're the new teacher, right?"

I nodded. "That's me. Sondre."

"Lilly." She extended her hand.

"Nice to meet you, Lilly."

"What brings you out of bed at this hour?" she asked.

"I heard a strange noise, so I got up to check it out. I thought it was right outside my door."

Lilly's expression changed almost imperceptibly — enough to make me suspect that she was wandering the halls for the same reason.

"And? Did you figure out what it was?"

"Probably just Mathilde," I shrugged. "She said she had work in the kitchen. We chatted briefly before she went back to her room."

Lilly remained silent for a moment, chewing on one of her piercings. "That's all?" She gave me a penetrating look, clearly unsatisfied with my answer for reasons unknown to me.

"Well, there was also a loud thud, like someone slamming a door or dropping something. But in a house this size, that's not unusual, even in the middle of the night."

Lilly raised her eyebrows. "Nothing surprises me in this house anymore."

"What do you mean?"

"Oh, just that. I've been here a while, and strange noises are as much a part of this house as snow is to winter. You get used to it."

"If it's not the noises keeping you up, then what is?" I asked.

She shrugged briefly and flashed a mischievous smile. "I just couldn't sleep, I guess. The gears up here sometimes work overtime, whether you want them to or not."

I should have returned to my apartment, but since I couldn't sleep anyway, I decided to continue talking with Lilly. There was something intriguing about her—something eccentric, yet also secretive and guarded—that made you wonder what was going on in her mind. She seemed to be around Jørn's age, and I imagined life here must not be easy for a teenager, especially for those already struggling before arriving. I couldn't help but wonder what Lilly had done to end up at *Fog Castle*.

"How long have you been at the boarding school?" I asked.

"Two years and four months."

"And? Do you like it?"

Lilly made a hissing sound. "Like it? Well, it's not like I couldn't imagine something better, but I didn't have a choice. It's not as bad as I first thought, though."

"Did you adjust to the new situation quickly?"

"More or less. Once you're here, you have to make the best of it. Otherwise, you sink like a shipwreck."

"Good attitude. I should adopt that mindset myself."

She frowned at me. "You mean you're not here willingly?"

"Of course, I am. But it wasn't an easy decision. It's quite different from my previous job."

"I can imagine. Well, some people here will certainly make things difficult for you. There are quite a few oddballs, but you'll find that out soon enough. Where did you teach before?"

"At a secondary school in Tromsø."

"And now you've chosen to teach in this godforsaken bay instead of in the city, where at least there's something to do?"

I laughed. "I'm not eighteen anymore. Clubbing is a thing of the past."

"How boring!" she said, shaking her head.

"Wait until you're my age. Quiet nights in front of the TV become much more appealing than wild nights out."

"That's why I'm enjoying my youth while I can. The problem is, there's no fun to be had here, far away from all the hotspots."

"You're still young. You've got plenty of time for fun."

She pulled a face. "I hope so. I'm not getting any younger."

A brief silence followed. Somewhere nearby, a cough echoed, then it was quiet again.

"You've chosen quite an unusual place to work," Lilly said eventually.

"Unusual? How so?"

"I've seen several teachers come and go. I doubt working as a teacher at this institution brings much happiness."

"It's certainly a challenge, and I was aware of that from the start. But nothing ventured, nothing gained."

"Have you heard the stories about this place?" she asked.

I nodded cautiously. "If you mean the suicides, then yes. I don't know many details, though."

Lilly puffed herself up. "The details!?" she said louder than intended. She bit her lip and looked around nervously. "The so-called details no one knows. At least, no one I've met. But among us students, there's talk that those deaths weren't suicides—they were murders!"

I raised my eyebrows and looked at her skeptically.

"Don't look at me like that! I'm convinced there's something to those stories. Sure, a lot of it is probably made up, exaggerated, or outright lies, but somewhere in there, there must be a grain of truth."

"What kind of truth?" I asked, frowning.

"That those students were killed."

"And what makes people think that?"

"I don't know. That's just what people say."

I chuckled. "Rumors are dangerous. It's easy to draw false conclusions."

"Fair enough. But a lot of people here believe there's something to it. According to the stories, none of the girls seemed like they were planning to take their own lives. None of them stood out as particularly troubled. Isn't that a bit strange?"

"Not necessarily. Many suicide victims don't give any indication of their intentions. They don't convey their feelings to friends or family. And yet, they go through with it."

Lilly pulled a face again. "That's exactly what the psychologist tried to convince us of, too."

During my time in law enforcement, I had dealt with suicides often. Family members of the victims frequently claimed they would never have suspected their loved one of such an act. It didn't necessarily mean anything if friends or acquaintances were unaware of someone's dark thoughts. Often, these decisions were made impulsively.

"Sometimes, it's impossible to peer into the depths of a person's soul. It's only logical that their darkest thoughts remain hidden," I explained.

Lilly shook her head slowly, almost in slow motion. "When I first arrived here two and a half years ago, I met a girl on my very first day. Her name was Linnea. She became my roommate. Linnea was such a cheerful person—always positive, friendly, caring, and funny. You know that feeling when you meet someone and instantly feel a connection? That's how it was with us. I couldn't imagine what a girl like her was doing here. One night, when neither of us could sleep, she told me she had lost her father in a car accident a little over a year ago. Since then, she had rebelled against everything and everyone. She wanted to be alone, neglected school, friends, and family, and easily got provoked. Eventually, she got into a fight at school and broke another girl's arm. That was the last straw for her mother, who was overwhelmed with her behavior. The school psychologist referred her here. It took her months to adjust to life here."

Lilly paused, swallowed hard, and cleared her throat before continuing.

"When we became best friends, we often walked along the beach after class, making plans for the future. We talked about our dreams and made a pact not to let anyone or anything take them from us. Linnea dreamed of seeing the world. She wanted to go to America, photograph cacti in the desert, walk across the Golden Gate Bridge, and eat cotton candy on the Santa Monica Pier. She wanted to go to Australia or New Zealand—anywhere as far away as possible. That dream, that thought, was always with her. I believe she would have spent ten more years here if it meant she could do all those things afterward."

Lilly stared into the distance, her voice soft as she continued. "One morning, I woke up and noticed Linnea wasn't in her bed. That was unusual because normally, I had to practically drag her out of bed in the mornings. I'd never met anyone who slept so deeply. Anyway, I started searching the building for her. She wasn't in any of the washrooms, the kitchen, or the classrooms. Not even on the beach where she loved to spend her time. No one knew anything or had seen her. So, I informed the school administration. The next day, the police arrived and began an extensive search. During that time, I was a wreck. I couldn't stop crying and spent all my time in bed. Sigrid tried to force me to attend classes, but I refused, and eventually, she left me alone. Two days later, we got the news: they had found Linnea at the base of a cliff. Dead."

Lilly wiped a tear from the corner of her eye.

"That's awful," I said.

Lilly's gaze drifted down the hall, her hair falling into her face. "Do you know what the worst part was?" she asked in a whisper. "Nobody believed me when I said Linnea didn't jump off that cliff willingly. I tried to tell them she would never do something like that—never! But no one cared."

"Did the police conduct any further investigations?" I asked.

Lilly pursed her lips. "I don't know. They asked me some questions, but after that, I never heard from them again. Of course, I asked Sigrid about it, but she was tight-lipped. All she told me was the same story she told everyone else: Linnea had psychological problems and probably saw no other way out. She also claimed she needed to respect Linnea's privacy and couldn't discuss her personality with anyone."

"Strange," I said. "Assuming she didn't take her own life—who do you think might have been responsible?"

Lilly shrugged, her expression a mix of frustration and sadness. "I don't know. I really don't. But something isn't right here—it wasn't then, and it still isn't. I'm sure of it."

"That does sound extraordinary," I admitted, my instincts as a former policeman stirring. Should I tell her about my law enforcement background? Probably not. The fewer people who knew about my past, the better. If I wanted to investigate these rumors further, anonymity might work in my favour.

Lilly suddenly waved her hands in front of my face. "Are you still with me?"

"Yes, sorry. I was just lost in thought."

She nodded and stifled a yawn. "I should head to bed now." Turning to leave, she added, "And you could use some sleep too."

"Quite right."

"See you around then."

I nodded in farewell, watching her disappear into her room before heading back to my apartment. Her story echoed in my mind, lingering long after I'd climbed into bed. It followed me into the restless sleep that finally came, some two hours later.

Chapter 17

After his mother had gone back upstairs, he had slept for a while and was now rested enough to give his princess his full attention. He threw back the covers, yawned loudly, scratched his belly, and took a sip of tea from the cup his mother had left on his nightstand. A growing warmth filled him as he gazed at his princess, but he noticed that she wasn't dressed like royalty.

That wouldn't do. She had to be dressed like a princess.

The problem was, he no longer had the dress—not for some time now. It had disappeared that night along with the princess and all her belongings. The heat from that night surged back into his mind—the searing throat, the burning skin. He could hear the roaring and crackling of the fire, and right in the midst of it all—his princess.

He hated that image so much. It refused to leave him. And whenever it surfaced, he would squeeze his eyelids shut as tightly as he could, until it hurt. When he opened them again, the image was gone. But he knew it wouldn't last long. The pictures always came back, like waves on the shore. There was nothing he could do about it. He was at their mercy, day and night, awake or dreaming. Sometimes, though, he felt that he needed those images — that he could only continue living because of them. And when they faded, he mourned their absence and wished them back.

Now, the pictures were gone, and he got up. He approached the sleeping girl on the bed beside him and looked her over, head to toe.

She felt the suffocation, the dizziness, and the paralyzing fear. She saw the man's face just inches from hers, felt his hot breath and the prickly stubble on her skin. She saw him trace her body's contours with his nose, snorting like a beast in twilight.

"Get away from me, get away, you monster!" she shouted in desperation, trying to break free. But she couldn't move her arms or legs. It was as if she were suspended, with no sense of up or down. All she could do was scream. She opened her mouth, tightened her abdominal muscles, and screamed louder than she ever had in her life.

But nothing happened.

No sound came from her throat. She opened her mouth again, and once more, her throat felt constricted. She couldn't breathe. The pressure in her chest grew stronger, dizziness and nausea overwhelming her.

At that moment, she opened her eyes, not knowing where she was. The last images from her nightmare dissolved like morning mist. The surroundings, blurry at first, gradually came into focus. She saw a door, a wardrobe, two chairs. Her right eye began to burn and water up. She wanted to rub it, but as she raised her hand, she felt a strange pressure on her wrist and heard a loud metallic clink. She turned her head and saw a figure standing a short distance from her bed.

The figure just stood there, staring at her. Unsure if she was still dreaming, she looked into its two jet-black eyes as they came closer. Instinctively, she recoiled and tried to scream, but the figure placed a rough hand over her mouth. A muffled cry escaped through the thick fingers, and she saw the figure put a finger to its lips. A wave of nausea hit her, and she feared she might vomit. She had no air left in her lungs, and her scream died out. She noticed the smile on the man's face and had the strange feeling she had seen that terrible visage before. But it was like the memory of a dream, one you strain to retrieve from the depths of your mind.

Suddenly, he reached out for her, and the stench of his hands hit her nose. She suppressed a gag reflex, and at the same time, she saw him pull out a white cloth. He pressed it against her nose and mouth. A sickly-sweet scent spread around her, and as she tried to pull away from his grip, the dim light in the room faded to black.

Chapter 18

After the short night, I woke up the next morning with a mild headache, staring half-deliriously at the ceiling. My thoughts had been spinning around Lilly's story about the suicides. Every few minutes, my eyes darted to the clock, and afterward, I cursed myself for letting such thoughts consume me in the middle of the night. But self-reproach didn't help—the troubling images in my mind came and went as they pleased.

I had breakfast standing up—a piece of toast with strawberry jam, a slice of cheese, and a cup of coffee. Once I washed down the last bite with coffee, I walked to the window and lit a cigarette. I inhaled deeply, held the smoke for a few seconds, then released a bluish haze into the icy morning air. The inner tension faded, and the winter chill did the rest.

I thought about the day ahead. It would bring many new challenges, especially when it came to the students' behaviour. Jori had warned me that some students had issues with authority and prided themselves on making life difficult for the teachers.

A few weeks ago, he had sent me a folder with behavioural guidelines. It outlined potential situations I might face and how best to handle them. Naturally, I was sceptical that a few pages could prepare me adequately for this job. Jori had reassured me, explaining that I would receive further in-depth training. I found that odd, but apparently, that was how things worked at this boarding school.

When this training would begin, however, he hadn't said.

My thoughts wandered to Jørn. Since his early childhood, I had always hoped he wouldn't stray off course. Whenever I saw teenagers in the city with red, green, or purple hair, smoking and exuding an air of discord with life, a knot would form in my stomach. So far, I had been lucky—Jørn was more interested in sports than parties or drugs. But he was still young, and interests could change overnight. The fact that I didn't have him around me all the time only amplified my fears. I rarely knew where he was, what he was doing, or what he planned to do. This sense of exclusion drove me half-mad.

A knock at the door pulled me out of my thoughts. I stubbed out the cigarette, closed the window, and walked to the door. It was Jori.

"Already awake, I see?"

What a stupid remark—classes were about to start!

"Indeed. I'm about to head out."

He shook his head. "Not just yet. Sigrid has called an emergency meeting. In ten minutes."

"But classes are starting soon," I replied, unsure.

"Don't worry, it's all arranged. If you'll follow me, please."

I stepped into the hallway and followed him downstairs. Some students were loitering in the corridors, whispering or casting meaningful glances our way. A heavy atmosphere hung over the house, as if everyone knew what was going on—except me.

Jori stopped at an open door and gestured for me to enter. Some of the teachers were already seated and scrutinized me from head to toe. A few nodded or offered brief smiles, but little was said.

I sat in one of the armchairs and took in my surroundings, amazed. The room looked more like a cozy living room than a staff lounge. There were three sofa sets and several armchairs. Each sofa had a coffee table and a floor lamp. A small kitchenette held a fridge, a coffee machine, baskets of shiny apples, and bowls of cookies. The floor was covered with a thick carpet, making it feel like walking on clouds. The walls were adorned with intricate art pieces, and every window had a lamp, making the room feel even more inviting. It felt like sitting in a royal chamber.

I was about to make a remark to the teacher next to me when Sigrid entered the room briskly, stopping in the centre. She always gave the impression of being perpetually charged with electricity.

Clasping her hands, she surveyed the room. "Good morning, everyone," she began, clearing her throat. "I hope you all had a restful night and are ready for the challenges of the day."

If only you knew…!

"First, I apologise for calling this early meeting. But there's a good—no, a concerning—reason for it." She paused theatrically, letting her words sink in. The room responded with a few grunts and indistinct noises.

"This morning, Mona informed me that her roommate was neither in their room nor anywhere else to be found. Usually, she's up before Mona, but today the bed was empty. Mona couldn't find her in the bathrooms or the dining hall either."

"Which student are we talking about?" Jori asked, his toothpick bobbing as he spoke.

"Tiril," Sigrid replied.

I froze.

"Have the police been contacted?" Jori pressed.

Sigrid shook her head. "No, it's too early for that. I'll wait until tomorrow morning. It's entirely possible that Tiril just ran off and will return. As you all know, this isn't uncommon."

As a former police officer, several questions came to mind. Was Tiril missing in her pajamas, or had she dressed warmly? Had her room been searched for clues? Did she have any known issues that might explain her disappearance? Had she argued with anyone recently?

The questions burned on my tongue, but I hesitated to speak up as the newcomer. "Do we know if Tiril disappeared in her pajamas?" I heard myself ask.

So much for restraint!

Sigrid's sharp gaze shot in my direction, her olive-green eyes seeming to pierce straight through me. She stared for a few seconds, and I regretted asking.

"We don't know," she finally said. "I'll follow up with Mona after this meeting to see if she noticed anything unusual during the night."

Again, my police instincts flared, and I wanted to offer my help. But none of the other teachers, except Jori, knew about my previous career, and they might find it odd if the new guy started volunteering to assist the boss on day one. It would seem disingenuous. So I bit my tongue and nodded vaguely.

Sigrid clapped her hands theatrically. "All right, ladies and gentlemen, that's all for now. I'll keep you updated." With that, she strode out of the room, leaving me slightly bewildered. My colleagues immediately began chatting animatedly.

"She probably just ran off!"

"She wouldn't be the first!"

"About time, really!"

These were some of the comments I overheard.

Jori got up from his chair, approached me, and said, "Let's get you to your class."

He led the way, and I followed. He didn't seem inclined to discuss Tiril's disappearance. My curiosity, however, wouldn't let it go. "Does this happen often?" I asked, catching up on him.

"What happens often?"

Either he was feigning ignorance or genuinely didn't know what I meant. "Students going missing?"

He shrugged. "It happens. Some of the kids here have personal issues. That can lead to this kind of thing."

"Shouldn't we be looking for her?" I pressed.

He shook his head. "Others are handling it. Our job is to keep things running smoothly." He winked—a gesture that seemed entirely out of place for him or the situation.

"What others?"

He gave me an exasperated look. "Kjell and Sander. Sander was Tiril's main teacher, and Kjell is the psychologist."

"You know I used to be a police officer. I could help."

"I know, but your priority now is your class. They're waiting for you. Here we are. Have a good first day. If you need anything, I'm two rooms down."

He shook my hand and disappeared into his classroom. I watched him go, shaking my head.

"Have they found Tiril yet?" one of the students called out as I entered the room.

I shut the door behind me. After addressing the student's curiosity, I began the lesson. I had spent the past few days preparing the material thoroughly. It was similar to my previous school, but the pace here was noticeably slower. Disruptions were more frequent, and as Jori had warned me, some students' intellectual levels meant progress was limited.

The rest of the day left me little time to dwell on Tiril's disappearance. I resolved to let my thoughts unravel later that evening.

Chapter 19

Mikkel Hansen stood before the basement door on the ground floor, rummaging through his pockets for a key. After ensuring no one was nearby, he unlocked the door and disappeared into the darkness. He didn't need light on the stairs—he knew the way by heart.

The sound of dripping water echoed faintly in the stillness of the basement. He stopped before an unassuming niche in the wall, slipped his right hand into a small opening, and pulled a lever. A barely audible click followed, and moments later, the stone wall slid aside as if moved by an invisible hand. Mikkel entered the small, square chamber beyond and opened another door.

Dim light illuminated the vaulted cellar ahead, and he could hear loud snoring accompanied by faint whimpering. The air reeked of rancid grease and unwashed bodies. His eyes fell on a sleeping man, sprawled on the floor nearby. Beside him lay a young woman, her hands and feet bound. She, too, appeared to be asleep, though soft, intermittent whimpers escaped her lips.

Mikkel approached her bed, studying the helpless figure closely. After a moment, he reached out and gently stroked her cool cheeks. She flinched slightly but did not wake. Carefully, he examined the leather cuffs securing her wrists, checking her skin for signs of injury but finding none. Satisfied, he placed her hand back on the bed, cast a glance at the sleeping man, and slipped out of the room as silently as he had entered.

When he returned to the basement door upstairs, he heard voices. Opening the door slightly, he saw several students loitering in the entrance hall. Seeing no sign that they would leave anytime soon, he quietly shut the door and descended back into the basement. He passed through a long corridor and eventually emerged outside the building. Snow was falling, blanketing the bay in a white shroud.

Thoughtfully, he watched the waves lapping at the nearby shore. His mind lingered on the girl in the basement—the torment she must be enduring, the uncertainty haunting her every waking moment. There wasn't much he could do, aside from waiting and hoping that everything would be resolved soon.

Unlike before, he was optimistic that the end was near, that the suffering would finally end and the uncertainty would dissipate for good. For years, he had yearned for this moment, pursued it relentlessly. It had robbed him of peace, kept him awake at night. Now, all that remained was patience.

Chapter 20

Tiril hadn't shown up by evening, which, to me, was not a good sign. After eating dinner in front of the television, I sat down at my desk and turned on the internet. All day, I had been wondering if there might be more information to uncover about this mysterious boarding school.

After twenty minutes, I had to admit that this place was more enigmatic than anything I had ever encountered. I couldn't even find reports about the suicides. The only way I might get relevant information was through the police— or rather, my former colleagues. The problem was, I had no idea who had led the investigations back then.

After pondering a phone call for five minutes, I picked up my mobile and dialed the number of my friend Roald.

When he answered, I instantly recognized his deep, nasal voice.

"Hey, Sondre! What a surprise. How's it going, old friend? Still tormenting students?" He laughed, followed by a fit of coughing.

"Something like that. But I'm no longer in Tromsø."

"Is that so? Where are you now?"

"Near Tromvik."

"The countryside, eh? Fancy that!" He laughed again, punctuated by another cough.

"I work at *Fog Castle*."

There was silence on the other end of the line. I was about to ask if he was still there when he spoke again. "*Fog Castle*? How on earth did you end up working there?"

"Long story," I replied curtly, not wanting to go into the details. "I need some information from you. Could you tell me who used to investigate in this area?"

Another pause, then Roald cleared his throat. "Uh… let me think. That would've been Jon Martin. Want his number?"

"Yes, please."

After ten more minutes of chatting, I hung up and stared at Jon Martin's number. Should I really call him? He wouldn't be able to tell me much — legally speaking — even if he knew all the details and the cases had long been closed.

Still, it was worth a shot. I dialed his number, and on the third ring, he picked up. He recognised me immediately, which surprised me since we hadn't worked together often.

"So, how's the new life as a teacher?" he asked.

"A bit dull, I must admit."

"I can imagine. Once a cop, always a cop, eh?"

"Exactly!"

"What can I do for you, Sondre?"

"Well, here's the thing: I'm now working at *Fog Castle*."

I waited for his reaction, which didn't come immediately.

"*Fog Castle*?" he finally said, almost whispering.

"That's right."

"My God. I know that place all too well." He exhaled audibly.

"I thought you might. That's why I'm calling. Roald mentioned that you investigated the suicides there?"

"Yes, I did," he replied seriously. "I was there many times. It involved two different girls, both under eighteen. Awful business."

"Did you notice anything unusual during your investigation?"

"Unusual? How do you mean?"

"Did you have any reason to doubt the suicide theory?"

It took a moment before Jon Martin responded. "Well, at the start of the investigation, we couldn't rule out foul play, of course. We questioned a lot of people, but nothing came of it. Those who didn't sleep alone had alibis for the time of death. As for the others—well, we couldn't prove anything against them, nor verify their alibis. But that didn't automatically make them suspects. We also found no plausible motives to suggest a crime."

"So, you assumed it was suicide?"

"As I said, not at first. But after all the fruitless interviews, it was the most likely explanation. If someone had wanted to kill those girls, they'd have weighted their bodies so they wouldn't surface. But that wasn't the case."

"I see. Did the coroner find anything unusual about the bodies?"

"Sondre, you know I shouldn't be sharing this information with you."

"I know, I know. But could you make an exception? The cases are closed, after all."

He sighed heavily. "You'd better keep this to yourself—understand?"

"Of course, you can count on me."

"The bodies were examined, naturally. Since we found them in the water near that steep cliff, the cause of death was likely the impact with the water. There was no fluid in their lungs, meaning they weren't breathing when they entered the water. The issue was the low temperature—three to four degrees Celsius. That made the examinations more complicated. We couldn't definitively determine the time of death."

"Was it possible to rule out foul play—pushing, for instance?"

"No, we couldn't. But we didn't find any evidence of it either."

"I understand. What about the victims' friends? Were they surprised by the suicides?"

"Yes, especially in the second case. The first victim didn't have friends at the school—she was a loner, reportedly quite peculiar. The second victim's friends, as you said, were shocked by her apparent suicide. But you know how it is with such cases; victims rarely announce their intentions. The school's administration assured us that some students had grappled with suicidal thoughts even before enrolling, so the incidents weren't entirely unexpected."

I mulled over Jon Martin's words. It wasn't surprising that the police had concluded these were suicides; much pointed in that direction. If the school administration had backed their claims with psychological reports, there wouldn't be much to add.

"Sondre? Are you still there?"

"Yes, sorry. I was just thinking."

"Ah. Has there been another incident?"

I hesitated, unsure if I should tell him about Tiril. Sigrid wouldn't be pleased if I informed the police prematurely. But I'd look foolish if Jon Martin found out about her disappearance tomorrow. "A student disappeared last night. Sigrid thinks she's probably just run away. She plans to notify the police soon. Please don't act on this yet. If she hasn't contacted you by noon tomorrow, you could call her and say you got an anonymous tip."

"That does sound worrying," he said with a sigh.

"I know, but I shouldn't have told you."

"Then we're even," he said, laughing.

"Touché!" I chuckled too.

After hanging up, I went to the window. Outside, it was now pitch dark. A silver crescent moon hung on the horizon, soon to vanish.

I thought about Tiril, and unease washed over me. Had she suffered the same fate as the other girls? Or had she harmed herself?

I could still picture her, guiding me through the building. At no point did she seem depressed or withdrawn. Then again, I knew how easy it was for some to put on a façade to avoid questions or scrutiny.

I sighed, returned to the couch, and picked up my book.

Chapter 21

The next morning, around nine o'clock, the police showed up at Fog Castle. I was in the copy room and watched as two police cars pulled up and four officers got out. They were greeted outside the building by Sigrid and Jori. I recognized one of the officers. His name was Kristen. We had started working in the police force on the same day, though we had never been on patrol together. He was a nice guy, had two children who went to the same school as Jørn. I would have liked to talk to him, but since my class was about to commence, I had no opportunity.

Back in the classroom, I could barely focus on the lesson. My mind was racing, trying to figure out a way to slip away for a moment to talk to Kristen. Sure, it would have been easy to make up some excuse for the students. But given my very short tenure at the boarding school so far, I didn't want to cause trouble within my first days. So, I clenched my teeth and continued teaching until the lunch break.

At a quarter to twelve, I locked the classroom and headed straight to the ground floor. The officers were nowhere to be seen. Looking out the window, I spotted their patrol car still parked outside, meaning they were still on the premises. I went to the dining hall and searched for uniforms. Finally, in the farthest corner, I spotted one of the officers talking to Sigrid. But it wasn't Kristen.

I returned to the lounge, stood by a window, and looked out at the bay. On the beach, I spotted three officers standing close together, seemingly deep in discussion. I turned on my heel and headed outside. From a distance, I immediately recognized Kristen. He was lean, had medium-length blond hair, and wore a beard. I jogged toward them, slightly out of breath by the time I reached them. All three officers looked at me with questioning expressions.

"Good day, everyone," I panted. "My name is Sondre Iversen, I'm a teacher at the boarding school."

They returned my greeting.

"Sondre?" Kristen stepped forward and extended his hand.

He hadn't aged a day—not something I could say about myself. Only a few gray hairs had crept into his beard.

"I can't believe it. You? Here? I thought you were working in the city?"

I shook his hand. "I was, up until a few weeks ago. I just needed a change."

Kristen raised his eyebrows. "You had a hand injury, right?"

I held out my left hand. "That's right. A complicated fracture and joint stiffening." I shrugged. "Too serious for police duty."

Kristen nodded. "I'm sorry to hear that."

"It's okay, thanks. Now I'm giving teaching a shot," I said, nodding toward Fog Castle.

"You've got your hands full with some... let's say, special people here."

"That's for sure."

He gestured toward his colleagues. "Let me introduce you: Tune and Viggo."

I shook both officers' hands. "Can I ask you something?"

"Of course, go ahead," Kristen replied.

"You're surely aware that this isn't the first case like this, right?"

The three exchanged a brief glance.

"We're aware," Kristen said.

"A few days ago, a student told me some interesting stories about the boarding school. Lilly—that's the student's name—told me that her former roommate also disappeared and was later found dead. The victim was Linnea. She had been Lilly's best friend, and Lilly said that Linnea had never shown any signs of suicidal thoughts. They had even talked about what they wanted to do after boarding school."

Kristen raised his eyebrows. "That's not unusual. Many suicide victims don't reveal their intentions to family or friends. Many can't explain it, and yet it happens. And the teenagers here aren't exactly clean slates."

"That's true. Still, I think the suicide theory is a little too convenient."

Kristen tilted his head slightly. "I can assure you, we're doing everything in our power to shed light on this matter."

I nodded. "Of course, I'm sorry. I'm not trying to accuse you of anything or tell you how to do your job. It just seems strange that things like this keep happening here."

"We think so too. But even in the current case, the school administration told us this morning that Tiril had psychological problems. Suicide isn't out of the question."

"I met Tiril on my first visit here. She seemed pretty composed to me."

"Which doesn't mean anything," Kristen countered.

"I know. Still, I have a bad feeling about this."

Viggo placed a hand on my shoulder. "The search for Tiril is in full swing. The coast guard has been alerted. A helicopter and a search dog team are also on their way. We'll find her. Don't worry."

"Let's hope so!" I said, glancing back at the house. Someone was standing by the dining hall window, looking in our direction.

"Well, we have to get going," Viggo said, shaking my hand, as did Tune.

Kristen patted my shoulder. "Take care, Sondre! We're doing our best."

I nodded. "I know you are."

He gave me a friendly slap on the upper arm and followed his colleagues. I watched them for a while as they walked along the beach and eventually disappeared into the northern cliffs.

Deep in thought, I returned to the house.

***

With a wary gaze and an uneasy feeling in her stomach, she watched Sondre run toward the beach. Was he heading for the police officers? What did he want from them?

She saw him stop by the officers and start a conversation. What on earth were they talking about? Who did he think he was, meddling in the investigation? She had already seen him sneaking around the house last night. Either he hadn't been able to sleep, or he was up to something.

The fact that he was sticking his nose into matters that didn't concern him greatly displeased her. She would keep an eye on him, and if he became a threat, she would have to take care of the problem.

Chapter 22

Tiril had been lying awake for hours in her prisoner's bed, listening to the sounds of her tormentor while pondering ways to free herself from this dire situation. She wasn't even sure if she was still in Mist House. She couldn't tell if she had been lying here since yesterday or for an entire week. She had lost all sense of time.

Desperately, she looked around the room. The only light came from the burning candle on the nightstand. Next to it lay the sleeping monster. Disgusted, she turned away from him and examined the leather cuffs on her wrists. She tugged at them, quickly realizing that while they weren't excessively tight, they were secure enough to make escape impossible. She bit her lip, noticing how chapped they were. She was thirsty—terribly thirsty. She longed for water, for milk, for anything.

Her eyes fell on a full water bottle beneath the man's bed. She saw bubbles rising inside, and her mouth instantly felt even drier. She was so close to the lifesaving liquid, yet she might as well have been miles away from it.

Everything felt like a nightmare. If only she could wake up in her bed, in her room. Far away from this dreadful place and this eerie figure. How had she even ended up here? She couldn't remember. She only knew that she had gone to bed and, half-asleep, had heard her roommate doing the same. After that, her memories were as empty as the bookshelves of an abandoned library.

She felt her throat tighten, and she began to cry — quietly, so the monster wouldn't wake.

A movement at the edge of her vision made her freeze. The man had turned in his bed and was now facing her. His eyelids were closed, but she could see his eyeballs darting wildly behind them.

What a dreadful creature, she thought.

His skin was like ivory snow under moonlight. His lips were cracked and crusted, his hair unwashed and greasy. He had pulled the blanket up over his right ear, but in the dim candlelight, she could make out a scar running up to his forehead. It looked old, mostly healed, yet on his pale skin, it stood out like a fresh scalpel wound.

***

Helpless and desperate, he stared at the inferno unfolding before his eyes. Heat and smoke pressed against him, and sounds he had never heard before filled him with panic. He was too young to know what to do, too young to be a hero, too young to die.

Holding his arms up to shield his face, he entered his sister's room. The air was so hot he feared it would burn his lungs. The smoke thickened, making it harder to breathe. Suddenly, a deafening bang rang out, and the next moment, part of the ceiling collapsed, burying him in a shower of sparks. He frantically brushed his hair, trying to extinguish the embers. When he looked up again, he saw that a beam had crashed onto his sister's bed, trapping her. The entire bed was a chaotic mess of fallen debris, ash, fire, blankets—and in the middle of it lay his sister. He saw her blackened skin, the blisters on her legs.

Gasping for breath, he opened his eyes. His heart pounded in his chest, his torso drenched in sweat. It took nearly two minutes for him to recognize his surroundings and shake off the last remnants of the dream. He sat up, rubbed his eyes and face. As he moved to stand, he noticed the girl in the opposite bed.

***

She felt his gaze on her, his dark eyes fixating on her like a wolf locking onto its prey. A wave of nausea surged through her, her hands grew clammy, and she barely managed to stop herself from wetting herself again.

She saw him suddenly throw back the blanket, stand up, and approach her. She recoiled in fear. He was still wearing his thick corduroy pants and a wool sweater. Both reeked of sweat and damp socks. Her nausea worsened, and she fought back the urge to gag.

When he stood beside her, towering over her like a polar bear, he fished a key from his pocket, unlocked both cuffs, and put the key back. Then, he retrieved a strip of tape from the nightstand and pressed it over her mouth. She writhed like a snake, but it was useless. She felt his hand stroke her hair, as if she were a cat. Then, he untied the rope around her legs, and warmth flooded into her limbs. She moved her feet once, twice—then she lashed out with her right leg. Her foot struck his upper arm, but he didn't even seem to notice. He only let out a grunt, then picked her up and carried her toward the door.

Tiril began to struggle, hitting him with her fists, but it had no effect. He only tightened his grip until she was nearly immobilized.

He stopped in front of a wall, pulled a lever, and the wall slid aside. A dimly lit underground corridor appeared. It smelled of dampness and dust. After a few meters, he stopped again and worked on another door. With a creaking sound, it swung open, and a blast of freezing air rushed into the corridor. They stepped outside. A bright crescent moon adorned the otherwise cloudless sky.

Tiril's gaze swept over the misty bay. She noticed the mountain slopes on either side and felt a fleeting sense of relief—she was still near the boarding school. Even though the cold burned her skin like a hot iron, she savored the fresh air for a moment. She felt the stench of the basement leave her lungs, easing her nausea.

The man locked the door and trudged toward the beach. Over his shoulder, Tiril looked back at Mist House, silently pleading with the few, distant lights behind its windows.

Even without the tape, she wouldn't have been able to scream—her mouth was so dry her tongue stuck to the roof. She began to tremble, but the man didn't seem to notice. He walked on, eyes fixed straight ahead, through the deep snow toward the beach. Despite the cold, beads of sweat formed on his forehead. His breath whistled through his nose.

They drew closer to the water, and with each step, Tiril's fear grew. She had no idea what he planned to do. Was he going to drown her? Crush her with a rock? Throw her off a cliff? Was this the end?

She didn't want to believe it, but she had no strength to resist. She started sobbing, gasping for air, until she thought she might suffocate.

"Shhh," the man hushed. "Shhh, princess..."

But Tiril kept crying.

After a while, he suddenly stopped. Motionless as a statue, he stared out at the sea. The wind tousled his hair. A tear rolled down his cheek.

Tiril barely dared to move, scanning the surroundings for someone—anyone. But there was no one.

She looked back at the house. Only a single light was still burning in a third-floor window. If only she could scream!

The man turned his head, his tear-filled eyes meeting hers. A weak smile spread across his face. And to her surprise, he suddenly set her down. He still held her wrists tightly. Her bare feet sank into the snow, the cold piercing her skin like needles.

A stiff breeze blew from the sea as she watched him close his eyes for a moment. He took a few deep breaths and let out a short grunt.

His grip loosened slightly.

Tiril realized—this was it. This was her chance to escape this monster. It might be her only one.

Her heart pounded as she watched his relaxed face, almost trance-like.

Her mind raced. In seconds, she planned her escape route, which entrance to take, where to find help.

If she could make it that far.

She kept still for another moment, and when his grip loosened a bit more, she wrenched herself free.

And she ran.

Chapter 23

Tiril's disappearance didn't create much of a stir at the boarding school. At least, that was the feeling I had. The cheerful students remained cheerful, while the more silent and seemingly depressed ones continued to keep to themselves. The faculty also didn't seem to dramatize the situation.

In the evening, I strolled through the hallways, searching for an explanation that seemed to be hiding from me. The prevailing indifference within these walls made me thoughtful and also sad. Of course, I had only been here for a few days, and the disappearance of students apparently wasn't a rare occurrence. Still, I struggled with the attitude of the school administration.

I paused by a window near the staircase and looked outside. I thought of Jørn and the times we used to go on ski tours together or went ice fishing. Those had been wonderful times—a time when I was still a part of his life. Today, it felt as if I had been excluded from the circle of his close friends. As if I had merely been a temporary companion who was no longer needed.

The memories of those times were becoming fainter, and I was afraid that one day they would no longer be retrievable at will, and those precious moments would be lost forever in the abyss of time. Perhaps this was also why I kept recalling those experiences over and over again, no matter how painful they were.

Sighing, I turned away from the window and walked into the entrance hall. There, I noticed a student sitting in one of the lounge chairs, reading a book. It was Lilly!

Our late-night conversation came to mind, and I wondered if I should join her.

"Are you planning to set down roots there?" Lilly suddenly called out, looking at me mischievously.

"Maybe," I replied as I walked over to her. "May I?" I asked, pointing to a chair.

She nodded.

I sat down and examined the cover of her book. *December Park* by Ronald Malfi. "Good book?" I asked, glancing at her from the side.

She shrugged. "Not bad. A bit drawn out, but it has a subtle tension in it."

"Do you read a lot?"

"I try to. But with studying, there isn't much time for it."

I nodded. "Do you get good grades?"

She closed the book and laughed. "If it were up to my parents, then no."

I raised an eyebrow, indicating that her answer wasn't sufficient.

"I'm barely passing in everything, if that's what you want to know."

"That's enough for me, thanks." I leaned back in the chair.

"Before I came to the boarding school," she continued, "I was failing in most subjects. I could never really concentrate on studying, and I simply wasn't interested in the material. That stupid arithmetic and geometry—who needs that stuff anyway?"

"Ask an architect." I made a face as I smiled.

"I will definitely never be an architect."

"What will you be then?"

She shrugged. "I want to do something with children. Maybe a social educator, a kindergarten teacher. Something like that."

"I think that's great," I praised her.

"Let's see if I even make it that far."

I looked at her silently for a while. "Why wouldn't you?"

"Well, as mentioned earlier, I wasn't always the brightest light in the classroom."

"That doesn't mean anything. If you have your goal in mind, you can focus all your energy on it. You'll manage. But it takes will and discipline."

"With you, it sounds so easy. I wish it were."

"Growing up while always keeping the future in mind is a difficult time. It was no different for me. But you'll see that, in time, paths will open up that you wouldn't even dare to dream of right now."

She sighed. "Maybe you're right."

"Can I ask you something?"

She looked at me with a mix of curiosity and boredom. "Do you want to know why I'm here?"

A bit surprised by her accurate guess, I nodded.

She made a face. "Then take a guess."

I scrutinized her and thought about my youthful mischief. It could have been almost anything — ranging from theft to armed robbery to fights. "I'll guess it's a smart mouth?"

She laughed. "Guess again."

"Stolen cars?"

She shook her head again.

I shrugged. "Robbed old ladies?"

"No!" she said, laughing. "Alright, I'll tell you." She placed the book on a table, tucked her legs under her, and cleared her throat. "Two years ago, I often hung out with my friends in a barn near my village. We met there after school. The barn was usually empty. The farmer kept a few horses there now and then. He had chased us off the property several times, but we weren't deterred and kept coming back, especially in the evenings when it was dark outside and he was sitting in the cozy living room with his wife, staring at the TV. One evening, however, the police suddenly showed up and took each of us to the station. We all got a fine, which we could work off with community service. Søren, the oldest of us, didn't want to accept the fine and planned a revenge campaign against the farmer. Sonja and I wanted to dissuade him at first, but we were the only ones in the group against it. Everyone else thought his idea was great, and so we let ourselves be pressured by the group and agreed. A few weeks later, we snuck back onto the property. Søren had brought a gasoline canister. When we arrived in front of the building, Sonja and I refused to enter the barn. Søren and the others didn't care. They left us behind and disappeared inside. Sonja and I considered just leaving. Unfortunately, we didn't do it." She shook her head. "In any case, a few minutes later, our friends burst out of the barn, laughing like hyenas, while behind them the glow of a fire was already visible. Sonja and I knew that there was no turning back now. We ran away as fast as we could, without looking back even once. That night, I didn't sleep a wink. I expected a loud knock on the door at any moment.

The next morning, the police showed up at the school and took us all back. They quashed our pathetic excuses right away, as none of us idiots could provide a plausible alibi, and eventually, our dam broke. They put us in front of the farmer, who, as we later found out, had housed his four Icelandic horses in the barn that evening. Unfortunately, they had been in the back, separated area, and so they were not noticed by Søren and the others."

I stared at her intently. For a moment, I didn't know how to react to her story. Loitering in a barn they weren't supposed to be in wasn't terrible, but the arson was another matter altogether.

Teenage recklessness that had ended tragically.

I knew from my own experience how quickly a prank could backfire. "And then you were sent here?" I asked her after a while.

She nodded. "My parents have a certain reputation in the community. This reputation was, or is, very important to them. They thought I would be best placed here temporarily." She shrugged. "Well, here we are talking about my stupidity."

I leaned back in the chair and crossed my legs. We were silent for almost a minute. A few students walked by us, but they didn't spare us a glance.

"When I was seventeen," I finally said, "my then-friend Sigbjørn and I went on a drinking spree together. Of course, we couldn't get alcohol legally at that age. Sigbjørn's brother was older and had a few beers hidden in his room. We got our hands on those and wandered the streets of Tromsø. At that time, I was living with my parents in the Lunheim district, and on our way home, we found a trailer in a garage entrance. We stored our sixth bottle of beer in the snow, we pulled the trailer out of the driveway and rolled it to the nearby intersection. There, we positioned it and let it rattle down the street. It made a hell of a noise, and we rolled around laughing. However, our laughter quickly faded when the vehicle swiped against a speeding cyclist at the next intersection and catapulted him several meters into the air. The trailer rolled on, narrowly missing a car on Tromsøsund Street, and finally crashed onto the premises of a company. The cyclist lay motionless on the ground. Sigbjørn and I stood at the intersection like mummies, frozen, realizing only after a few minutes what we had done. In an instant, we were as sober as a monk in morning prayer. We then simply ran away, each in a different direction, without looking back, without caring about the injured cyclist."

Lilly looked at me with her mouth agape. "Oh my God!"

I nodded. "Yes, you could say that."

"Did the cyclist die?"

"No, fortunately not. He sustained serious injuries, but he recovered soon after. Sigbjørn and I quietly ended our contact after that incident. We both knew that our friendship would now only be defined by those few seconds of utter stupidity. We could no longer roam freely and carefree. We would be trapped in those last images that bound us. Of course, we still saw each other on the street or at school. But we avoided eye contact, well aware of what was going on in the other's mind. Our action had, of course, made headlines in the local news. The police were in the dark, and to this day, I carry that secret with me."

"And what about Sigbjørn? Aren't you afraid he might suddenly tell someone the story?"

I shook my head. "Sigbjørn died five years later on a mountain tour in Lofoten."

Lilly looked at me with raised eyebrows. "Should this story cheer me up?"

"That was my intention, yes!" I replied with a hint of a smile.

"Do you regret the act?" she wanted to know.

I grimaced. "Of course. Every day. But you know as well as I do that you can't change the past. I've always found comfort in the thought that the victim didn't suffer any lasting damage. The act is long past, but that doesn't change the fact that I still blame myself today."

She nodded. "I know that feeling."

At that moment, Lilly turned her head, and her eyes followed a woman who marched past us and shot Lilly a scathing look. The woman had been introduced to me yesterday as Runa.

"What was that look about?" I asked Lilly.

"Runa is my geometry teacher. She can't stand me. And I don't like her either. But I'm not the only one."

"What do you mean by that?"

"No one likes her. She is discipline personified."

I laughed. "Well, a teacher should be a bit strict, shouldn't they?"

"A bit, yes. You all are. But it's different with her. She can be really nasty, even insulting. It's no secret that all the students in this boarding school carry some unpleasant history with them. That's just a fact. Runa exploits this fact, and she enjoys it too. If even one student gets a little rebellious, she threatens expulsion or predicts a life of crime for us."

"That's not very nice."

"No, not at all."

"Have you talked to Sigrid about it?"

Lilly puffed up. "What do you think? Of course! But you might as well teach a reindeer to dance. Sigrid doesn't believe a word we say."

The more I learned about the internal processes and events of this boarding school, the more I regretted my decision. I had only been here a few days and had already encountered the strangest things.

"Are you still there?" Lilly had leaned forward and was waving her hand in front of my face.

"Sorry, I was lost in thought."

"Oh? What were you thinking about?"

I waved my hands dismissively. "Nothing in particular!"

Lilly looked at me intently. "You're hard to read, you know that?"

"Is that bad?"

She shrugged. "Not necessarily. But it can be exhausting."

"You might be right."

She laughed and fell silent for a moment. Then she asked, "Have you heard anything about Tiril?"

Only now did I realize that Tiril's disappearance hadn't been on my mind at all in the last few hours. "No, unfortunately not," I replied. "Which surprises me a bit. I actually assumed that at least the teaching staff would be informed about the search."

Lilly shrugged indifferently. "I'm not the least bit surprised. Information is as scarce here as oranges at the Arctic Circle. If you want to find out anything, you have to get the information yourself. At least when it comes to missing students."

"I doubt anyone from the administration would tell me more about it," I objected.

Lilly looked at me thoughtfully. "I'll tell you what; as soon as it gets quiet in here, you and I will go look for her ourselves. Are you in?"

I didn't respond right away but pondered the pros and cons of such an action. There was nothing wrong with a night walk. I just didn't want to get caught with Lilly.

I looked around as if I were about to confide a well-guarded secret to someone. "Alright, we'll go look for Tiril. But this action has to, I repeat, has to stay between us. I'd be in deep trouble if anyone found out about these nighttime investigations."

"No one will find out," she assured me. "We'll meet at eleven o'clock down at the beach. About in the middle of the beach is a huge boulder that looks like it's growing out of the sand."

"Alright. But I don't think we'll find anything concrete. After all, the police have already searched thoroughly for Tiril."

"I know that. But they can overlook something too."

I shrugged. "Who knows."

"Well then, I'm going to my room now. I still have schoolwork to finish. Runa's trapezoid calculations won't solve themselves!" She rolled her eyes and stood up. "See you later."

I watched her leave with a tightening in my stomach, hoping I hadn't just made a mistake. To further intensify my guilt, I noticed Sigrid standing in the doorway to the dining hall, watching me. As our eyes met, she turned and disappeared between the tables into the darkness. I frowned. Had she overheard our conversation? No, impossible! The distance was too great, and Lilly had only whispered our plan. Still, I felt like a little boy caught sneaking a snack right before dinner.

I stayed seated for a while, listening to the sounds of the house. Most of the residents had retreated to their rooms, and it had grown quiet. A few students entered the lobby, shivering, and loudly disappeared upstairs. Then it was quiet again, only the occasional cough or distant footsteps could be heard. Further down the hallway, a clock ticked. The sound nearly put me in a trance, and for a moment, I drifted away, away from Fog Castle, away from the bay and the mountains, and I saw myself sitting at my son's hospital bed, holding his hands. I saw his pale skin and heard the incessant beeping of the monitors. I smelled the hospital's scent and heard footsteps in the corridor. No matter how much I tried to push these thoughts away, I also tried to hold onto them. They belonged in my life, just like Raik belonged in my life.

I forced myself to turn back, back to the bay, back to Fog Castle, back to the here and now.

Just before eleven o'clock, I sneaked through the main entrance to the outside of the building. I felt as if I was about to commit a crime, which of course was complete nonsense, since nighttime walks weren't forbidden. In front of the building, it was rather dark by Norwegian standards. A few lights illuminated the pavement leading to the parking lot. Otherwise, there were no light sources on the property.

I circled the house and trudged through knee-high snow toward the beach. The cold air awakened my weary spirits, and I felt the inner tension easing a bit. After a few minutes, I reached the beach and stopped near the high tide line. With my flashlight, I scanned the surroundings and fixed on a dark mound that jutted out of the sand about twenty meters in front of me. Lilly stood a little away from the rock, her arms crossed over her chest.

"Ready for a bit of adventure?" she asked as I joined her.

"I'm always ready for adventure," I replied.

"I suggest we split up. You search the beach and the water toward the south, and I'll go northward."

"Is there a reason we're searching for Tiril specifically at the beach?" I asked.

"The previous victims were always found in or near the water."

"But we don't even know if Tiril is a victim. Maybe she just ran away." It sounded unconvincing.

Lilly shook her head. "Something happened to her, I'm sure of it!"

I sighed. "The police have already searched everything here," I interjected. "But not the surrounding mountains."

"Do you want to wander through the mountains in the dead of night? I don't!"

"No, of course not."

"Exactly. Besides, she might have washed ashore by now."

I nodded hesitantly and let my gaze wander over the beach.

"As you say," I conceded. "Then let's go, and good luck." I turned around and strolled along the beach with my flashlight held out. I swung the beam back and forth in a 180-degree arc, like a blind person using their cane as a substitute for their eyes. The snow had melted from the seawater, which was unfortunate because a body would have provided a better contrast against a light background. On the other hand, walking on the sand was much easier than trudging through knee-deep snow.

The clouds from the afternoon had dissipated, and the sky was dotted with stars. They fell into the sea on the western horizon, and in between, two greenish bands of northern lights snaked across the sky, completing the nocturnal painting. Even though I was used to this sight, I still enjoyed it anew, and along with the deathly silence, I felt utterly alone, like on a foreign planet.

I directed my thoughts to Tiril. Admittedly, I had little hope that we would find anything tonight. On the one hand, I was still uncertain whether Tiril had simply taken off. On the other hand, the police had already searched for her. Until around nine o'clock, I had watched boats plying up and down the coast, illuminating the water's surface and the adjacent shore with their powerful searchlights. Around ten o'clock, it was clear that the search had been called off, and it had grown quiet in the bay.

I remembered that during my active service, I had been involved in one or two missing person searches. In an area like this in northern Norway, it was the proverbial search for a needle in a haystack. Tiril could be anywhere. If she had hiked over the pass, she could be hiding somewhere in Tromvik now or have already moved on. However, I considered that option unlikely.

I approached the southern end of the beach. From there, a slope led steeply up to a rocky ledge that jutted out into the sea like an anvil. I stood dumbfounded because at the edge of the rock, I thought I could make out the silhouette of a person. I switched off my flashlight and squinted. The figure clearly stood out against the pale background. It stood still and seemed to be gazing out at the sea. Judging by its size and stature, it had to be a man. But it was too dark, and the figure was too far away for me to identify him.

For a long moment, I watched the man and wondered whether he was simply enjoying the view or if he stood there for another reason. Was he perhaps also searching for Tiril? He apparently hadn't noticed me, as he was looking in the opposite direction.

Suddenly, the man moved and left the rocky edge toward Fog Castle. I noticed that he was wearing a hat, similar to the one worn by Australian farmers.

A hat!

Where had I seen someone with a hat recently?

It had been at the top of the stairs when Tiril and I were touring the building. He had stared at me, and I nearly stumbled down the stairs. But within five seconds, he had already disappeared without a trace.

A shiver ran down my spine as I watched the figure slowly move away from the rock and disappear behind a hill. I turned my flashlight back on and retraced my steps. At the other end of the beach, I could see the bobbing light of Lilly's flashlight and headed toward it. I found her standing at the high tide line, the light directed toward the sea, her eyes fixed. I joined her and followed her gaze to the horizon. The northern lights had become so bright that the snow around us glowed emerald green. Lilly wrapped her arms around her body and looked up. The northern lights moved faster and changed colors between green, ivory white, and a slight reddish-violet hue.

I glanced over at Lilly and noticed that she had tears in her eyes. I gently touched her shoulder, and she jumped.

"I'm sorry, I didn't mean to startle you," I apologized.

"It's okay," she said, shaking her head sadly. "Maybe you're right, and Tiril really did just take off, even though it's hard for me to believe that."

"It doesn't make sense to dwell on that right now. Speculating won't help at all. The police will resume the search tomorrow, and I'm sure they'll find her. If not here, then perhaps somewhere on the run."

"I hope you're right." She wiped her nose on her jacket sleeve. "I just don't think they'll find her alive."

I didn't respond to that. The likelihood was high that she was right. In silence, we watched the swirling Northern Lights as they wove their patterns in the sky. Each of us was lost in thought, and I was sure that our thoughts couldn't have been darker. Lilly must have been aware that Tiril had likely become another victim of Fog Castle. A thought that should have instilled fear in the young women at the boarding school, for who was to say that one of them wasn't next? And Lilly knew that.

"Do you believe in life after death?" she suddenly asked.

I pondered her question for a while. Not because I didn't know the answer, but because I had consciously avoided this question.

"No! I don't believe in life after death," I finally replied.

"And why not?"

"There are various reasons."

"I have time," she said, giving a faint smile.

I turned to face the sea and crossed my arms over my chest. "Actually, it's quite simple. I have a naturalistic worldview. For me, the natural sciences, astronomy, and evolutionary theory matter. I've read many scientific treatises on the topic of life after death. I even spoke with a scientist who provided convincing evidence against life after death. But ultimately, everyone must decide for themselves. The upbringing one receives from ones parents certainly has a significant impact on our later way of thinking and believing. Many are indoctrinated with faith. They are blinded to other truths, and I find that problematic. That's why it's good for everyone to determine their own way of thinking."

She studied me from the side for a while before responding. "Don't you think there's more to our world than we believe we know?"

"That may be true. But no one can prove it. Death makes way for the new. That's how nature has functioned since the Big Bang, and that's how it will continue to function long after you and I are gone."

"Isn't your theory terribly boring?"

I laughed. "Boring? I find it rather terrifying."

"Why terrifying?"

I put away the flashlight and looked at the sky. "You know, sometimes I wish I could believe in life after death. It would take away my fear of my own death. To know that after all this, there's simply nothing left, that one moment you can think, see, and smell, and the next moment you can't anymore. That has haunted me since my youth. And there's nothing I can do about it, except perhaps believing in an afterlife. But I'm sure that will never be the case, unless perhaps I'm convinced of the opposite after my death."

I felt Lilly's gaze on me. She was silent for a while. Then she said, "I believe in life after death," she said almost in a whisper. "I don't believe in a God or anything like that, but I'm still sure that there must be something after my life. This can't be all there is."

"And what if it is? What gives our lives here any meaning if we transition to another world where everything is supposed to be so much better and more beautiful?"

Again, she took her time with her response and chewed on one of her lip piercings. "Maybe we have to earn our next life, to determine whether it goes toward heaven or hell."

"And who decides whether you go to heaven or hell?"

She smiled and shrugged. "I will see my grandmother again, someday, in the distant future; that's all I hope for my next station."

"And I envy you for that!"

The tide had come in, and the water was now almost reaching our feet. "Come on, let's go in," I said to her. "We could both use a little sleep."

"Go ahead, I'll stay a few more minutes. It's just so beautiful."

I glanced at her briefly, touched her shoulder, and made my way back to the house.

Chapter 24

The following afternoon, I had some free time from lessons. I should have been preparing for upcoming classes, but I procrastinated, convincing myself that I needed to retrieve a few things from my apartment in the city. To be honest, I simply craved being around people, in restaurants, looking for a distraction. The fact that I had only been here for a few days and was already missing the city made me a bit reflective.

On my way to the parking lot, I heard a loud, dry cough. A man was kneeling by one of the path lights, fiddling with some tools. He wore a brown, yellowed leather jacket, beneath which peeked a gray wool sweater with completely frayed sleeves. His leather shoes had seen better days, and with all the scuffs and holes, they looked like they had been worn during World War II. I wondered how his feet didn't freeze in these temperatures.

But what struck me the most was the leather hat he wore. "Good day," I greeted him.

The man turned around in surprise. "Good day. I didn't hear you come in. I'm engrossed in my work. Sorry."

His voice sounded old, much older than he actually appeared. If I had been blind, I would have sworn an ancient man stood before me. "No need to apologize," I replied. "We haven't met yet. I'm Sondre, the new teacher."

"Nice to meet you. I'm Mikkel."

"Are you like the janitor here?" I asked him.

The man was already back to his work. "Yes, something like that."

"There must be a lot to do with a property like this."

"You have no idea. I could work twenty-four hours a day and still not finish. But I don't care about that anymore. I'm old; I do what I can."

Even though his voice sounded older than he probably was, I wondered if the guy should have been retired by now. I estimated he was at least seventy, if not older.

"How long have you worked here?" I wanted to know.

He gave me a brief, meaningful look. "Too long!"

I nodded. "You must have a lot to tell from your time here!"

"Pfff!" he said. "I could fill a book."

"Apparently, you like it here. Otherwise, you wouldn't have stayed so long, right?"

He looked at me sideways while he fiddled with a screw. "You could say that," he said flatly.

I realized that I couldn't get much sense out of this guy. He hadn't really answered any of my questions yet. Still, I asked him another: "Could I talk to you about Fog Castle?"

He gave the screw a hard twist with the screwdriver, cursed, and stood up. "You want to talk about the boarding school?"

I nodded. "Only if you don't mind."

He wiped his dirty hands on a handkerchief and looked at me somewhat suspiciously under his hat. "What do you want to know?"

"Well, for one, I'm interested in the history of the house," I began. "So far, no one has been able to provide me with any real information."

Mikkel studied me while still rubbing his hands with the handkerchief. After a while, he tucked it into his trouser pocket and said, "I don't have time now; I need to finish this." He nodded towards the path light. "Come to the rock ledge down in the bay at nine o'clock tonight."

The bay! Why the bay? Couldn't we just have a cozy coffee in the dining hall? "I can manage that," I replied instead.

Mikkel crouched down again and continued working, which I took as a sign to make my exit. "See you later, then."

Mikkel muttered something to himself that sounded like "all clear."

Confused, I walked to my car, got in, and started the engine. A few minutes later, my car struggled up the snow-covered road, and I directed my thoughts back to the conversation I had just had. I had noticed the way he had looked at me. His eyes seemed so tired and old, as if they had already lived two lives. His gaze reminded me of my late grandfather's. From him, I had learned everything about surviving in the wild and what truly mattered in life. Thanks to him, I got to know the world in a way that my own father had withheld from me. My father had been solely focused on his career and never recognized the beauties of life. He only cared for his family on the side, which ultimately led my mother to file for divorce, and since then, I have had no contact with him. Neither he nor I seemed to miss each other. The same went for my brother, who lived in Hammerfest with his family and also maintained no connection with him.

My grandfather had taken it upon himself to raise my brother and me after his son's failure as a father. He had become a father figure to me—someone I looked up to, whom I admired, and hoped I would be like one day. He had lost his wife early on but had refused to pursue any other woman since. I still remember what he told me a few years after her death: There was only one true love in life. I have always felt lucky to have known her. She was an enrichment, an inspiration. She was my companion on the journey; without her, my life would have turned out entirely differently. Your grandmother will be in my heart until the end of my days, and no one can replace her.

The end of his days came fifteen years ago. He died unexpectedly, peacefully, but alone in the bed of his weekend cabin by Nakkevatnet. I had loved that cabin. It had been a refuge for me, a place where I preferred to be as a little boy, rather than home. In the summer, I could swim in the cold water of the lake, and in the winter, I could go ice fishing. When it snowed at night, I would shovel the snow early in the morning and then return to the cabin, where grandfather would be waiting for me with hot chocolate. I remember the starry, cold nights when he showed me the northern lights in front of the cabin and told me stories of the Sami legends. I remember the reflections of the lights on the water, the snow-covered mountains, and the bubbling, crystal-clear streams as if it had all been a dream.

When I received the news of his passing, I felt like a child who had lost his hero. From that day on, I feared death like the devil fears holy water. When my son passed away as well, it seemed like my world had finally come apart at the seams. The joy of life had become a burdensome attachment. The minutes after waking in the morning were torture. The hours at work dragged on as if they wanted to inflict additional pain. My ex-wife sought help from the church and seemingly found it. From then on, she found comfort in the thought that our son was now in a better place, watched over by God. I was envious of her faith, of her way of dealing with death. I was envious of the solace she seemed to have found in the Holy Scriptures, while I was searching for answers that I have yet to find. I only knew that life was not fair for everyone.

I shook a cigarette from the pack and lit it. As I reached the highest point of the mountain road, the valley with the nestled fjord opened up before me. The sun hung in the lower third of the sky, transforming the water into a play of millions of sparkling gems. Occasionally, I enjoyed the seclusion of our home, the tranquility, and the almost untouched nature. However, when the psyche was fragile, the North—with its dark winter days and endless expanses—could hit one hard, especially if you didn't know how to cope with it. After Raik's death, I longed for a big city, bright and bustling with thousands of people, where the noise of life drowned out the harrowing thoughts, and where one could be as anonymous as a commuter in a crowded subway. Yet, I remained loyal to Tromsø and could not imagine living anywhere else in a million years.

An hour later, I stepped through the door of my city apartment and called Jørn.

"What are you doing right now?" I asked him as he answered with a grumpy voice.

"Mom made me clean my room," he replied.

"Sometimes it has to be done."

"I see it differently."

"If Mom thinks it should be tidy, then that's just how it is."

"Yeah, yeah!"

"Why I'm calling, son, I'm in the city. Do you have time to go get a drink?"

"Can't. I'm meeting Eirik in a few minutes. We're going to Nerstranda."

Nerstranda was a shopping center in the city center. In the afternoons, it was packed with teenagers who met there to chat or shop.

"I could drop you off later," I tried to persuade him. "I'd rather go right away."

"Alright, as you wish." It was frustrating. I really wanted to see Jørn; I missed him. But this feeling seemed to pertain only to me. So I came up with another strategy. "Would you like to spend a weekend with me at the boarding school? We could go snowshoeing together?" Silence!

"Jørn, are you still there?"

"Yeah, I'm still here. Isn't it super boring out there?"

"So far, I can't complain about boredom. The area is beautiful. I'm sure you'd like it."

"I don't know."

I tried to put myself in the shoes of a seventeen-year-old. Would you want to spend a weekend with your father in a small apartment in the middle of nowhere, without a shopping street, without friends? I thought back to my youth and concluded that I wouldn't have hesitated for a second if I had faced the same decision. However, my father would never have extended such an invitation. I remembered a trip when I was not yet ten years old, when he took us on a mountain hike, and we got lost and almost froze to death had a helicopter not rescued us from the predicament. After that, I never went anywhere with him again.

I sighed inwardly. "Oh come on, Jørn, we would surely have a lot of fun." It almost sounded pathetic. Again, there was silence for a while until he audibly exhaled. "Alright. I'll join for one night."

"Wonderful." I couldn't expect more.

"This weekend?" he asked.

"Whenever you want, I'm fine with it."

"When and where?"

"I'll pick you up on Friday around noon."

"Okay. I have to go, Dad. Bye!"

I threw my phone onto the sofa and sat down at the dining table. In front of me lay a pack of cigarettes. I was just about to take one out when I thought better of it. Annoyed, I threw the pack against the wall, put on my jacket, and left the apartment. I walked to Storgata, Tromsø's shopping street, and strolled past the shops. I desperately needed new books. My current reading was nearing its end, and I had no stock left, which was rare. I stopped in front of my favorite bookstore, located between a burger restaurant and an optician's shop, and inspected the display. Where once only old, almost antique books collected dust, there was now modern literature as well. A few weeks ago, a colleague had told me that the owner, a certain Yorick, had recently employed his nephew, who apparently had introduced modern literature into the bookstore empire.

I entered the store and was immediately glad that the scent of the book paradise had not vanished along with the old books. I remembered some interesting conversations I had had with Yorick. He was a man who, certainly because of his profession, was very well-read and thus knowledgeable about almost everything. He was one of the most interesting contemporaries in the city for me.

"Good day," chirped a somewhat stocky, middle-aged man who just emerged from the back row of shelves. "I didn't hear you come in."

His voice sounded somehow too high for a man. He wore nickel glasses and had straight blonde hair, parted in the middle and reaching just below his ears. His face was dotted with stubble, and his chin was adorned with a short goatee. Despite the warmth in the store, he wore a thick green sweater and brown pants that were far too loose for his thin frame.

"Are you looking for something specific?" he asked after placing the books on a side table. "No, not really. I need to stock up on books. I'm just looking around."

The bookseller smiled and said: "If you need help, just let me know." He grabbed another stack of books and disappeared among the many shelves, which, like the display in the window, had changed with the times. The front of the shelves was labeled with the respective genres, making it easier for customers to search for the right book. Despite the increased selection, the store had not lost the original charm of an old bookstore, and the dark, worm-eaten wooden shelves still gave me the feeling of having dived into another time, into another place. The silence in the store had survived the transformation, and even when several customers were present, the tranquility was respected, almost as if one were in a church.

After half an hour, I balanced seven books in my hands towards the cash register when the bookseller emerged from behind one of the shelves.

"Let me help you," he said, grabbing the top four titles. I followed him and placed the books on the counter. "The selection of books has changed a bit since I was last here," I noted.

The bookseller shrugged. "One has to keep up with the times. My uncle knows hundreds of authors but never offered their works here because they were either too modern or too poor for him. The store simply didn't generate enough income to make a living. I hope to increase the income again with a broader selection. Even bad books can sell!"

"That's true!" I inquired about Yorick's whereabouts. His nephew nodded towards the back of the store. "He's in the office reading."

"May I?"

"Of course, go ahead. I'll set the books aside." I made my way to the back of the store and stopped in front of a door labeled "Office." I knocked and gently opened it. Yorick was sitting in an armchair. A wool blanket lay across his legs, and in his hands, he held a leather-bound book. He looked much older than during our last meeting. Perhaps it was just the dim light that made him look old. His gray hair was thin on his head. He wore reading glasses that were probably older than I was. When he noticed me, he looked up from his reading and stared at me with wide eyes. I was about to say hello when he raised his hand. "Wait, don't tell me." He closed his eyes for a moment, and after a few seconds, he snapped his fingers. "Sondre! Right?"

"Absolutely right!" I said, impressed. "Good to see you, Yorick. How are you?"

He shrugged and closed the book. "Can't complain. But the bones aren't getting any younger. That's especially noticeable in the mornings when I get up. Otherwise, I'm in perfect health." He broke into a broad smile. "The store has changed, hasn't it?"

"Yes, indeed."

"I guess I haven't been keeping up with the times, as they say."

"It's not just you. But the tried and true has its charm. Sometimes more than the new!"

"I completely agree."

"Still, I think the spirit of the old shop has been preserved. When I stepped over the threshold earlier, I felt as if I was transported back in time. And that's what matters to me, and certainly to many others who appreciate this kind of bookstore."

He grimaced. "Maybe you're right. Well, Arne knows what he's doing. I don't spend as much time in the shop as I used to. I need a little more peace and quiet." He raised a cup to his mouth and noisily took a sip. "Do you want a coffee?" he asked after putting the cup down. "No, thanks. I'm trying to cut down on my coffee consumption," I replied.

"I still drink my eight to ten cups a day," he said proudly.

"Yes, I used to manage that too!" I responded with raised eyebrows.

He laughed and took another sip. After putting the cup down, he studied me for a moment and said, "Are you still a teacher? Not bored yet? With your background as a police officer, I mean?"

He knew me. "Well, what can I say? My new job isn't exactly adrenaline-fueled. I do miss the excitement a bit. But that's how life is. Beautiful moments are fleeting."

"Well said," he nodded. "Where are you working these days?"

"At Fog Castle!"

Yorick's eyelids twitched at the mention of the boarding school. He looked at me for a while, scrutinizing me over his glasses. "Fog Castle," he whispered, more to himself than to me. "How did you end up working there?"

I found the question a bit odd. "Well, I needed a change in my life, different people, different spaces, a different area."

"And you chose that old place?"

I shrugged a bit uncertainly.

"Don't take it personally; I didn't mean to offend you."

"No problem. I didn't take it as an insult. The old building is a bit strange, I'll admit that. But that's exactly what fascinated me when I first entered. As soon as you step through the door, you're gripped by a suffocating feeling, as if you were crossing a cemetery at midnight. Do you know that feeling?"

"Of course. It gives you goosebumps from your neck to your rear!"

I laughed. "That's one way of putting it."

Yorick adopted a more serious expression. "Are you familiar with the history of the house?" "I wanted to find out a bit about the house beforehand, but it wasn't as easy as I initially thought. It almost seems like the house wants to remain invisible to the outside. Even though it actually has quite a lot to tell." Yorick raised his eyebrows significantly. "Don't you want to sit down?" He pointed to a chair, adjusted his wool blanket, pulled his glasses a bit closer to his eyes, and leaned back in the armchair. "A few decades ago, Fog Castle wasn't a boarding school. The house was built, if I'm not mistaken, in 1980 by an Englishman named Blake Hargrave. He was a wealthy industrialist who made a fortune producing alcohol. He moved here with his wife Eleanor and their two small children, Ashlyn and Colton, from England and resided in Fog Castle from then on. A year later, he bought hundreds of acres of land, and the area around the house became private property. The residents of the nearby village of Tromvik initially resisted. They didn't want a rich Englishman buying up their land. But the community needed money, and that was that. Mr. Hargrave was received with hostile glares in the village afterward. In the shop, his family was only served with disdain, and they were ignored in church. For a while, Blake watched this game with feigned indifference until he finally had enough and devised a plan. He had no friends here, no business partners, no drinking buddies, nothing. He had only one thing: money! And along with it, of course, came great power. So he donated a significant sum of money to the community, with no conditions, no repayment contract, just out of goodwill. With the unexpected windfall, the village finally invested in much-needed renovations of the school and the church. A new warehouse was built at the harbour, as the old one was on the verge of collapse. And lo and behold, overnight, the Hargrave family was accepted. Blake occasionally organized parties at his estate to which the entire village was invited. This earned him even more respect, and in the following years, Blake donated several more sums of money to the village. At that time, rumours circulated that our town also benefited from his money. To what extent that is really true, I don't know. I only know that he built a good relationship with the mayor and other figures in the town." Yorick cleared his throat and took a sip of coffee. "A few years later, around 1984, there was a landslide in Tromvik that severely damaged several houses. Among others, a mother with two children lost everything with her two children. They temporarily stayed with acquaintances in the village, but this was not a long-term solution. They didn't have money for a new house anyway, and the insurance seemed to cover only part of it. Blake then promised the family help, and he kept his promise. Not two weeks later, he began building a house not far from his estate, which he gave to the impoverished family upon its completion."

"Quite generous, this Blake!" I interjected.

"You could say that."

"I just find it a bit strange that he had the house built in the bay instead of down in the village."

Yorick's rugged face twisted into a mischievous smile. "The family whose house fell victim to the landslide had two children; a boy and a girl. The father was no longer alive. The children were about the same age as the Hargrave offspring. Blake always wanted playmates for his children. Fog Castle was too far from the village for his children to quickly run to the village to play with their friends. By having a family living just a few meters from his own house, he would solve that problem." He paused briefly and adjusted his wool blanket. "This fact was the official reason for the house being built near Fog Castle."

"Officially?" I asked, puzzled. "And unofficially?"

"Back then, it was rumored that Blake had an affair with the mother of the two children, and this was before they moved into the new house. Whether that's true or not, I can't say. Rumors are as common in small villages as fish in water. The thing is, Blake's wife Eleanor left Fog Castle with Blake's children shortly after the family moved into the house. It was rumoured that she returned to England. But nobody knew for sure, and Blake kept quiet. After that, the industrialist was rarely seen in the village. A servant did all the shopping, so Blake didn't even have to leave his estate. He even hired a private tutor. From then on, the children of his mistress went to school at Fog Castle. The new woman in his life withdrew from village life just like

Blake. They were only seen when they drove down the mountain road and continued toward Tromsø. Blake continued to donate money to the village when necessary, but no parties or other events were held at his estate. About a year and a half later, believe it or not, a disaster occurred at Blake's estate. The house he had built for the family burned down completely. The mother, whose name was Ailin by the way, was not at home at the time of the fire. No one knows where she was. However, her children were asleep in their beds and were caught by the fire. The boy survived; the girl perished in the flames."

I swallowed awkwardly. I was hearing about this event for the first time today. But I wasn't particularly surprised. Apparently, there were only a handful of people who seemed to know anything about Fog Castle. Yorick was one of them. "Why was Ailin still living in the house next door with her children when she could have lived in Fog Castle?" I asked him.

He shrugged. "In the village, it was said that the children couldn't stand Blake. But whether that was really the reason, I can't judge. Rumours, you see?"

I nodded. "How did it happen that Fog Castle was converted into a boarding school?"

"Well, Blake wasn't the sole owner of Fog Castle. His business partner and best friend, John Birch, was involved in the purchase at that time, although not to the same extent as Blake. After the tragedy regarding Ailin's child, neither she nor Blake were ever seen again. Not even their car was ever spotted again. They had disappeared without a trace. His business partner took over Fog Castle that same year and soon transformed it into a boarding school. To this day, he has remained silent about the whereabouts of Blake and Ailin. However, it is believed that Blake left the country with Ailin and her son. The postman at the time told the village that he occasionally had to deliver a letter from England to Fog Castle. Therefore, it is suspected that Blake retreated there with his lover. But no one knows for sure. And really, it doesn't matter. It's nobody's business. The villagers were not satisfied with mere speculation. Some of them would occasionally sneak onto the estate and observe the house from a distance. But they saw neither Blake nor Ailin. Only the servant would occasionally walk around the house.

"A truly eerie story," I commented. Even though I didn't believe in ghosts, I wished at that moment that the two were haunting the house as spirits. That would add some spice to the whole tale. "But the burned-down house wasn't rebuilt, was it?" I asked Yorick. "At least I didn't see any other buildings nearby."

"No. The rubble was cleared away, and the land was left to nature."

I nodded and wondered where this house could have stood. I recalled the image of the building and its surroundings, but I concluded that the house could have been anywhere. Yorick's story fascinated me. These were tales for a book. He clearly knew a lot about Fog Castle and its fate. Therefore, I assumed he must have heard about the deceased students as well. "You've certainly heard about the deceased teenagers from the boarding school, right?"

Yorick's eyelids were half-closed, and his gaze drifted past me. I wasn't sure if he was tired or pondering my question. He blinked a few times, then his gaze returned to me as he crossed his arms over his chest. "I've heard about it," he said, nodding.

"And what do you think about it?" I pressed further.

"A tragic story."

"Do you know anything interesting about it?"

Yorick looked at me inquisitively. "Do you know anything about it?"

"Not much," I replied. "Back when I was with the police, I certainly caught wind of it. However, since I was never involved in the investigations, I don't know the details. I only know that since the beginnings of the boarding school, students have repeatedly died, and it was assumed that they had taken their own lives."

"That's right."

"Strange coincidences, don't you think?"

He shrugged. "One thing is certain; the teenagers who go to school there are not clean slates. You know that best yourself. One or two of them must have struggled with their fate. So suicide isn't out of the question."

"That may be true. Still, I have the feeling that something is seriously wrong there. I just don't know what."

"You're not the only one," he said with raised eyebrows.

"What do you mean?"

He cleared his throat. "An acquaintance of mine worked as a teacher at Fog Castle for a while. However, after half a year at the boarding school, she quit her job and moved back to the city. She told me some very strange things about the school."

"Strange things?"

"Janne, that's my acquaintance's name, is a bad sleeper, which is why she often roams around at night. It was the same at the boarding school. She told me about strange figures she saw wandering through the house or on the beach in the middle of the night, aimlessly and without intentions. At first, she assumed it was someone like her who couldn't sleep well at night. Unfortunately, she could never find out who they were. The figures disappeared as quickly as they had appeared."

Without meaning to, I had to smile. Janne's sightings sounded like ghost stories and phenomena that the brain conjures up at night.

"Yes, I also smiled at first," Yorick said, and I felt caught.

"I'm sorry, I didn't mean to make light of it. It's just that the brain often plays tricks at night."

"I agree. In Janne's case, though, I doubt that. She continued telling me that one night a student disappeared from her room. No one had seen her leave; no one knew where she was. The boarding school administration didn't take the incident seriously enough, in Janne's opinion, so she wanted to investigate it herself. Two weeks later, she woke up in the middle of the night, and when she turned around, she saw a figure standing by her bed, its face covered by a cloth. An ice-cold hand covered her mouth, and she was told to let the matter be. If not, she would float in the sea like an iceberg. Then the figure disappeared, leaving Janne completely terrified. The next day, she handed in her resignation."

For a long moment, it was quiet in the back room of the bookstore. Two questions arose in my mind: Was the figure, or the figures, the same person? Had a student played a prank on Janne?

I noticed Yorick's questioning expression.

"Do you think I could talk to this Janne?" I asked him.

"I think so," he replied. "I can give you her address. Hand me some paper and a pen from the desk over there."

After I had given him both, he scrawled the name and address on the paper. Janne Hermansen, Beryllvegen 4, Lunheim.

"Do you know her address by heart?" I asked in surprise.

"I may be old, my friend, but my brain still functions very well."

"I can see that, I'm impressed."

We chatted a bit longer without mentioning Fog Castle again. After about half an hour, I said goodbye to him, paid for the books with his nephew, and stepped back out into Storgata. Tourists and locals strolled or hurried past me, and I headed toward the harbour. The sun was only a finger's breadth above the southern mountains, and the last rays of the day flooded the streets and alleys with golden light, almost as if someone had directed a giant spotlight on the town. The water of the strait sparkled in the evening light, and the shrill cries of seagulls echoed across the square. I made my way to my favorite café, The Bean, and saw from a distance that my regular seat by the window was occupied by some guy in a wool sweater with his laptop open. Gritting my teeth, I sat at a different table and waited for service. Svea, the barista and bread seller, came out from behind the counter and approached me with a smile. I already knew her from my numerous visits to the café, and I thought she was one of the friendliest people I had ever met. Her cheerful demeanor lifted my spirits during every visit. She portrayed a person who was completely satisfied with her job, and the same probably applied to her life. She had indeed managed to lift my gloomy mood in a matter of minutes several times, and that meant something.

Two minutes later, she served me a steaming coffee and a pastry filled with vanilla. As I let the wonderfully fragrant coffee flow down my throat, I thought about my conversation with Yorick. I rummaged for the note with Janne's address and stared at the crumpled piece of paper. A visit today was out of the question. I had to return to the boarding school. Whether Janne would even receive me was another matter entirely.

I put the note back in my pocket and looked out the window. On the opposite side stood a fishmonger hawking his fresh goods. I thought of Marit and how often she had prepared fish that Jørn, Raik, and I had caught. They had always been so proud when they could bring their catch home.

I watched a young mother trying to gather her out of control children, which proved to be no easy task. I saw two teenagers about Jørn's age wandering across the square with their heads down and cigarettes in their mouths, making faces as if they were heading to an exam.

I thought of Jørn and our relationship, which seemed to be getting more complicated rather than simpler. I sensed that he was drifting further away from me, and I feared that one day he would move so far away that we wouldn't be able to find our way back to each other. Of course, I had to factor in his age, and in three to four years, things might look better. But four years in the life of a teenager felt like twenty at my age. I wished Marit would contribute her part and talk to Jørn a little about it. Instead, she seemed to enjoy it when our son made friends with her new love interest. At the thought of that scoundrel, the hair on my neck bristled, and I would have loved to throw my coffee cup into the display window.

After twenty minutes, I said goodbye to Svea, grabbed a few things from my apartment, and made my way back to Tåkevik.

Chapter 25

Tiril gagged and coughed. The hand covering her mouth reeked of a mixture of garden waste and dog faeces. With every breath, her nausea worsened, and she feared she would be sick at any moment. After escaping her tormentor, she encountered him again, and less than ten seconds later, she felt an ice-cold hand grasp her mouth. She was lifted up, her legs pressed together as if caught in a gigantic vice, and then she was taken back to the cellar. When the woman opened the door, however, it was not the familiar room with the two beds that came into view; no, this room was completely empty and devoid of any light. The man surprisingly set her down gently, took a few steps back, and finally stood next to his mother. Tiril couldn't see their faces; the room was too dark, but she knew they were both staring at her.

"Instead of lying in a cozy bed, you can spend the night in this dungeon and think about whether you want to attempt an escape again. I guess that you'll soon come to realize that it wasn't worth it." She turned to leave the room when her son began whimpering like a young puppy.

She grasped his arm. "This is what happens when you defy the rules. I've told you countless times; your princess must not go outside!"

He whined even louder.

"Well, let it be. You'll see her again tomorrow." She shoved him out of the room. With his head hanging low, he stepped into the corridor, and she locked the door. Tiril lay in complete darkness. She felt the cold and dampness of the stone floor through her thin pyjamas and leaned her back against the wall. Shivering, she pulled her legs up, rested her head on her knees, and began to cry. Just moments before, she had believed that the nightmare had finally come to an end, that she could raise the alarm, take a shower, and then crawl into a warm bed. Instead, she was huddled here, alone, trembling from the cold, and without any hope. Her stomach growled, and her throat was parched.

After her crying fit had eased a bit, she leaned back against the wall and tried to regain control of her breathing. She directed her thoughts to her childhood home. She saw the fishermen casting their lines from their boats. She saw the warm lights of the nearby village, and she saw her parents sitting at the dining table playing cards. She heard her own angry voice as she had rebelled against her parents so many times. She recalled numerous situations and moments in her life that she wished she could take back, moments she wanted to undo. But now it was too late. Time had moved on, the deeds were in the past, and in the present, there was no warm blanket she could pull over her head to escape the world for a brief moment. Here, there was no dog to hug and share her worries with, no grandmother to fulfill her every wish. Here, she was left to fend for herself, forgotten and lost. For a while, she indulged in the memories, and at the same time, she felt her pulse gradually calm down and her breathing become shallower. She contemplated what she could do. Screaming would do nothing; the walls seemed too thick. The only way out was the door. But the woman had locked it.

Nevertheless, she stood up and felt her way along the wall until she could touch the door. Gently, she pressed the handle, but as expected, nothing happened. She shook it a few times, but it didn't budge an inch. In daylight, she could have attempted to run into the door. But in complete darkness, that was an impossible endeavor. Resigned, she buried her face in her hands and cried quietly. She felt tired and drained; all she wanted was to sleep. But the floor was so uncomfortable that she wouldn't find any sleep on it. Besides, she urgently needed to use the toilet, but of course, there was none here either. She knelt down and crawled forward until she reached a corner of the room. There, she squatted and relieved herself on the floor. Afterward, she crawled back, laid her head on her knees, and closed her eyes. With regular breaths, she tried to put her body into a kind of short sleep. She knew she had the ability to sleep for a few minutes anywhere and at any time. But she doubted she would manage it down here. She listened to the rhythm of her heartbeat and heard the steady dripping of water that came from somewhere in the darkness.

Drip...drip...drip...!

She relaxed her neck muscles and felt her head grow heavy and press down on her arms. The dripping faded into a distant echo, and the rush of blood in her ears subsided like a dying storm.

***

Tormented by guilt and fear, he sat on his bed, rocking his body back and forth. He missed his princess, even though he knew she was very close. But she was not with him. He could not understand why Mama had taken her away from him. She knew how much he needed his princess.

His gaze fell on her empty bed. The blanket at the foot of the bed was neatly folded, the body warmth gone from it.

His gaze clouded, his eyes became fixed, and he saw his sister's bed before him, as the blanket caught fire; the mattress began to burn, he saw the glowing beam lying across his sister, and he felt the paralyzing powerlessness that overwhelmed him. For a long moment, he remained motionless. He forgot the pain radiating from his burned facial skin, he forgot the burning in his lungs, and he forgot his parched throat. Suddenly, under the rubble, he saw a hand protruding, with a silver ring on the index finger, which Elida had received as a Christmas gift. Determined, he fought his way forward, stumbling over parts of the blanket and burning wooden beams, and finally managed to grasp her hand. At the same moment, he noticed a tuft of her hair, singed, peeking out from under the blanket. He reached for it, hoping to pull Elida's head out from under the rubble, but the hair tore out, and he was left holding only a handful. Panicked, he tugged at her arm, but the beam was just too heavy; she didn't move an inch. In a deathly fear, he screamed Elida's name until another beam crashed into the room and knocked him backward. When he looked up, he saw the empty bed in front of him, holding the strands of his sister's hair in his hand, and he knew that this time he had to save his princess.

***

Tiril jolted awake, feeling dazed, her eyes burning. She noticed a light source in the room, and as she lifted her head, she saw a figure standing in the doorway, motionless and eerie. She couldn't make out its face; the brim of its hat concealed almost its entire face. The figure was tall and sturdy, but not as broad as her captor. For a horrifically long moment, she stared into the shadow under the hat and dared not move or breathe. In fear, she squeezed her eyes shut, rested her head back on her knees, and stammered, "Stop! Stop! Stop! PLEASE!" She began to sob and pulled her legs even closer to her body. She didn't know what was going to happen to her now. She didn't know who or what this figure was or what it wanted from her. She waited for the cold hands to pull her from the ground and drag her off to who knows where.

But nothing happened!

After a while, she opened her eyes, lifted her head, and to her astonishment, the light source had vanished, and the figure was gone.

Darkness!

Was the person still in the room with her? She couldn't see anything, not even her hand in front of her face. "Let me go! Let me go!" She waved her arms in front of her. But it remained silent; no one approached her or grabbed her. She tried in vain to penetrate the darkness, but everything remained black.

Then suddenly she heard the click of a lock, and immediately a beam of light fell into the room. She blinked, and in the dim light, she recognized the man who had brought her here. Shuffling, he came towards her, his hands outstretched. She recoiled but bumped against the wall. One hand covered her mouth, and then she was lifted up and carried out of the room. The man brought her back to his chamber, laid her on her bed, covered her up, and secured both wrists to the iron chains. After that, he sat on his own bed and looked at her with a smile. His eyelids moved almost in slow motion as he blinked, making him appear almost gentle.

Tiril avoided his gaze and noticed a cup on the nightstand, looking at him pleadingly. "Thirst!" she croaked.

The smile on his face vanished, and he frowned at her. She pointed to the dresser again. He followed her gaze and seemed to understand. He reached for the cup and approached her bed. With the caution of a surgeon, he lifted her head and brought the cup to her mouth. Tiril inhaled the tea-scented liquid and felt her dry throat bloom, like a desert that could finally absorb rain after years of drought. She choked, began to cough and gag. The man helped her sit up and patted her back.

"Thank you," Tiril whispered, out of breath. Gently, he laid her back on the pillow, returned to his bed, and took off his shoes. With a long sigh, he crawled under the blankets, and no more than a minute later, Tiril could hear his deep breaths. With a mix of disgust and curiosity, she observed the man, trying to understand what must be going on inside him. He was an adult, yet he behaved like a little boy. His face, even if it was disfigured, radiated something warm and caring. His movements reminded her of a worried father taking care of his sick child. She let her gaze wander to the ceiling and felt the fatigue take hold of her body. Her head lay heavy on the pillow, and her eyelids felt like they weighed a ton. She tried to stay awake, fearing what might happen to her in her sleep. She listened to the soft snoring. She heard the dull sound of her heartbeat, and when she opened her eyelids again, she heard the distant opening of a door and was instantly wide awake. The candle on the dresser was almost burned down, and in the dim light, she could see the woman entering the room, glaring at her angrily. Marching briskly, she approached her son and woke him roughly from his dreams. "What is this?" she hissed at him. "Didn't I tell you she stays where she is?"

The man jolted awake, looking frightened, as if he expected to be hit, which seemed almost ridiculous considering his size. He mumbled something unintelligible and glanced fearfully at his mother.

"Didn't I tell you?" There was a loud bang, and he fell back onto his pillow. A faint whimper escaped his throat, and Tiril felt a pang of sympathy, even though she couldn't quite understand this feeling.

The woman stormed out of the room and slammed the door behind her, while he held his hands protectively over his head and quietly sobbed to himself. Tiril wondered if she should say something but dared not. She fell back onto the pillow and felt a stabbing pain in her stomach. She hadn't eaten in hours, perhaps days; she couldn't say for sure. With a pained expression, she held her hands over her belly and groaned softly. The man turned to her, and his red eyes wandered to her stomach and back again. "Hunger?" he asked.

Tiril nodded uncertainly.

He pulled back the bedcovers, slipped on his shoes, and left the room.

Tiril looked uncertainly at the door, wondering what would happen next. Was he going to get her something to eat?

A few minutes later, the door flew open, and he returned.

Chapter 26

At five to nine, I closed the front door of the boarding school and made my way to the west side of the building. All evening, I had been eagerly anticipating what Mikkel wanted to tell me about the boarding school.

I reached the slope near the beach, stopped, and looked for him. To my left, the rock ledge emerged from the darkness. Like a sentinel, it loomed over the bay, a witness to ebb and flow, to harsh winter storms and gentle summer breezes.

I followed the path to the southern end of the beach. Waves lapped against the shore, and I enjoyed the soothing sound. I remembered my parents' first house. It stood on Kvaløya right by the strait. From the window of my room, I could see the dark water and the white mountains of the mainland. In the summer, I left the window open at night and let the sounds of the water lull me to sleep. I had never fallen asleep as well as I did in my first house.

When I reached the end of the beach, I climbed along the side of the rock until the path ended at the cliff edge, revealing the sea below me. I looked up at the sky, which was as dark as the sea beneath it. There was no beginning and no end; they merged into one another as if they were one. I lost myself in the lights of the stars. There were so many that I felt small and insignificant. I thought about the darkness, how beautiful it actually was, and what a privilege it was to still know the darkness of the night. I felt pity for those who lived in big cities and did not understand this tranquility and simplicity of the night. They did not know the silence it brought; it was as foreign to them as the city noise was to this bay.

I lit a cigarette and thought at that moment that I should really quit. I had been dragging this vice around for too long, and all my previous attempts to stay away from the cigarette had failed miserably. If Jørn lived with me, I would have given up smoking long ago. However, his absence had even increased my consumption.

Standing on this rocky ledge and gazing out at the sea, I wondered where I had gone wrong in life and what path I should have taken instead. The transformation from a happy family man to a lonely loser had torn me from my normal life and had given me many dark hours. From one day to the next, I found myself alone in an apartment, with no one to share dinner with, to watch a movie with, or to lie in the same bed with. I had to learn that acceptance of this situation seeped in only after months, if not years, and even then only painfully slowly.

The wind picked up, and the air became damp, as if descending into an old cellar. From the beach below, wisps of fog climbed the cliffs, and the lights of the boarding school disappeared one by one behind an impenetrable curtain. I glanced at my watch. It was three minutes past nine. There was no sign of Mikkel. The thick fog worried me. Hopefully, I would be able to find my way back to the house.

Suddenly, I heard the crunch of footsteps. With my flashlight, I shone it on the path and paused at a shadow emerging from the fog. The scene felt almost ghostly, and I felt a tingling in my neck. I recognized the hat, and at the same moment, I noticed how sluggish Mikkel's gait appeared, almost as if he were carrying years of worries in a backpack.

"Good evening, Mikkel," I said as he approached within earshot.

"Good evening," he replied, tipping his hand to his hat brim. He joined me and looked out at the sea. The fog grew denser; the beach was already invisible. However, the rock we stood on towered above the fog like a high-rise in the city.

"This fog is pretty thick!" I remarked.

"Always has been."

"Is that why it's called Fog Castle?"

Mikkel nodded. "The wind blows in from the sea and brings moist air, which condenses on the slopes behind the beach, creating the fog. Sometimes, we can have four days of fog in a row, especially in the autumn months."

"Have you ever felt lonely here?"

He raised his eyebrows and took a deep breath. "Loneliness isn't tied to a place — it's tied to the person. In my life, I had everything I needed. At least, up to a certain point. Today, I live on memories; there is no place for loneliness there."

I let his words linger on my tongue. There was something true in them, even if I wasn't sure I had understood him correctly.

I looked at Mikkel from the side, and again the question about his age arose. I couldn't gauge him. "I don't want to intrude or offend you," I said, "but shouldn't you already be retired?"

Mikkel raised his eyebrows again, still looking out at the sea, and a melancholic smile lay on his lips. "Let me tell you a story. In the 1980s, I lived with my wife Vilda and my daughter Malin in Tromvik. We owned a small house near the harbor, where I also worked at the time. One day, the then-owner of Fog Castle, John Birch, came to the harbour and asked my boss if he knew anyone he could hire as a caretaker for his property. My boss directed him to my coworker Einar, who declined the position. I was not far from the three of them, so I caught the conversation. Since I wasn't entirely satisfied with my job at the harbour anyway, I approached the gentlemen and offered my services to the landowner. However, my boss didn't realize at the time that this would be a full-time job; otherwise, he probably wouldn't have suggested his own employees." Mikkel smiled mischievously. "Anyway, a month later, I started my new position at Fog Castle. I liked the work. It was varied; not only was the pay much better, but so were the working hours. For the first time ever, I was able to provide my wife and daughter with things I hadn't been able to afford before. We went out to eat or went to the movies in Tromsø. A year after I started at Fog Castle, the deputy principal of the boarding school, Sigrid, called me into her office. She offered my daughter the opportunity to attend school at the boarding school. The school had excellent teachers, and she was sure that Malin would benefit compared to the public school. I wouldn't have to pay any school fees. I thanked her for the generous offer and discussed it with my wife. A few days later, we presented the proposal to our daughter, and a week later, I accepted Sigrid's offer. Shortly after, Malin moved to the boarding school. So that we wouldn't have to drive back to the village every evening, which was especially difficult in winter, we got an apartment in the house. We loved our little paradise in the attic. We spent a lot of time together. I read Malin stories from the past, told her about my youth when life in these latitudes was much tougher, and I told her the story of how I met her mother." He paused briefly and took a deep breath. "A few months after we moved in, in January, Malin suddenly disappeared after school. No one had seen her or knew where she was. I immediately began searching for her. When I hadn't found her after two hours, I asked others to help me search. At midnight, the police were finally called, and some of the villagers also came out to look for my daughter. For four days, we turned over every stone, looked behind every bush or rock, but found nothing. Vilda and I were sick with worry. Even though you never lose hope as a father in such a situation,

I slowly began to fear the worst. I remember sometimes standing in the middle of nowhere and shouting Malin's name as loud as I could. My desperate calls went unanswered, and I never heard Malin's voice again. On the fifth day, the police came to our home. They had found Malin — dead."

I was so absorbed in his story, in his voice that sounded so deep and melancholic, that I had become oblivious to the sounds of the bay. Mikkel had not turned his gaze from the horizon the entire time; his eyes were fixed and empty. I recognized that look all too well. The images that shot through my mind and simply wouldn't go away. It was so familiar to me, so omnipresent. And I was sure that Mikkel too had not received an answer to the question of why to this day.

I placed my hand on his shoulder. "I'm sorry, Mikkel. Really, I am. I'm not just saying that. I know what I'm talking about."

He briefly twisted his mouth but said nothing.

"Where was she found?" I asked instead.

He pulled himself away from the horizon, moved to the edge of the cliff, and pointed down. "There, between the rocks."

I leaned over the edge, but due to the darkness and the fog, I couldn't see anything. "How did she get there?"

"The police told us she probably slipped on the cliff and fell into the depths."

I looked at him, confused. "Slipped? And that was four or five days after she disappeared?"

Mikkel shrugged. "That's what they told us. The current might have carried her into the sea and later washed her back ashore. They couldn't determine the time of death accurately since her body had been in the water for a long time."

I shook my head in disbelief. "I find that explanation a bit odd, if I'm honest."

"You're not the only one."

"A crime was ruled out?" I wanted to know.

"After a while, yes. They questioned all sorts of people, but no one could say anything more precise. After that, they settled on an accident as the cause of death."

In that moment, countless questions raced through my mind, but I didn't want to burden the man further. It was already hard enough for him to talk about his dead child. Still, I wanted to ask him one particular question and hoped he wouldn't take it badly. "May I ask if Malin had any problems?"

"No, she had no problems. She was a wonderful girl, cheerful and kind to everyone."

I nodded.

"My wife got worse week by week," he continued. "She couldn't cope with the loss. I wasn't doing any better myself, but I threw myself into work, and that kept my mind occupied. However, I soon realized that the peace of the bay could also be a curse. Memories and images feel more alive, closer, and more intense in the silence. On some days, I almost broke under them. A father's heart is strong, even if it's just for his own child. But once it's broken, there's nothing in this world that can mend it. You live constantly on the edge and don't know whether to take the final step or not. We tried to live with our daughter's death for three years, three sorrowful years that were worsened by Vilda's severe illness. In the fourth year, I finally buried my wife too." He paused, and I swallowed hard.

"The bay was Malin's home," he continued after a while. "Every day, I wander through the house, hoping to catch a whiff of her scent, hear her voice, or recognize her face among the many people in the house. Every night, I come to this rock, my head full of memories, my heart full of sorrow. It's all that's left to me."

Above us, the northern lights danced, and for a while, neither of us spoke a word. So many things raced through my mind, so many questions I still wanted to ask. But the moment felt wrong. I wondered if I should tell him about my pain. I wanted to say that I knew exactly what dark place he had been in for years and how hard it was to find a way out of there.

But I remained silent. I felt that no further words were needed, that Mikkel would much rather linger in the stillness of the moment. I imagined how difficult it must be to confront the fate of his family day in and day out in this secluded bay. With every walk around the house, with every glance out the window, seeing the place that had taken his child. Out here, there were no distractions in the form of busy streets or restaurants, of ships entering the harbour or cultural events. Here, one was left to oneself.

I was sure I would have broken under such circumstances.

Suddenly, Mikkel turned to me and looked deeply into my eyes. "This place isn't lonely; you're only lonely inside." He tapped his finger on my chest. He winked at me, gave me a gentle tap on the arm, and turned his back to me. Light-footed, he followed the footpath down from the cliff and was swallowed by the fog a moment later. I stood there, a bit perplexed on the rock, gazing into the mist, hoping Mikkel would return. But he didn't.

His voice echoed in my thoughts for a long time as I looked out to sea and thought of his Malin. What would she tell us if she could return to the land of the living? Would she confirm that she had slipped and fallen into the waves? Or would she tell a completely different story? Would she tell the same story that the other dead girls would have to share?

Whatever had been going on in this bay for years, there had to be something evil behind it.

I turned away from the horizon and followed the path back to the house. Halfway there, already enveloped by the fog, I noticed a bouncing beam of light shimmering not far from me through the mist. Alarmed, I stopped.

"Hello, is anyone there?" I called out.

"It's me, Runa. Who's there?" Her voice sounded sharp.

"Sondre," I replied.

"What are you doing here?" she asked suspiciously as she approached me.

I was about to respond that I could ask her the same thing, but I held back. "I was taking an evening walk. That's not forbidden, is it?"

"It's dangerous by the rocks, especially at night."

"I'm aware of that."

"You wouldn't be the first to fall down there."

"I'm aware of that too."

Runa looked at me with narrowed eyes. "Is anyone else with you?"

"No, I'm alone. Why?"

"Just wondering."

She shined the flashlight around the area.

"Are you looking for someone?" I asked.

"No. I just saw the beam of your flashlight and wanted to check if one of the students was wandering around out here."

"I was alone," I lied.

She nodded. "Alright then. I'll go back inside. Goodnight." She turned around, and the light of her lamp disappeared into the fog with her. Shaking my head, I watched her go.

What an unpleasant person.

Before walking on, I noticed the outlines of a rock formation in a clearing in the fog that stood out as a dark spot against the snow. I left the path and approached the rocks. When I stood in front of them, I looked up and saw the cliff where I had just stood with Mikkel. So this had to be the place where Malin had been found. It was unimaginable how a body must have looked upon impact here. A cold shiver ran down my spine.

With my flashlight, I illuminated the rocks. They were partially snow-covered and looked slippery. Nevertheless, I climbed a few meters up and stopped at the top. Spray splashed into my face, and I had to be careful not to lose my grip. I looked around, not knowing what I was searching for up here.

As I let the light glide over the surface, I stopped at something shiny. Carefully, I balanced from one stone to the next until I stopped in front of a small indentation in the rock and knelt down. I shone the flashlight into the small rock opening and noticed an object that seemed to be wedged between the stones. I reached in and felt something cold and metallic. It barely moved, so I shook it until it loosened enough for me to pull it out. I placed the flashlight between my teeth and examined the strange object. It was a silver, slightly dented box, adorned with lines and faded trolls. There were small clasp locks on three sides that opened easily. Carefully, I lifted the lid and found a transparent plastic bag containing a folded sheet of paper. Curious, I took the paper out of the bag and held it in the beam of the flashlight. It was clearly a letter, written in blue ink and, judging by the handwriting, from a man.

My Dearest Daughter

When the stars twinkle over our bay and the Northern Lights trace their paths, when the snow falls gently and the sounds of the world succumb to the white winter cloak, I feel close to you, as if you have never been gone. Every day, I see your smile in front of me, your sparkling eyes, and I smell the almond oil in your hair, which reminds me so much of your mother. I feel your delicate hands seeking mine while we walk, and I hear the echo of your voice, which now reaches me from so far away that it pains me immensely.

Living without you is like a life without breath. Memories are the only things left of you, and that's why I imagine us sitting together on the shore, waiting for a fish to bite, while I answer your innocent questions, even if you've asked them a dozen times before. I stand by your bed and listen to your breathing, and in those moments, I always realize that I need nothing else in my life.

These daydreams, which rob me of sleep at night, are both a blessing and a curse. I am incredibly grateful that all the memories of you are still so vivid, and at the same time, I try to suppress them. Please do not think poorly of me for that. Seeing your face before my eyes is sometimes so hard to bear that I wish I would never have to endure even a single thought of you. I wish I were where you and Mama are now. I know you are waiting for me, but I have not yet fulfilled my role in this story. I must stay here a little longer. Do not worry, be confident, and filled with joy. I will soon join you, and then we will be reunited—forever.

  Your Papa

I realized I had been holding my breath while reading. I inhaled the sea air into my lungs, and at the same time, I swallowed a lump that felt as thick and dry as a ball of yarn.

The letter clearly came from Mikkel. I read it once more, and with each word, I could feel his pain within myself; the same thoughts about my own life flared up, like a fire of memory that no water could extinguish.

I put the letter back in the bag, placed it in the box, and secured it back in its rightful place. Then I stood up, took one last look over the beach, and went back to my apartment.

Chapter 27

On the morning of the next day, I left the classroom during the break, made my way to a small balcony at the end of the corridor, and allowed myself a cigarette. The relaxing effect of the first puff pushed the anger I had felt during the last hour with the students into the background. The lack of focus in the class that day was hard to bear. I had to repeat almost every question, and there was constant chatter in between. Two female students even got into a fight, and I almost had to intervene with a chair. I promptly banished both of them to Sigrid, where they would receive a warning.

Now it was finally break time, and I could breathe again. Last night had not been a highlight in terms of sleep. The words in Mikkel's letter would not quiet down, and I wished I could talk to him about it again. After all, we had endured similar fates in our lives.

Suddenly, the balcony door opened, and Elin, a fellow teacher, stood in the doorway. "Sondre, you need to come to the staff room. Sigrid has information about Tiril," she said, out of breath.

I was startled.

Hastily, I stubbed out the cigarette and followed her into the staff room, where most of the colleagues were already present. I didn't feel like sitting down, so I leaned against the back wall and glanced around the room. My eyes landed on Runa, who was observing me in turn. When our gazes met, she looked away.

What was up with her?

After another two minutes, Sander, Inge, and Skadi finally arrived, and the faculty was complete. Sigrid stepped to the front, her posture as stiff as ever.

"Good morning, everyone. Thank you for taking a moment. I wanted to update you on the progress of the search for Tiril." She held her hands, like a preacher at prayer, in front of her stomach. "Unfortunately, the police have not been able to report significant progress. Yesterday, together with volunteers, they searched the area for Tiril, but had to call off the search shortly after nine o'clock. They resumed the search early this morning, and it is still ongoing. You can share this information with the students. I know many are expecting the worst, but I remain hopeful that Tiril will turn up somewhere."

That had to be a joke, I thought. "May I ask something?" I interjected.

Sigrid's icy gaze shot in my direction. "Sondre?"

"If I'm correctly informed, Tiril disappeared in the middle of the night?"

"That's correct."

"She was only wearing her pyjamas."

"Possibly, we don't know for sure."

"Maybe I'm the only one here who finds that strange. But what kind of person would just run away in pyjamas in the middle of winter? Especially in this wilderness?"

She didn't respond immediately, but I could tell my questioning was greatly displeasing to her. "Unfortunately, many of our students are psychologically troubled. You never know what they are capable of. You'll realize this soon enough." She shrugged and turned away from me.

I couldn't believe what I was hearing. This couldn't be serious! "Wait a minute," I pressed on, much to her displeasure. "According to what I've heard, Tiril wasn't actually doing badly. Her friends have confirmed this as well. I consider it rather unlikely that she ran away." I looked into the faces of my colleagues, hoping for some support. But far from it. Most looked bored, only Jori nodded at me. Fine, I thought, then I would have to deliver a monologue. I wanted to ask more questions when Runa stepped forward.

"Sondre, you haven't been here long. You will soon realize that many students have problems that run deeper than what is visible from the outside. We've dealt with many very unusual incidents. Often involving students whom you'd never suspect of such strange behaviour. I think Sigrid is right, and we can trust in Tiril's return." She smiled at Sigrid.

If she had crawled any further up Sigrid's backside, she could have scratched her throat!

"Thank you, Runa," Sigrid said, nodding at her. "That's all. I will inform you at the appropriate time. I wish everyone a pleasant day."

She strutted out of the room, leaving us behind. A few colleagues cast a glance at me, ambiguous whether in agreement or disapproval. Runa briefly glanced my way, grabbed her documents, and left the room as well.

Jori approached me. "Let it go, Sondre. Sigrid is a tough nut to crack; she's not worth losing sleep over, you'll need them here." He gave me a pat on the arm and went outside. I looked at the clock. I had ten minutes left until the break was over. I felt my stomach growl, demanding food. So I left the staff room and hurried up the stairs to my apartment. Just before my floor, I heard footsteps from the fourth floor. I looked up over the railing but couldn't see anyone. Instead, I heard a door open. Then there was silence.

Could that be Mikkel?

I climbed another floor and found an empty hallway. The first door on the left was closed, the one next to it was too. The only door that was ajar was the chapel's. The hallway wasn't carpeted, so I feared the old wooden floorboards would betray my presence. On my fifth step, the floor beneath me let out a terrible creak. In the dull silence of the fourth floor, it sounded like a gunshot. My body froze, and I listened with a pounding heart to see if anything stirred. A minute passed with nothing happening, so I cautiously moved on. When I reached the door, I peered through a crack into the room. A woman was kneeling in the front row of the chapel, seemingly praying.

It was Sigrid!

Quiet murmurs escaped her lips, and I wondered for whom or what she was praying. I would have liked to tell her that she would do better to take Tiril's disappearance a bit more seriously. That would have helped the poor girl far more than her empty words.

Suddenly, Sigrid turned around, and our eyes met for a split second. Startled, I darted behind the wall and stood there indecisively. I could have kicked myself. What was I thinking, watching her while she prayed?

I considered whether to stay put to explain my presence or to simply run away.

I chose to run away.

In a rush, I made my way to the stairs, practically flew down the steps, and reached my class out of breath. A minute later, I resumed the lesson, expecting Sigrid to knock and summon me to her office at any moment.

***

Just before eleven o'clock at night, Lilly slipped out of her room. She wanted to call her friend Sonja, who had just texted her that her boyfriend had left her and that she needed someone to talk to. She couldn't make the call in her room because her roommate was already asleep. So she had no choice but to make the call from somewhere outside the building, which was a big risk. Students were not allowed to be outside their rooms after ten o'clock at night, unless they needed to go to the bathroom or the nurse. Lilly had been out after ten many times before. Twice she had been caught; a third time would end her stay at Fog Castle. For some, being suspended from the boarding school might seem like the perfect solution. However, one had to consider the consequences. What would her parents say? Where would she go to school after that? Who would take her in?

So, following the rules was much easier, at least in theory!

The circumstances today called for an exception, and she disregarded the rules. To avoid being caught again, she took much more time this time. She stopped every few meters, listened for any suspicious sounds, moved on, stopped again, listened, and thus she carefully made her way until she finally reached the entrance hall. She carried her shoes in her hands, as moving in socks was much quieter. It took her almost ten minutes to get from her room to the entrance hall. Tonight, however, she would not use the front door as usual, but the door in the kitchen, which led directly to the west side of the building.

The kitchen was dark, with only a few small lights from the dishwasher glowing in the back of the room. Lilly sneaked between tables and countertops and finally stopped in front of the door. She put on her shoes and stepped outside. Clouds of fog swept past her, and she felt the moisture on her face. She closed the door and trudged off. The wind picked up, causing the temperature to drop even further. Shivering, she zipped her jacket up to her chin and adjusted her hat. The fog made the whole scene even creepier, and she had difficulty finding her way. Fortunately, there were already tracks in the snow. At least she could follow those. After a few minutes, she noticed a gap in the fog and saw the ash-gray sea about a hundred meters ahead. The surface of the water was choppy from the wind, and the air smelled of algae. Just before she reached the high-water mark, she stopped, rummaged for her phone, and called Sonja.

"Hey, Sonja. I couldn't get in touch earlier. You know how it is here."

"It's fine. I can't sleep anyway."

"What the hell happened?"

"That jerk left me," she sobbed.

"Why? Everything was going well!"

"Yeah, I thought so too. But he met someone else."

"Seriously? Who?"

"No idea!" She blew her nose noisily. "I only know that her name is Helen."

"Doesn't ring a bell."

"She's from the city. Apparently, he met her in a disco."

"What a jerk. I'll kick his ass the next time I see him."

"Oh, just let it go. He's not worth it."

At that moment, Lilly heard a noise. Startled, she listened intently.

"Lilly, are you still there?" Sonja asked.

"Shh... be quiet for a second. I think someone is struggling through the snow."

"What? Who?"

"No idea, wait a minute." Again, she heard the noise. "I think someone is walking through the snow."

"Then get out of there!"

"Where to? It's pitch dark here."

"Do you see anyone?"

"No. I only see the sea and the beach. Everything behind me is shrouded in fog. I better hang up, Sonja. I'll get back to you later. I'm sorry." She ended the call and tucked her phone away. With her heart pounding, she looked around but saw only darkness. The fog had swallowed the boarding school and the lights in the windows. The noise was getting closer. Anxiously, she turned around once but couldn't see anyone. Her pulse quickened.

Had her nighttime excursion been discovered?

She needed to get out of there, and there was only one way: along the beach, to its end, and from there back to Fog Castle. She left her position and followed the high-water line. After about a hundred meters, she stopped and listened into the night. At first, she only heard the wind and the waves, but then a strange, animal-like snorting mixed in. All the hairs on the back of her neck stood up. She would have preferred to run, but it was simply too dark for a quick escape.

She hurried on as fast as she could and reached the south end of the beach after another three minutes. From there, she turned at a ninety-degree angle and followed the footprints toward the house. She walked faster and faster. She felt panic seize her, almost taking her breath away. She had no idea whether the person in the dark was just a teacher wanting to confront her or if it was a psychopath who wanted to kill her.

Suddenly, a boulder appeared in front of her, and she took a deep breath. Her heart was racing wildly, and she was sweating despite the freezing temperatures. Exhausted, she crouched down and listened to the darkness. The wind had died down a bit, and she could only hear the rhythmic splashing of the waves. She tried to calm her breathing and wished she hadn't left her room.

Desperately, she searched the surroundings for a saving light, but there was none. She considered pulling out her flashlight but decided against it. The light would be immediately noticeable. She searched for the footprints and hoped they were still leading toward the house.

A cough very close by made her jump. Gripped by fear, she ran, trying to stay in the tracks and hoping that finally a light would pierce through the darkness and the fog. Her thighs were burning like fire by now. But she ignored the pain, stumbled on, and could barely breathe. Once she tripped over a bush and landed face-first in the snow. She felt a pain on her left cheek and a warm trickle running down her neck. Groaning, she picked herself up and ran on. Her lungs ached from the icy air, and she knew she couldn't keep running for much longer. After a few meters, she thought she could see a faint glimmer of light in the fog, which became clearer the closer she got. Finally, she recognized the pathway lighting that led to the house. She summoned her last reserves of strength, finally collapsed onto the pavement, and from there, continued toward the front door.

Just twenty meters!

She reached the door, pressed down the handle, but it was locked. She tried a second and third time, but the door wouldn't budge. With her fists, she hammered against the solid wood and simultaneously screamed for help. She heard footsteps behind her. Without turning around, she ran again, along the facade, until the next corner of the building. There she turned left, sprinted to the side door, pushed it open, and jumped inside with one leap. She dashed through the kitchen, past the lounge, into the entrance hall and up the stairs, taking two steps at a time until she finally reached her room. She collapsed onto her bed and started to cry. First quietly, then louder and louder, and only after a while did she notice her roommate standing next to her with a shocked expression on her face, touching her shoulders.

Chapter 28

A cloudless sky promised much-needed sunshine for my vitamin D intake. I often found myself distracted in class, which made me susceptible to the eccentricities of certain students. I had to rein myself in at times to ensure that the police officer in me didn't emerge, reprimanding the deliquents in an overly authoritative tone, but rather the trained and composed teacher that the position required. Fortunately, classes only lasted until midday today. After that, the students had to retreat to their rooms to study. I wanted to take the opportunity to visit Yorick's acquaintance in Tromsø that afternoon. I had already tried to get Janna's phone number beforehand but couldn't find it anywhere. Her mobile number didn't seem to be listed, and she obviously didn't have a landline.

After lunch, Lilly approached me and told me that she had been followed by someone at the beach during the night. I could hardly believe my ears and asked her to recount the whole story from the beginning. She had put her stay in Fog Castle at risk with her actions, and what was worse, she might have put her life on the line, for which I admonished her.

After Lilly dejectedly retreated to her room, I left Fog Castle behind and drove eastward. My thoughts revolved around Lilly's night adventure and Tiril's whereabouts. I was increasingly doubtful that Tiril had disappeared of her own volition. Without warm shelter, she would have frozen to death in no time, and there was none to be found in the immediate vicinity. The only way I could still consider a voluntary disappearance would be if Tiril had received help from outside—someone who had picked her up and brought her warm clothes. However, this theory was out of the question for Lilly, and she definitely knew Tiril better than I did. So, if flight and suicide could be ruled out, only a crime remained. And this could perhaps also apply to the earlier cases. The investigators might not have succeeded in finding the necessary evidence so far, which can happen in criminal cases. If it was indeed such a case, then the perpetrator or perpetrators must come from the ranks of the boarding school. Someone with access to the premises, who knew the building, the students, and their rooms. This fact alone excluded an outsider. Perhaps Tiril was still hiding in Fog Castle, somewhere concealed, in a room, in a closet, in the attic...!

The question was, who knew the building best? The answer was simple: Mikkel, of course. He had worked at the boarding school for decades. He must know every nook and cranny, every hidden corner. But what motive would drive him to commit such an act? He had had to bury his daughter. What satisfaction would it bring him to make girls disappear at random or even to kill them? Sure, he was a strange fellow, his soul surrounded by darkness, but I did not see him as a murderer. Not yet! Perhaps something would crystallize in another conversation that would make him seem suspicious.

I didn't know the other boarders well enough to form a judgment about their lives and intentions. So far, I had exchanged only a few words with hardly anyone from the teaching staff and hadn't spoken to the psychologist at all. Only Runa had stood out to me negatively. Her suspicious glances and her sudden appearance at the rock outside seemed very strange to me. However, I doubted that she could physically manage to abduct a girl from her room and drag her through half the house, which didn't mean she couldn't have received help from someone.

In summary: I had a house full of suspects. But it was impossible for me to discreetly check each and every one. There simply wasn't enough time. I crossed the Sandnessund Bridge and instead of taking the tunnel system, I drove up the Tverrforbindelsen. The road led over the higher central part of the island and descended on the other side down to the shores of Tromsø Sound. The water lay like a mirror between the island and the mainland, and the mountains behind glowed in orange-yellow light. Some boats were plowing north or south through the sound, including a Coast Guard ship.

After I reached the other side of the island, I drove through Tromsø Sound Tunnel onto the mainland and a few minutes later turned onto Beryllvegen. I drove slowly past the houses, searching for house number four. I eventually found the house a bit further up the road. A grey Volvo was parked in front of the garage. The house was generously built, about thirty meters long, and had two floors. A covered balcony ran along the entire west side of the building, and a few meters apart, ceiling lights burned, which now barely showed in the sunlight.

I parked my car next to the Volvo and got out. During the drive here, I had prepared some questions and hoped that Janne would be willing to talk to me about the boarding school. Perhaps she had put the past in Fog Castle behind her and didn't want to say another word about it.

With mixed feelings, I climbed the steps to the entrance. The doorbell read Janne + Aksel Helland. I pressed the button, and an annoying melody immediately penetrated through the front door. It took almost a minute for someone to fiddle with the lock. I heard the jingle of a keyring, a brief curse, and then the door was flung open to reveal a somewhat stocky woman staring at me, breathless. I estimated her to be about sixty years old. Her hair was packed with curlers, and a towel was draped around her neck. She had a hooked nose, and her lips were chapped in many places. Her forehead had an unusually high number of wrinkles, which was further accentuated by her facial expression.

"Good day, Janne," I greeted her. "My name is Sondre Iversen. Yorick from the bookstore in town gave me your address. He told me you worked at Fog Castle some time ago."

Deeper wrinkles formed on her forehead. "I did, yes."

"I have recently started working there as a teacher."

Her eyebrows shot up. "Oh really?" she replied, and from her tone, I could tell that she didn't think much of it.

"I wanted to ask if we could briefly talk about the boarding school?"

"Now?" She looked at me in shock.

"N-no, it doesn't have to be now," I stuttered, hoping she wouldn't send me away from the threshold. "I was just in town and thought I'd try my luck. I don't expect you to drop everything right now."

Janne sighed and ran her fingers through her hair. "I'm busy, as you can see. But since you didn't drive here for nothing, you can come in, provided my appearance doesn't bother you."

"No, of course not," I reassured her.

She stepped aside and let me enter. "Have a seat in the living room. I'll be right back. Can I get you something? Water, coffee?"

"Water would be lovely." I sat down in an armchair near the window and looked around the living room. A large flat-screen TV hung on the wall. In the corner, a floor lamp cast warm light, and the floor was covered with thick rugs. From my chair, I had a wonderful view of the mountains on Kvaløya and Ringvassøya. I noticed dark snow clouds on the northern horizon.

Janne returned to the living room, holding a glass of water in each hand. She had taken off the towel but not the curlers. She placed the glasses on a small table and sat down on the sofa. "Well, how can I help you?"

"As I mentioned, I've recently started working as a teacher at Fog Castle. I like the job, even if it's definitely different from my previous school. As you know, the students at the boarding school can be a bit difficult at times."

Janne nodded and simply said, "Oh yes!"

"The boarding school is, in my opinion, an interesting but also somewhat strange institution, if I may say so. From the first day, I felt this—how shall I put it—oppressive atmosphere."

Janne made a grimace, nodded slightly again, but said nothing.

"I believe this melancholic atmosphere is not without reason. Two days ago, a student vanished without a trace overnight." I watched her facial features, which briefly tensed at the mention of the missing student. "A large-scale search operation was initiated, but so far, they haven't been able to find her."

Janne shook her head sadly. "That poor girl."

"Yes, it's terrible. Especially for her parents and friends."

"Has there been any clue about her whereabouts?"

"As far as I know, no. The police are investigating but haven't found anything concrete yet. In any case, we haven't heard otherwise."

"It's a wild area out there. She could be anywhere."

I nodded in agreement. "Yorick told me you had some strange experiences at the boarding school. Would you be willing to share them with me?"

Janne looked at me thoughtfully for a moment. I could see that my question unsettled her, and I feared she might refuse my request.

"What exactly did Yorick tell you?" she finally asked. "That you had seen figures sneaking through the house at night and that someone had visited and threatened you in your room."

Janne nodded. "That's correct."

"Do you know who visited you?"

She shook her head. "No. It was dark. I could only see silhouettes, and the face was obscured by a veil. The person was relatively slim, not very tall. What I mainly remember are the ice-cold hands that were pressed over my mouth."

"Were they large hands?"

"No, not necessarily. I felt like they were women's hands."

"Women's hands?" I asked, surprised.

"I think so, yes. But I can't say for sure. I was so panicked that I might not have perceived some details correctly. Also, the unknown person only whispered."

"Did the person have any distinctive features?"

Janne shook her head. "Like I said, it was dark, and I was too frightened to pay attention to details."

"Yorick said that they threatened you with violence if you didn't leave the boarding school."

"That's right. I have never been so scared in my life. I was paralyzed; I couldn't even scream."

"Do you know if it was the same person you saw sneaking through the house?"

"I can't say that with one hundred percent certainty. The night figures were usually too far away for me to see any details. But I believe the person that night was bigger and stronger."

"So probably a man?" I speculated.

"I assume so."

Mikkel flashed through my mind. He was tall. "What is the name of the missing girl?" Janne suddenly asked.

"Tiril!" I replied.

"Did you know her?"

"She showed me around the boarding school on my first day. But that was all. She seemed very nice to me."

Janne nodded.

"When you worked at the boarding school, another girl also disappeared, right?"

"Frida," she said, nodding. "She went to bed at night, and the next morning, there was no trace of her."

"Did she ever turn up again?"

"Yes, but dead!"

"How long was she missing before she was found?"

"Two days, if I remember correctly."

"Where was her body discovered?"

"I believe near the beach. The body was half in the water."

"This has happened to other girls before her, hasn't it?" I continued.

"Indeed."

"Did all the girls go missing for two days before they were found?"

Janne looked up at the ceiling. "I believe so. But I'm not sure. Do you think that's a coincidence, or is there more to it?"

I shrugged. "Good question. As a former police officer, I see more of a pattern. But we won't know the reason until the case is solved. If it ever gets solved."

"You were in the police?" she asked, surprised. I nodded.

"Well, you have a better foundation than I did back then to get to the bottom of this."

I shrugged again. "We'll see. Right now, I still don't see through the matter. There are so many people in this boarding school, but I haven't been able to find any motives so far."

Janne leaned back on the sofa. "You know, there are a lot of odd kids at the boarding school. The students have all gone through difficult times; otherwise, they wouldn't be there. Frida, for example, I knew from class. She had three lessons of English with me each week. I liked her. She smiled often, much more than most of her classmates. And she was curious and polite, which aren't exactly common virtues at the boarding school. The reason Frida was at the boarding school wasn't as dramatic as one might assume. She was caught using cannabis a few times. For me, that's not a big deal. I was high more than once as a teenager. In any case, I could hardly believe it when they announced after her death that she was supposed to have committed suicide. I couldn't imagine that, not with Frida. I subsequently sought a conversation with Sigrid and the psychologist, whose name I unfortunately forgot, and tried to express my doubts about the cause of death. The psychologist wasn't really forthcoming, after all, the conversations between him and the students weren't meant for outsiders. He only said that people are often misjudged, that there is often a simmering unrest behind their facade, and that they might do something unexpected or thoughtless." She shrugged briefly. "And Sigrid supported the psychologist's theory by claiming that Frida was suffering from cannabis withdrawal and that she was feeling bad because of it. She also made it clear to me that although she appreciated my concerns, the matter was none of my business." She shook her head. "You see, I was met with deaf ears regarding my suspicions. However, I was quite unsettled after that conversation. I wondered if I was overreacting and turning a molehill into a mountain. But the more I thought about it, the more certain I became that my doubts were justified, especially since this wasn't the first time something like this had happened." "What do you think could have led to the deaths?"

"If I knew that, you wouldn't be here, would you?" She laughed broadly.

"That's probably true!" I replied with a smile.

"When I first heard about these deaths, I started doing my own research. I asked various people questions, made observations, or searched the house for hiding spots. Most of the teachers had been at the boarding school for too short a time to know anything more about the incidents. And those who had been there longer couldn't help me either. One night, I think it was in November, Frida finally disappeared. From then on, I was sure someone was playing a dirty game in the house. The police interviewed everyone involved in the house, including me, and I told them about my observations and suspicions. They found it very interesting, but at the same time, they asked me why I was sneaking around the house at night. So I told them about my sleep problems. I can still see the looks on the officers' faces; they probably thought they had a gossiping old lady before them who was vying for attention. But that wasn't the case. Anyway, they dismissed me from the questioning, and after that, it seemed like the matter was closed. The next day, I asked some people questions again, and someone probably felt cornered. Two weeks after Frida's death, I received that visit. After that, my career at the boarding school was over."

"Do you remember which people you had asked questions to?"

"Which people?" She looked at me questioningly.

"Exactly. I just want to know if any of them still work at the boarding school today."

"Oh, I see." She looked back up at the ceiling. "Let me think. There were a few…! Teachers, the psychologist, the cook…!"

"Do you remember the names of the teachers?"

"I believe there were Jori, Tyr, Inge, and Runa. Yes — I think that was them. Are they still at the boarding school?"

"They are."

"Good for them," she said with a sarcastic undertone.

"Have you ever met a man named Mikkel at the boarding school?" I continued.

Janne furrowed her brow. "Mikkel? The name doesn't ring a bell."

"Strange. He seems to be the caretaker. You must have known him."

"There was a caretaker, yes, but I'm not sure if he was called Mikkel."

"He always wears a hat."

Janne pondered. "No, I can't remember that, I'm sorry."

"It's fine, no worries."

A pause ensued while Janne adjusted one or two curlers. She looked at me and finally laid her hands in her lap. "If I understand you correctly, you want to get to the bottom of the events at the boarding school. Am I right?"

"I want to try, yes."

She nodded. "I can only approve of that, but I want to warn you at the same time. Something strange is happening within these walls, and it's not good. It could be dangerous for you, just as it has been for me. Someone there does not want the truth to come to light and is trying to prevent it by any means necessary. So be careful." I knew she was right. However, the looming danger would not deter me from further inquiries. On the contrary; after this conversation, I was more motivated than ever. "I'll take care of myself, don't worry." I set the glass of water on the table and stood up. "Thank you very much for talking with me. I'll let you get back to your hair care."

Janne briefly touched her hair and said with a grin, "I have a lot to do."

On my way to the door, I asked her, "You hardly find anything about the events at Fog Castle in the media. Isn't that a bit strange?"

Janne let out a dry laugh. "The school administration tries to avoid bad publicity at all costs. They are dependent on the students. If they stayed away, it would spell the end of the school. That's why very little gets out to the public. Nevertheless, the local newspaper published a report several years ago about a suicide at the boarding school. But it remained just that one report. Everything else could be swept under the rug."

"I couldn't find any reporting on that online." "You won't. The notice from that time exists only in printed form."

"And where would I find this publication?"

"In the library. They have a section with old newspaper reports. I'm sure you'll find what you're looking for there. If I'm not mistaken, the article was published in the spring of 1990. Somewhere around March."

"Wonderful, thank you for that information. Hopefully, it will help me."

"Anytime. If you find out anything, let me know."
"Of course."

We said our goodbyes, and I returned to my car. I glanced at the clock and decided I still had time for a quick stop at the library.

Chapter 29

Never in her life had Tiril devoured her food as she did at that moment. It was everything her heart desired. Reindeer meat in currant sauce, rice and cauliflower, along with a piece of fresh bread. At first, she was afraid that the food might be poisoned, but hunger triumphed over fear, and now she savored every bite. The person who had brought the meal sat on his bed, watching her eat. It was an uncomfortable feeling, but she didn't care. The main thing was to eat!

"Good?" he suddenly asked.

Tiril nearly choked on her bite. Startled, she looked at the man. A gentle smile played around his rugged lips. His voice sounded so hoarse and old, as if he hadn't used it in decades. Although Tiril was glad that the guy broke the terrible silence down here, she didn't want to answer his question. So she just nodded and continued eating.

"You have beautiful hair." He pointed at her hair with his thick finger.

Again, she looked at him, confused, and put her food down. She didn't know what to make of his sudden words. All she managed to say was, "Thank you!"

The left corner of his mouth stretched back, contorting his entire left side of the face in a bizarre way. It almost seemed as if there was not enough skin. A horrific yet sad sight.

Until now, Tiril had been terrified of him. Just the size of this man would make anyone afraid. But now, after he had served her these delicacies and shown human traits with his own words, the fear lessened a bit. At the same time, many questions arose in her mind. Why was she being held down here, why did this man live alone in this hole, what was his relationship to her? Was she his mother?

She longed to ask him these questions, but she was too afraid of his reaction. However, her situation couldn't get much worse, and who knows, maybe a conversation would soften him up, and she could find a way to escape. "Can I ask you something?" she said quickly, biting her lip.

The man tilted his head, his gaze fixed on her. Tiril already regretted her hasty decision.

He nodded.

Tiril breathed a sigh of relief. "Why am I down here?"

***

His gaze dropped to the floor, and he began to swing his legs back and forth. Almost two minutes passed, during which he alternated between looking at her and the ground. Two minutes that felt like an eternity to Tiril.

"You are my princess."

Tiril frowned. "I'm not a princess."

He nodded, but didn't say anything else.

"Why are you keeping me locked up here?"

Now he raised his head and looked at her. "You are safe here, I can protect you here."

"From what?"

Again, he lowered his gaze but didn't answer her.

"What do you need to protect me from?" Tiril asked again.

With his hands, he kneaded the mattress. "From the fire."

"The fire? What fire?" she asked, puzzled.

"From the fire above," he said again. "It can't burn down here."

Tiril didn't know how to respond to that. She didn't understand what he meant by the fire. But when she looked at his scars, she could see a connection to fire. "Why are you down here?"

"Mom wants it this way," he answered.

So she was indeed his mother!

"But she can't do that. You can't lock people up, especially not your own child."

The man lowered his head. "But Mom takes care of me." He started to play with his fingers and appeared almost ashamed.

"But why do you have to live down here? It's much nicer up there?"

He rocked back and forth, and a tear rolled down his cheek. "It's too dangerous up there."

"Dangerous? Why? Because of the fire?"

He nodded.

"Your mom is up there too. Isn't it dangerous for her?"

He shook his head. "She's not in the fire."

Tiril understood less and less. But she also realized that it made no sense to question him about reasons. He obviously had a completely different perception than she did.

She thought about her next question, but he suddenly continued.

"Mom loves me."

"Of course she loves you."

"But she shouldn't love me."

Tiril frowned. "Why shouldn't she love you?"

He looked at her with a furrowed brow, and in his gaze was a profound sadness that she had never seen in any other person. His eyes seemed like two windows, providing a glimpse into his bleak and dark life, witnesses to his grim thoughts.

With barely audible voice, he said, "I was naughty."

At that moment, Tiril didn't know whether to laugh or cry. From his mouth, it sounded as harmless as a mouse's squeak, yet it reflected, for this boy in an adult's body, the fate of his existence. Whatever he had done in his past, it must have been something terrible.

"What happened to you?" she asked after a while.

He showed no reaction for a long time, just staring ahead and playing with his fingers. She waited, wondering if she should say anything else, waited a little longer, but he said nothing more. "You can trust me, I won't tell anyone."

He shook his head vigorously.

"How long have you lived down here?"

He shrugged. "I don't know."

"Don't you ever get bored?"

His eyes searched hers, and like before, his mouth twisted into something resembling a smile. "You're here. You're my princess."

Tiril tried to force a smile, but she couldn't manage it. She couldn't assess this person. Did he want to harm her, or did he simply need company? So far, he hadn't hurt her, but that could change at any moment. "Do you have friends?" she asked.

He shook his head. "No!" At the same time as he answered, more tears rolled down his cheeks.

A pang of pity surged through her, even though her insides resisted this feeling. If a little boy were sitting here, she would have taken him in her arms and comforted him. "I could be your friend," she said to him, hoping to win his trust.

"No, you can't!" His voice sounded much brighter and clearer than before. His eyes fixed on her, and he suddenly stood up abruptly, walked toward her, and stretched out his arms.

Tiril flinched, scooted back a bit, and held her arms protectively over her head.

"Don't be afraid!" he whispered to her.

She felt him pry her arms apart and gently stroke her hair, almost as if he wanted to comfort her. "I'm so sorry, Princess—so sorry!"

She looked into his deformed, sadly smiling face and let him continue, every muscle in her body tense.

"Shall we go for a walk?" he asked suddenly.

For a moment, she didn't know how to respond. Didn't he see that she was only wearing pyjamas? And had he already forgotten his mother's scolding?

At that moment, the door flew open, and light flooded into the room. His mother stood in the doorway with her arms crossed, her gaze could have frozen the Indian Ocean.

Chapter 30

I parked my car right behind the library in the tunnel parking. The sky had noticeably darkened by now, and this was not only due to the low-hanging sun but also because of the approaching cold front.

I entered the glass building and inquired at the information desk where the old newspaper articles were kept. A middle-aged lady with rust-colored hair directed me to the first floor, second shelf from the south, labeled Newspaper Archive. I thanked her and made my way upstairs.

The library was packed with students, either sneaking along the shelves or deeply engrossed in their reading. After some initial searching, I finally found the right shelf and sifted through it for the year 1990. The newspaper issues were all in thick volumes about eighty centimeters tall.

The six books containing the 1990 issues were at the end of the shelf. I took them out one by one and dragged them to a nearby table. Sighing, I opened the first book and immediately reached the issue from January 1st. The first four pages of the *iNord* daily were dedicated to world news, followed by two pages of news from Norway, and then five pages of local events. If anything had been reported about the events at Fog Castle, it had to be found on one of those five pages. The first book contained the months of January and February, so March had to be in volume 2. I searched for the corresponding book and began my research with March 1st. In the local news, the disappearance or death of a boarding school student was not a topic, so I sifted through the days of March 1990 until I came across the newspaper from March 22nd, where an article shone like the Northern Lights in the dark night.

Police Investigate Fog Castle

As iNord has learned, the police have been investigating a death that occurred at the boarding school Fog Castle, near Tåkevik, for the past two days. According to initial reports from the police, it is most likely a suicide. A farewell letter was found at the scene. The deceased is seventeen-year-old student H. A.

I paused.

Farewell letter?

That was something new. I read the article a second time. It truly seemed that Henriette had committed suicide, if, as stated here, a farewell letter had indeed been found. The realization took some wind out of my sails. Why hadn't Janne mentioned this?

I searched through the remaining newspapers from March, but I couldn't find any other articles about Henriette Abramsen's death. I closed the book, went to a computer at the adjacent table, and searched online for entries about Henriette. The search engine returned several hits. However, none seemed to refer to Henriette Abramsen. I wondered if she was from the Tromsø area. If so, I would have loved to talk to her parents. First, though, I would need to locate the address, which wouldn't be easy.

Lost in thought, I gazed through the enormous glass front outside. The sun had vanished, and the snow clouds were poised to enter the city. The streets in front of the library were illuminated by the warm light of street lamps, and the first business people streamed out of their offices. I got up, carried the newspaper volumes back to their designated places, and left the library. As I stepped onto the street, the first cotton ball-sized snowflakes fell from the sky, transforming the city into a scene straight out of a Christmas card.

A few minutes later, I got into my car and left the city towards Kvaløya. The sky north of Sandnessund Bridge was thick with snow clouds, while in the south, the sun spread its last light over the land below the horizon, mingling with the snowy curtains over the fjord. When I reached Kaldfjord, the wind picked up, sweeping snow across the car and the roadway, and just before Tromvik, I could hardly distinguish the road from the sky. At the last moment, I noticed the turnoff to Tåkevik and, twenty minutes later, stood exhausted in front of the entrance door of Fog Castle. A bustling scene welcomed me in the lobby. The study hours seemed to be over, and the youths were attending to their other commitments or socializing with friends in the lounge. I couldn't spot Lilly anywhere. I made my way to her room, knocked on the door, and waited a few seconds until she finally opened it, a bar of chocolate in her hands.

"You look busy," I greeted her.

"I need to raise my blood sugar; this damn studying is making me dog-tired."

"A walk would be healthier than chocolate," I said with a wink.

"Maybe for you. I prefer the unhealthy method." She waved the chocolate in front of my face.

"Do you have a moment?" I asked.

"Of course. Come in."

"No, not in your room."

Lilly smiled mischievously at me. "Are you afraid someone might get the wrong impression?"

"Of course, what else? Come on. And take your jacket."

"At your service, Colonel!"

Lilly closed the door behind her and followed me outside. I led Lilly to the wind-sheltered south side of the building, where we stopped under the awning of a side door. I was about to light a cigarette when I remembered that smoking wasn't allowed on the premises. Especially not in front of students. So I put the pack away again.

"Shall we smoke one together?" Lilly asked, putting on a puppy dog face.

"Not a chance. What do you think would happen if they caught us here?"

"Oh come on, just one."

"Forget it and listen to me. I was just in town. I spoke with a former boarding school teacher..."

"What's her name?" Lilly interrupted me.

"Janne."

"Don't know her."

"Doesn't matter. What matters is what I learned from her. During her time here, a death occurred among the students. A girl named Frida was the victim. Does that name ring a bell?"

Lilly shook her head.

"Never mind. Janne told me that after this death, she conducted inquiries within the boarding school. She wanted to get to the bottom of things because she felt that the school management wasn't doing enough to clarify the case. Apparently, someone didn't like her questioning, because two weeks after Frida's death, Janne was visited in her room at night and intimidated. After that, she resigned and left the school."

"That's a scandal!" Lilly said indignantly.

"Indeed."

"And she just put up with that?"

"I wondered the same, but that's her business. In any case, she sent me to the library. She told me I would find a newspaper article from March '90 there reporting on the death of a student. Her name was Henriette, and she seems to have been one of the first victims at the boarding school. This was one or two years after its founding. And now hold on; apparently, a farewell letter was found on site."

Lilly raised her eyebrows. "Really?"

I nodded. "According to the report, yes. That certainly casts a different light on the whole matter. So suicide did play a role after all. But that doesn't mean that the same happened with the other four. As far as I know, no farewell letters were found in their cases."

"I've never heard anything about farewell letters."

"Exactly. That's why I'm not letting this go. The farewell letter could have been forged too. Maybe she had to write it under the threat of death, who knows? The only way we can get a clearer picture of this is by talking to Henriette's parents. And that's where you come in."

Lilly looked at me in surprise. "Me? How so?"

"The school management must have archived all student records somewhere. Do you happen to know where this archive is located?"

Lilly laughed briefly. "What do you think? Of course, I know. They're kept in Sigrid's office."

I nodded and looked at her suspiciously. "And how do you know that, if I may ask?"

"If you mess up here and get caught, you have to go see Sigrid or Jori. I've had to see Sigrid twice already." She rolled her eyes. "That's when I noticed a distinctive filing cabinet in her office. The student files are in there."

I recalled Sigrid's office, and indeed, I had noticed a filing cabinet back then. The question was, how was I going to get access to these files? I couldn't exactly ask Sigrid for Henriette's dossier.

What are you planning?" Lilly asked.

"I need Henriette's file. That's the only way I can get her address, and it's the only way I can make progress in this case. If I have Henriette's file, I'll surely find Frida's and Tiril's as well. Maybe I'll recognize a connection between the cases—a pattern."

She looked at me questioningly. "A pattern?"

"Yes, a pattern. It's like with a serial killer. You have to recognize a pattern to track down the perpetrator."

"So you're convinced it's a crime?"

"I didn't say that. I'm just exploring every possibility."

"Sure! I can see that you don't believe in the suicide theory."

I didn't reply to that.

"And how do you intend to break into the office?" she asked, looking at me askew.

"I'm not breaking in; I'm just retrieving my pen that I lost in there."

"Sure, everyone will believe that. If you get caught, you'll lose your position."

"I won't get caught."

She raised her eyebrows and shook her head slightly. "I have another idea. I shouldn't tell you this, but it's not the first time I've broken into Sigrid's office."

Now I raised my eyebrows. "Do I want to know why?"

"Sigrid had a proof photo. I had smoked on school grounds; that was at the beginning. She took a picture of me and then summoned me to her office. Of course, I denied it, but when she showed me the photo, the lies were over. After that, I wanted to delete the photo from her computer. So, I got access to the office, tried to log into the computer, but of course, I couldn't figure out the password." She shook her head. "What I really wanted to say is: I know how to get in without a key."

"Absolutely not. I don't want you putting yourself in danger. If you get caught, you'll be expelled from school."

"I won't get caught."

"Many thought that here; otherwise, they wouldn't be here, right?"

Lilly looked at me reproachfully. "Do you already know how you're going to get in?"

No, I really didn't know that yet. But I'd think of something.

When I didn't respond to her question, she said, "See, I thought so. Let me handle it, and tomorrow you'll have your files."

I shook my head, unconvincingly. "I can't — drag you — into this."

"Stop it. I'm already in the thick of it. Tiril was a friend; I owe her that. Please, let me handle it!"

I chewed on my lower lip, unsure how to get out of this. Telling her no made about as much sense as telling a child they couldn't go into a toy store. "Fine, you pest. If you insist. But for heaven's sake, be careful; don't take any risks, got it?"

"Yeah, yeah, okay. I'm not a little girl anymore."

"Even big girls can get caught."

"I know what I'm doing. Trust me."

"Let's hope so. Come on, let's go back to our rooms."

***

Behind a tall houseplant near the entrance, Runa watched as Sondre came in with Lilly and how they said goodbye at the door. The wink exchanged between them didn't escape her watchful eyes. She looked after them thoughtfully, wondering what was going on. She hadn't liked the guy from the beginning. He came here, acted like he knew how things worked, and now it seemed he was even interested in one of the students. That needed to be stopped.

She left her hiding place and headed for an office on the ground floor.

Chapter 31

On the evening of the same day, Mikkel stood in a dark nook beneath the stairs, observing the comings and goings in the corridors of the ground floor and the entrance hall. Most of the students were already in their rooms, and slowly, calmness returned. A few were still lounging in the chairs of the lounge. Mathilde, the cook, apparently had had enough of her workplace and hurried out of the house through the main entrance, with Jori following her two minutes later. Shortly after, a woman sneaked down the stairs, glanced around the entrance hall, brushed a red strand of hair from her eyes, and disappeared into one of the corridors. He followed her at a distance, watching as she tampered with Sigrid's office door. Once she paused, looked up and down the hallway, then continued.

Not a minute later, he saw her disappear upstairs with a satisfied smile, unaware that she had been watched. Pleased, he left his hiding spot, crossed the entrance hall, and stepped outside, where he ducked behind curtains of snow.

A few hours later, as the house lay in deep slumber, Lilly stealthily descended the stairs and headed toward Sigrid's office for the second time that day. She pressed down the handle, the door swung open, granting her unhindered access. She slipped inside and quietly closed the door behind her. Once in the office, she took out a flashlight, clamped it between her teeth, and made her way purposefully to Sigrid's desk, rummaging through a drawer until she unearthed a small key. With this, she approached a large filing cabinet, unlocked it, and pulled out the second-to-bottom drawer, labeled "1998 and older." The files were arranged chronologically, but ended with the year 1992.

What a mess!

Where were the records from the preceding years? Had they already been destroyed?

In the upper drawers, she found documents from 1999 to the present.

Nothing to show!

The bottom drawer was unlabeled. Curiously, she opened it and stared at a chaotic mess. Papers and old newspapers lay scattered haphazardly. Vases leaned against the back of the drawer, empty of flowers, a bottle of fertilizer was stuck to the bottom, and countless light bulbs were stacked on top of one another. Beneath a yellowed folder, she noticed a torn hanging file that had the word POLICE written in capital letters. She shoved the folder aside, brought the file into the light, and opened the cover. The first thing she saw was a photo of a blonde girl smiling warmly at the camera. The photo was attached to an old entry form, its print faded and barely legible. However, the name stood out to her as if highlighted with a neon marker: Henriette Abramsen!

Lilly's pulse quickened. With trembling fingers, she laid the file before her on the floor and began reading. The first form was the same document she had had to fill out upon her entry. The same questions, the same legal disclaimers, the same rules. She flipped to the next file and found another photo of a young woman. Only this one had hair as black as night and a button nose. She lifted the photo and read the name underneath, but it meant nothing to her. In the next two files, she also found photos and documents about former students.

And suddenly, her breath caught in her throat.

In one of the photos, Linnea Rolvsson was looking back at her. Her expression just as Lilly had known her, with a bedroom gaze and the left corner of her mouth curled up into a timid smile. Lilly looked up, her hands trembling so fiercely as if she had been standing in the biting cold for hours.

All these files in front of her pertained to deceased students. The police must have requested them from Sigrid. Why she kept them so disrespectfully among the garbage was beyond her understanding.

Suddenly, a clicking sound like a lock came from the direction of the office door.

Startled, Lilly dropped the flashlight. The clattering noise echoed through the house like thunder. Her heartbeat momentarily ceased, and she turned toward the door. With wide-open eyes, she saw it slowly opening. Quick-thinking, she grabbed the flashlight, turned it off, and quietly closed the drawer. She tucked the documents into her waistband, searched for a hiding spot, and finally decided on a houseplant behind the door. Holding her breath, she crouched down and waited for Sigrid to enter the office.

But no one came.

The door was now fully open. A weak, shadowless beam of light fell into the room. It was utterly silent. Lilly could hear neither someone breathing nor footsteps approaching.

Had the door opened by itself?

Her pulse pounded faster, and a tingling sensation ran down her back like a swarm of ants. Feverishly, she considered what to do next. She couldn't stay here forever; that much was clear. If she were caught, it wouldn't matter if she was found here behind the door or when leaving the office. It would make no difference to her expulsion.

Again, she listened to the silence. But all she heard was her own blood rushing in her ears. With utmost caution, she stepped out from behind the plant and approached the door. At any moment, she expected someone to grab her by the collar and confront her with the situation.

But no one jumped out from hiding, no one called her name in a stern voice. She wondered if she should simply run out with her sweater pulled up and disappear into her room. If someone was indeed waiting for her outside the office, they might not recognize her that way.

The hallway was only dimly lit. With a quick glance, she checked the floor for a telltale shadow but found none. At the pace of a dormouse, she stretched her head out into the hallway, first looking left, then right—and realized the hallway was empty. She didn't know whether to feel relieved or worried.

Why the hell did that damned door open by itself?

She stepped into the hallway, closed it as quietly as possible, and sprinted toward the stairs. She took two steps at a time, reaching the first floor in record time. On the second floor, she bumped into someone and fell to the ground. She heard an expletive, scrambled to her feet, and looked into Runa's angry expression. She was also on the floor, holding her elbow.

"Damn it, what's that about?" she scolded. "Are you out of your mind?"

"I'm sorry, I didn't see you."

"What are you doing here?"

"I needed some fresh air. I'm not feeling well," Lilly replied quietly.

"And why are you running around the house, then?"

Lilly tried to hastily come up with a plausible explanation, but her thoughts were a jumble, and she could barely think clearly. "I..., I was cold, I just wanted to get back to bed as quickly as possible."

Runa hoisted herself up with a pained expression. "Don't give me nonsense. Are you meeting someone?"

"No, certainly not." Lilly also stood up.

"Don't lie to me," Runa hissed angrily.

"I'm not lying."

"You seem to get along quite well with that Sondre, don't you?" Her voice dripped with sarcasm.

"So what? Is that forbidden?"

Runa stared at her suspiciously. "Just don't get cheeky. Otherwise, I'll drag you straight to Sigrid. I was actually on my way to her anyway."

Normally, Lilly would have fired another cheeky retort in Runa's direction, but she just wanted to get back to her room. "I'm sorry. It won't happen again."

"Come on, back to your room."

Nodding, she hurried past Runa and walked to her quarters. She stopped in front of the door and took a deep breath. The T-shirt stuck to her back, and her legs felt as if she had just swum from Spitsbergen to Tromsø.

Suddenly, she remembered the documents. She pulled them from her waistband and was relieved they hadn't fallen out during her collision with Runa. That would have been a disaster—she couldn't even imagine it.

Deep in thought, she looked at the file in her hand. In truth, she longed for her bed, but she couldn't keep the discovery to herself until tomorrow. She had to present her findings to Sondre.

Chapter 32

For hours, I lay awake in bed, rolling from one side to the other, checking the clock, getting frustrated, rolling back, and hoping that morning would soon break. No matter how hard I tried to switch off my thoughts, it just wouldn't work. I thought about Jørn and that he would soon be here with me. I was immensely looking forward to the few hours we would get to spend together, but I was also a bit afraid of the uncertainty that such a weekend could bring. I wasn't sure if Jørn was looking forward to it as well or if it was just an annoying obligation for him. I had planned to talk to him about our cooled-off relationship, but at the same time, I had some reservations. His reticence was unlikely to just vanish over the weekend.

When I wasn't thinking about Jørn, my thoughts drifted to Lilly's nighttime expedition in Sigrid's office. The guilt gnawed at me like woodworm on a church bench.

Automatically, my thoughts turned to Tiril. The hope of finding her alive dwindled with every passing hour. As a father who had buried a child himself, I knew what such a time of uncertainty could mean for parents. It was an unending nightmare, a long and dark tunnel with no light at the end. One drifts into a world that seems so foreign and malicious at the same time, and yet one does not allow any other thoughts. One barricades oneself behind the pain and suffering, behind a transparent wall that no one can penetrate. And in doing so, one fails to notice that one has already retreated from life, that the earth continues to turn, while one remains stuck in place. A state that is hardly bearable!

At that moment, there was a knock at the door. I opened my eyes and wasn't initially sure if someone was really standing at my door.

Before I could pull back the blanket, there was another knock. Surprised, I got up, went to the door, and found Lilly standing in the hallway, pale as a ghost. With her red hair and pale skin, she looked like a dancer from the Moulin Rouge. She cast a quick glance at me, slipped past me uninvited, and collapsed onto the sofa, hands covering her face. I went back to my bedroom, pulled on a pair of sweatpants, and sat down in an armchair. "You look pretty worn out. Did something happen?" I asked, expecting the worst.

Lilly looked at me as if I had just asked the dumbest question in the world. "Happened? That's the understatement of the year!" She let her head fall back onto the sofa.

"Would you like something to drink?"

"Vodka neat, please!"

"First of all, I don't keep that kind of stuff, and even if I did, I certainly wouldn't offer it to you. Water, tea, or coffee?"

"Well then, water it is."

I filled a cup with water in the kitchen and watched her down it in one go. "More?" I asked.

"No, that's enough," she replied, still out of breath.

"Tell me," I urged her.

She sat up, took a few deep breaths, and set the cup down on the side table. "As promised, I gained access to Sigrid's office..."

"How did you manage that?" I interrupted her.

"The door is still intact, if that's what you mean."

"I hope so."

"I slipped a small wooden splinter into the lock the night before while Sigrid was still in the office. After that, she couldn't lock the door from the outside anymore."

I had to suppress a laugh.

"So I entered the office, found the key to the archive cabinet, but then discovered that the older files aren't kept there. Either they are in another, unknown location, or they have already been destroyed. I was about to give up when I noticed an unmarked drawer. At first glance, it looked like just trash, but upon closer inspection, I spotted a folder that was at the very bottom. When I checked it, it had POLICE written in big letters on it."

I became alert.

"I took the folder, opened the first page, and lo and behold, Henriette's dossier was right on top." She paused.

"But that's not all. In addition to Henriette's dossier, I found records of at least two other girls, and I assume they are the deceased students."

I widened my eyes, and Lilly just nodded. "Where are the documents now?" I wanted to know.

"I'll get to that. Now comes the scary part: I was just about to go through the files when the door opened as if by ghostly hands."

My heart sank. She had been caught!

"I almost fainted. I barely managed to hide behind a houseplant, waiting for the inevitable. But no one came. I waited a few minutes, already envisioning myself packing my bags in my mind. But nothing happened. Finally, I worked up the courage to leave the office anyway and was even more astonished when I found no one in the hallway either. So I ran away as quickly as possible, up the stairs, to the first floor, where I collided with Runa."

"Oh no!"

"Oh yes! We both fell flat. Runa cursed and then cornered me. I managed to talk my way out of it somewhat skillfully, but I'm not sure if she bought it." She shrugged.

"What did you tell her?"

"That I didn't feel well and needed fresh air."

"Hopefully, she doesn't report that to Sigrid," I interjected worriedly.

"I don't think so."

For a moment, I didn't know what to say. Lilly had been incredibly lucky. If she had been caught, I would have had to take the blame. "Did you leave the records in the office?"

"What do you take me for?" She dramatically lifted her hoodie and pulled out a folder. She slammed it down on the table, her expression like that of a victorious general.

I looked at the folder, which had POLICE written in bold on the front.

"So, boss!" Lilly said, clapping her hands on her thighs. "That's it for tonight. I can't take it anymore. I need to go to bed, even though I'm almost dying of curiosity, but that has to wait. You will tell me everything tomorrow, right?"

I nodded. "Of course!"

"Well then, good night, and don't stay up too late."

She pushed herself up from the sofa, slapped her hand on my shoulder twice, and left my apartment. I watched her until the door closed behind her.

What a little devil!

Shaking my head, I opened the folder. I looked into the face of a young woman with blonde hair. She was smiling, even if it seemed forced. I lifted the photo and found the name of the girl underneath: Henriette Abramsen. Just below the name, I saw the address: Bergheimvegen 23, Kvaløya.

I skimmed through the rest of the admission form but found nothing of significance. In the other documents, there were some reports and notes that I wanted to save for the next day. I set Henriette's file aside and moved on to the next one. Again a student, but this time with black, curly hair, a round face, a mole on her right cheek, and a silver nose ring. Fenna Guldbrandsen was written on the form.

The next picture showed Frida Vinter, then Dagny Arnesen, and finally Linnea Rolvsson. On the latter, something black was pressing through the photo. I turned it over and looked in surprise at a drawn crucifix. I checked the other photos and found another crucifix on each one. A shiver ran down my spine.

I took Henriette's photo in hand and studied it for a while.

If only I knew what happened to you, girl!

I pulled out my phone and searched for the listed address. The house was in Kaldfjord, right between here and the city. The day after tomorrow, I had to pick up Jørn. That would give me the opportunity to check the address on the way, as it was likely that the Abramsen family no longer lived in that house. After all, over twenty years had passed since then.

The oven clock read 1:15 AM, which explained my tiredness. I contemplated whether I should go to bed but decided against it. My curiosity about the files was simply too great, and the hope of finding something significant outweighed my desire for a restful night's sleep.

Yawning, I flipped through Henriette's file and found notes on grades, behavior, and progress in class. The teachers mentioned in their reports that Henriette was often withdrawn and not following along in class. She frequently needed to be reminded several times per hour to concentrate. Furthermore, I found a report about a conflict with a classmate concerning a boy. Lastly, I read the notes from a parent-teacher meeting where the issue of her lack of concentration was discussed. I didn't find any reports from the psychologist; they must have been archived separately if there were any regarding Henriette at all. The only clue I found interesting was the report about her inattention during class. If Henriette had issues and brought them into the classroom, it could shed light on a potential suicide.

The same picture emerged with the other students. Many documents were irrelevant to my investigation. The only conclusion I could draw from my research was that five students had disappeared or had been found dead. Except for Henriette and Tiril, all were found after about two days. However, it had now been four days since Tiril went missing.

I separated the photos from the admission forms and laid them out. One by one, I examined the photos closely, memorizing the facial details and considering connections to the others. What stood out to me first was Henriette's blonde hair. All the other girls had black hair. But was that significant? Or was it merely coincidental?

Exhausted, I leaned back and rubbed my burning eyes. It was high time to seek my bed. I put the photos back with the files, closed the folder, hid it under my mattress, and threw myself into bed.

Chapter 33

Startled, Tiril looked into the sparkling eyes of the woman standing just a few steps from her bed, her hands on her hips. Her son immediately turned away from Tiril and slipped under his blanket, where he began to whimper softly.

His mother approached his bed and ripped the blanket off him. "What do you think you're doing here?" she barked at him. "You know your princess isn't allowed outside. She'll get sick out there."

"I know, Mom."

She sighed loudly. "No, you apparently don't!" She brought her hands to her face and let out an angry scream. "Why can't you just listen to me?"

Tiril waited for a reaction from the man, but he merely looked down in shame.

"I warned you," his mother said to him. "You know what's going to happen now."

The man shook his head in a pitiful manner. "No, Mom, please not her! Not her!"

Tiril's stomach twisted.

"You should have thought about that beforehand. Come on, get up!" The woman waved her hands in front of his face.

He looked away.

"I said, get up!" Her voice grew angrier, and Tiril edged closer to the edge of the bed.

The man reluctantly stood up, his mother positioned herself beside him, crossing her arms. "Grab her!"

Tiril looked fearfully into his tear-streaked eyes. Hesitantly, he approached, and she scooted further away from him. "Leave me alone! Please! I haven't done anything to you!" she screamed.

He paused and looked uncertainly at his mother, who defiantly stared back at him. "Just do it," she commanded.

"Please, not her, Mom!"

"I won't say it again." She approached him threateningly.

He stepped aside in fright, torn between obedience and rebellion. But eventually, he grabbed her by the arms; his mother released the handcuffs and reached for a candle, examining Tiril's wrists. She tried to pull away from his grasp, but couldn't.

"Stay still, or you'll regret it!" the woman hissed at her.

"It's fine, nothing's visible," she said, placing the candle back on the dresser. "We can go."

The man shook his head vigorously.

"Come on!" she snapped at him.

"Please, leave me alone!" Tiril sobbed. "I haven't done anything to you." She tried to break free from the man, but his hands clamped around her like a vise. She kicked at his shins, only hurting herself. He pulled her from the bed and set her on her feet, then shoved her toward the door. In the hallway, he turned left, pushing her further until they stopped in front of a closed wooden door. Just as he was about to unlock it, Tiril elbowed him in the stomach. He flinched slightly but otherwise showed no reaction. She wanted to turn around and hit him, but he wrapped his arms around her, nearly immobilizing her.

"Please, don't fight me!" he pleaded with a half-choked voice.

"LET ME GO!"

"Shut up, you two!" came a booming voice from behind.

"LET ME GO!" Tiril screamed as loud as she could. "Leave me alone, you monsters!" A sharp pain shot through her body. The woman had stepped beside her and dug her fingernails into Tiril's jaw.

"Be quiet! I said QUIET!" Her eyes sparkled like two rubies, her voice sharp as a knife. With one last pressure on Tiril's jaw, she released her and ordered her son to move on.

As the door opened before Tiril's eyes, the whispering of the wind reached her ears, and the cold enveloped her. She suddenly realized she would become one of the missing girls. Only now, after all the hours and days in her prison, did this fact hit her. It had been so clear. Why it hadn't crossed her mind before, she couldn't explain. The realization struck her like a bomb. She felt her legs give way. But before she could fall to the ground, she was lifted up and carried like a child in someone's arms. Snowflakes landed on her face, and she heard the roar of the surf, far away, as if it were only in her memory. She felt the biting cold cut into her skin like a knife. She saw a few lights in the rooms above her and wished she could be lying in her bed now, sleeping, sleeping until all the fear, all the cold, all the dark dreams were just fragments of her imagination. She wanted to wake up to a dim morning, wanted to open the window and hear the seagulls screeching, drink fresh coffee, and take a cleansing shower.

The snowfall intensified, and the surroundings vanished in a cloak of white cotton. She heard the man's rasping breath, his gaze fixed on the path ahead. Behind him, she saw his mother, who was likewise lost in thought as she trudged forward.

They climbed a hill, further away from Fog Castle. The sound of the waves grew louder, and the cold increased. The dizziness subsided a bit, and the fresh air breathed new energy into her. She screamed for help but immediately felt the man's cold hand on her face.

"Shout all you want. No one will hear you out here," the woman said, coming to a stop. "That's enough; we're here!" She positioned herself next to her son and looked at him in a way that seemed like an unspoken command.

"No, Mom, please, I don't want to!" he stammered.

"You know what to do." She looked at him demandingly.

The man shook his head. "Not my princess, Mom. I don't want to be alone."

"You won't be," she replied. "She'll come back."

He sobbed loudly, sniffing back tears noisily, and looked at Tiril with pity.

"LET ME GO!" Tiril's voice cracked. "YOU BASTARDS!"

"Let's go now!" the woman shouted. "Or I'll do it…!"

The man let Tiril squirm but still held her tightly. With his thick fingers, he reached for one of her hair strands, pressed it to his nose, and took a deep breath with his eyes closed. Tiril broke free from him, causing him to set her on the ground and give her a kiss on the forehead. With his rough hands, he caressed her cheeks and smiled sadly at her. Just as she was about to break away, she felt a jolt and then heard a horrific roar that grew louder. A sensation like being on a roller coaster coursed through her body, and the world turned black and still.

***

Filled with fear, sadness, and loneliness, he remained on the rock. His princess, vanished into the darkness—once again. He was alone again, the bed next to him empty, without a breath, without the soothing scent.

All that remained of his princess were a few strands of her hair, which he now fished out of his pocket and smelled. He closed his eyes and once again saw his sister's bed engulfed in flames, her hand blackened, the rest of her body no longer visible. He picked himself up, stumbled over a piece of debris, fell, got back up, the palms of his hands scorched. His body was one aching wound, and it dawned on him that there was no rescue for his sister anymore. He had failed; he had let her down, the little princess. Screaming, he left the room, ran through the smoke-filled hallway, down the stairs, and out the door. He ran and ran until he could go no further and collapsed into the snow.

Even today, he hears his own voice calling for his mom, but the wailing merged with the roar of the fire, and he saw his sister being carried away by the sparks and the smoke out to the open sea.

Chapter 34

My night's rest didn't last long. After I had set the files aside and managed to get some more sleep, I was woken up a few hours later by a knock at the door. The lack of sleep weighed heavily on my bones, and I could hardly get out of bed.

I sluggishly dragged myself to the door. When I opened it, Lilly stood before me, crying.

"Henrik found Tiril!" she sobbed, entering the apartment. Judging by her complexion, this Henrik probably hadn't found Tiril alive. Lilly sat down on the sofa and buried her face in her hands. I went to the coffee machine, prepared two coffees for us, and placed the cups on the table. With trembling hands, she took a sip.

I sat down next to her. "Where did he find her?"

"Down by the rocks."

"Who told you?"

"I was just on my way to the dining hall when he burst through the door, completely distraught. He was shouting something incomprehensible and stormed into Sigrid's office. He banged on the door, but she didn't open it.

Sander came down the stairs and asked him what was going on. Then it all just spilled out of him."

"Damn it!" I cursed.

"Henrik was out for a walk when he found her at the southern end of the beach. Her body was supposedly still half in the water. He dragged her to the high tide mark, then threw up and ran back to Fog Castle."

"Were the police notified?"

"I think so. Sander called Sigrid and Kjell, then they disappeared into her office."

"I'd like to see the site where she was found, but I don't want to destroy any evidence. Footprints in the snow could provide a crucial clue. Hopefully, the whole boarding school isn't traipsing around the beach."

"Don't worry. Sigrid ordered everyone to stay inside. She has teachers stationed at the exits."

I went to the window and looked down at the beach. From my vantage point, I couldn't see the end of the shore. "How is Henrik doing?"

Lilly shrugged. "Not so well, I think. Kjell took him into his office."

"This will haunt him for a while."

"Can I have some more coffee?" Lilly asked, extending her cup to me.

I went to the kitchen and refilled it. "Do you want something to eat?"

"No thanks, I've lost my appetite. But I feel so shaky that a piece of bread might not be a bad idea."

"I think so too. Sit at the table; I'll make us some sandwiches." After I prepared a plate with bread and cheese for her, we sat in silence at the table, lost in our thoughts. Lilly chewed listlessly on her bread, her eyes looking tired and bloodshot.

So, Tiril's death was now a fact. Another sad chapter in the history of the boarding school. I was curious to see how Jon Martin would react. The fact that Tiril had only been found now, days after she had disappeared, clearly pointed to a crime. I didn't know how a suicide could be explained.

Lilly put her half-eaten bread back on the plate. "I can't eat anymore; I'm sorry." She grimaced in disgust and pushed the plate away. "What happens now?"

"I assume the police will be here soon. They'll cordon off the beach, the forensic team will do their work, and some people will likely be questioned here. Classes will definitely be cancelled today."

She raised her eyebrows. "At least something positive." She got up and placed her hand on my shoulder. "Thanks, Sondre. I'm going back to my room now. I want to lie down for a bit."

At that moment, there was a knock at the door. We looked at each other, both knowing she shouldn't really be here. She fled into the bathroom, and I went to the door.

Runa stood in the hallway, hands on her hips. "Good morning, Sondre. All staff members must report to the staff room in ten minutes."

"Is there a reason?" I asked innocently.

"You'll find out in the staff room," she replied snippily.

I nodded and made an effort to give Runa a smile.

"Do you have company?" She tried to look past me.

"How do you know that?"

"I thought I heard voices earlier."

"I was on the phone."

Again, she peered into the apartment. "Why are there two cups and two plates on the table?"

"Does that concern you?"

"If you have a student here, it could have serious consequences. I hope you're aware of that?"

"Completely aware," I said with a self-satisfied smile.

She stared at me scrutinizingly for a while.

"Anything else?" I asked.

"No." She turned and walked away with an air of importance.

I closed the door, and Lilly came out of the bathroom.

"That stupid cow!" she said angrily.

"Let it go. You'd better go back to your room now. I have to leave soon anyway."

"Will you let me know if there's any news?"

"Sure."

She walked to the door. "Where are the archive files, by the way?"

"In a safe place."

"Have you looked at them?"

"I have actually."

Lilly looked at me expectantly. "Do I always have to pull the worms out of your nose?"

"We'll talk about it later."

She rolled her eyes and left the apartment.

When I arrived in the staff room shortly afterwards, there was a subdued atmosphere among those present. Many wore long faces, and Annika and Inge were quietly crying. Liam was whispering with Sander, while Jori was absentmindedly pondering with a toothpick in his mouth.

Sigrid entered the room. Her expression was cool and emotionless. "I regret to inform you that Henrik found Tiril dead an hour ago. She was lying on the beach below. The police are on their way here. They're also bringing Tiril's parents. Classes are cancelled for the next two days. The students are now in their classrooms, and I will inform them there. Depending on what the police decide, students and teachers can have their time off. Of course, they are allowed to travel home unless someone needs to be available to the police. A bus will arrive in four hours to take the students to the city. Runa and I will hold the fort here. Everything should return to normal by Monday. I wish you all a pleasant day, despite everything."

She left the room, leaving us all, as far as I could tell, in shock. A deathly silence had descended over the room. Most of my colleagues stared blankly into space; Inga and Annika were still crying. No one said a word; there was nothing to say. Einar suddenly stood up and left the staff room, and most followed his lead. Runa shot me a scathing look as she exited.

I stayed seated for a few more seconds before I followed them out. Back in my apartment, I grabbed my jacket and went outside. Jon Martin would surely be arriving soon, and I wanted to speak to him before he began his investigations with the boarding school administration.

I got into my car, turned on the radio, and thought about Tiril's parents. From today onwards, their lives would never be the same. The gnawing uncertainty of the last few days had turned into a nightmare, a nightmare that would haunt them for a lifetime.

I heard a door slam and glanced in the rearview mirror. Einar and Skadi were pulling out of a parking space and disappearing over the mountain pass from my view. Half an hour later, the first police vehicles arrived. Jon Martin got out, and I approached him.

"Nice shit, huh?" he said as he walked up to me.

"Indeed."

"Can you tell me something important?"

"Not really. I barely knew the victim. I only met her briefly during my interview. She showed me around the building. That was about it."

"Did you notice anything suspicious in the last few days?"

"Everything here seems a bit suspect if you ask me."

"What do you mean?"

"I don't know. I have a feeling that something is not right. Lilly, a student, told me yesterday that she had been followed on the beach at night. But she couldn't see who it was. Too dark, too foggy."

"Could it have just been a prank?"

I shrugged. "Possible. But I find it unlikely."

At that moment, an officer led a sobbing couple past us and headed toward the house.

"What a mess," I cursed.

"This is going to be very difficult for them."

"I can empathize."

Jon Martin nodded and looked down.

"Are you going to interview all the residents now?"

He shook his head. "No, just those who were closest to her. Also, their main teachers and the psychologist."

"Tiril was in my class too. I only taught her twice. She didn't stand out negatively or anything. To be honest, she hardly stood out at all."

Jon Martin nodded. "Is the psychologist still here?"

"I think so. His name is Kjell."

"Do you happen to know if she was in treatment with him?"

"No idea. Unfortunately, I don't know the students well enough yet."

"I understand."

"Are you heading to the beach now?" I wanted to know.

"Of course."

"Can I come along?"

Jon Martin clicked his tongue and seemed to think. "If it were up to me, I'd love that. But you know the rules. We need to secure the evidence first."

I nodded through clenched teeth. "Of course."

"I'll call you when I know more, okay?"

"Sure."

He patted me on the shoulder. "Keep your chin up, I'll get in touch."

He went to two policemen and signaled for them to follow him. Like two puppies, they hurried after him and soon disappeared behind Fog Castle. I felt the fatigue spreading in my head and went back to my apartment. There, I lay on the sofa and stared at the ceiling for a while. I saw Tiril in my mind, showing me the empty room above me. I saw her mischievous smile, a smile that didn't seem forced or fake. I heard her voice as if I had just spoken with her. The ceiling of my apartment became blurry, my eyelids heavy, and the sofa softer.

When I awoke four hours later with a sore neck, my first thought was of Tiril again. I sat up, rubbed my eyes, and then went to the window. On the beach, I saw four policemen searching the ground with lowered heads. But Jon Martin was not among them. Had he found out something already?

I lit a cigarette in frustration and thought about Jørn's impending visit. The timing couldn't have been worse. However, I certainly didn't want to miss our time together. Who knows when the next opportunity would arise? I extinguished the half-smoked cigarette, put on warm clothes, and left the apartment.

As I reached the stairs, I heard a dry cough from the fourth floor and looked upwards over the railing. The cough sounded familiar.

Mikkel!

Instead of going down, I went up. In the dim hallway, I couldn't see anyone at first. However, I noticed that the door to the mysterious room was only ajar, and a weak beam of light was spilling out. Curiously, I moved closer, and just as I was about to push the door open, it suddenly swung wide, startling me.

Mikkel stood grinning in front of me. "Sorry, I didn't mean to scare you," he said in a raspy voice.

"No harm done," I reassured him.

"Are you on an exploration tour?" he asked.

"Actually, I was just on my way outside when I heard your cough."

"Is that so?" he said tersely.

"Is this your apartment?" I asked uncertainly.

"It is."

"Tiril told me on the first day that nobody knew what was behind this door."

Mikkel smiled faintly. "It's not quite like that. When I'm not in my house in Tromvik, I live here. That's why the door is usually locked, and the students aren't interested in me. I'm essentially invisible to them."

I lifted my chin to signal that I didn't quite understand. "How are you?" he asked me.

"I'm okay. The situation with Tiril is weighing heavily on me."

Mikkel shook his head sadly. "The house has taken another soul."

I frowned. "Do you think someone did this to her?"

He shrugged. "I don't know. I just feel sorry for her parents. Nothing worse can happen to someone."

I nodded slightly. "I know exactly how that feels. A few years ago, I lost my son, Raik. He had cancer."

Mikkel looked at me silently for a long moment. His eyes sparkled in the hallway light, and I was uncertain whether he wanted to say something in response. But he remained silent, instead stepping aside and inviting me into his apartment with a hand gesture. I followed his invitation and entered the mysterious room, which turned out to be the janitor's living room. As I crossed the threshold, I immediately felt as if the temperature had dropped a few degrees, almost as if stepping outside. I felt a prickling in my neck, and a slight dizziness took hold of me. The room was sparsely furnished. There were two armchairs that had obviously seen better days. In the middle stood a scratched dining table, against the wall was an empty bookshelf, and there was a small kitchen without pots, plates, or glasses. On the right side of the room was a door, but it was closed.

"Please!" Mikkel pointed to a chair at the dining table, and I sat down. He also took a seat, his hands folded on the table, his eyes directed at his hands. "I'm sorry about your son," he said quietly.

"Thank you," I replied. "From you, I know it's sincere."

For a long moment, we looked into each other's eyes. Two men who had lost everything important in their lives. Two men who would give anything, even their own lives, to bring another back. I saw the pain in his gaze, his eyelids heavy. And yet his expression was penetrating like that of a wolf. I tried to look away, but I couldn't. It was as if he was hypnotizing me. My eyes were already burning because I hadn't blinked in ages.

And then he finally broke free from me, turned his head to the window, his hands tense on the table, his knuckles white. In a calm voice, he said, "Time in this bay passes slower than elsewhere. It's as if one is in a time vacuum. The world stands still here; everything has its own laws and rhythms. Here, the memories of a life that once seemed so beautiful and carefree fade away. Every day, they fade more until they appear as an inconspicuous dot on the horizon in the distant future. How often have I wished that these memories would remain, preserved in my dark thoughts. One tries to hide them, to keep them in check, not to let them take over. And yet, one brings those thoughts into the light again and endures the pain until it becomes a constant companion, without which one cannot exist, because one feels alone, forgotten, and gone. It's a vicious circle, a labyrinth from which one cannot find a way out, or doesn't want to find a way out. The years go by, and what remains is a scar that finds no healing." I swallowed hard and had to clear my throat to even say a word. "What you describe mirrors my emotional state quite accurately. The grief overwhelms you. Day in, day out, the same thoughts. My wife and I sought psychological help back then. I wanted to do everything to get through this time together, for the sake of our second son, who needed our attention more than ever. However, life had other plans for us. My wife and I drifted apart, month by month, day by day, hour by hour, until in the evening, only two strangers lay side by side in the marital bed — the beginning of the end!"

Mikkel nodded, his gaze lowered. For a while, neither of us said anything. The sound of the waves drifted to us from outside. Somewhere a clock ticked, and muffled murmurs from the fourth floor reached us from far away. "How do you like it here?" he suddenly asked. "Actually quite well," I replied, somewhat surprised by the abrupt change of subject. "The circumstances are just a bit complicated at the moment.

"Because of Tiril?"

"Yes, among other things."

Again, he put on that penetrating look. "I saw you sneaking around at night."

I made a surprised expression. "Sneaking around? When?"

"I don't remember, it was a few nights ago."

"That's right. I couldn't sleep and went for a walk."

He nodded. "I heard you used to be a police officer?"

"That's true. But that was a while ago."

"Why teaching now?" He leaned back in his chair.

"I had an accident and could no longer pursue that profession."

"Accident?"

"Skiing accident. I injured my hand quite badly. TFCC rupture, the doctors said back then!" I shrugged. "In any case, I haven't been able to move my left hand properly since then."

"That's unfortunate," he said.

"Indeed. Since I had already thought about becoming a teacher before my police career, the time had come to switch paths. And now I'm here."

"And now you're investigating the dead students?" It sounded more like a statement than a question. A strange feeling crept over me. How did he know that? "I—well, I'm just curious about what's really going on here." Mikkel nodded thoughtfully. "And have you found anything out?"

"Not really. The school administration seems convinced that the students all committed suicide."

"And you don't share their opinion, if I'm judging your tone correctly?"

I hesitantly shrugged. I didn't want to talk to him about the school administration or my investigations. I didn't know him well enough and wasn't sure how loyal he was to the administration. While I was still searching for a suitable response, I noticed a reflection of light at the window. I looked over and noticed a locket dangling from the window handle, with a picture of a girl stuck to its front.

Mikkel followed my gaze. "That's Malin." He stood up, went to the window, and came back with the locket. He handed it to me across the table, and I took it as if it were a valuable piece of parchment.

Malin was a spitting image of her father. Round face, noticeably small ears, while her cheeks had a healthy color, which could not be said of Mikkel. Her nose was gently curved, her hair black and long. The color of her eyes was a mixture of brown and alabaster. You could lose yourself in her gaze. It appeared absent, thoughtful, maybe even simply childlike.

"Beautiful, isn't she?" Mikkel said with a smile.

"An angel!"

As I continued to gaze at the photo, I suddenly felt dizzy for a moment, as if I had experienced this moment before. As if I had spoken those same words, seen those same images, smelled the scent of old furniture before. Even though it was my first time in Mikkel's apartment, I felt something familiar, something comforting.

I looked into Malin's eyes. She looked back. The image blurred, and another image surfaced in my mind, and suddenly it struck me like a flash of insight. It wasn't the apartment, or Mikkel, or his words. No, it was Malin! That face, as if I had seen it before, in the past, or in a dream. I thought of the photos from last night, the photos of the dead students. I had been searching for similarities, for a connection, for the obvious. Now I knew what it was. They all looked similar. They all had round faces and dark, almost black hair. Only Henriette didn't fit the picture.

But what did this realization mean? Did it mean anything at all?

I tried to sort my thoughts, to make sense of them. Mikkel had lost his daughter, and all the dead students resembled Malin.

Was that a coincidence? Did he have something to do with it?

I looked up, our eyes met—mine uncertain, his cold and expressionless. He just sat there, his eyes slightly reddened, and on his lips, I thought I could see a faint smile. Had he read my thoughts? Did he know what suspicion was stirring within me?

An adrenaline rush coursed through my body, and my hands began to sweat. I handed him back the locket, and he accepted it. For a moment, he looked at his Malin, lovingly and dreamily. Then he stood up and hung it back in its rightful place. He remained at the window, gazing into the bay, his face as pale as the sky.

"You haven't answered my question yet," he said suddenly.

I couldn't remember the question. "What question do you mean?"

"Whether you share the opinion of the school administration?"

I raised my eyebrows. "Well, if I'm honest—no!"

"And why not, if I may ask?"

"Gut feeling."

He turned around but stayed by the window, his hands in his pockets. "So, gut feeling. What do you think happened to these students?"

I shifted uncomfortably in my seat. I felt like I was in an interrogation. "Someone must have pushed these girls off the cliff," I finally replied.

"And you think someone from the boarding school is responsible for it?"

I shrugged. "I don't know. It's plausible, but I can't say for sure."

Mikkel sat back down at the table. "Who would be capable of such a thing?"

"That escapes my knowledge as well. I don't know the people here well enough yet. But all these incidents seem very strange to me, to put it mildly."

"I agree with you there."

"Were you all interrogated by the police when they were investigating the deaths?"

"Of course. At least those who were closest to the deceased."

"Were you questioned too?"

"Yes. I don't have any contact with the students, but I've been here since the beginning, and not many can say that."

I frowned. "Who else has been here since the start?"

"Runa, Sigrid, Mathilde," he listed.

"Do you know if any of them were suspected?"

"I'm not sure. I believe Runa was questioned several times back then."

"And Sigrid?" I asked further.

He hesitated and shrugged. "Sigrid is a strange person, if I may put it that way. Even though I've known her for years, I don't know what's going on behind her facade.

She's like a ghost to me, unfathomable, mysterious, unattainable."

"I feel the same way."

An uncomfortable silence ensued. Mikkel's gaze lingered on me, and I felt the urge to look elsewhere but couldn't manage it again. So I searched for a suitable continuation of the conversation. "If it really is about a crime, who would you consider as a perpetrator— or perpetrators— in this case?" I held my breath.

Mikkel leaned forward. "I've been here too long, Sondre. In this house, anything is possible. Over the years, I've seen many individuals come and go; none were like the other. But one thing has remained the same all this time—the house. It has a will of its own, feelings, moods. Its numerous nooks and hidden rooms are like the dark corners of a soul."

His words echoed in the small room, like in a knight's hall. "What do you mean by hidden rooms?" He looked at me, amused. "English buildings, like Fog Castle, have hidden rooms. In the past, these rooms served as accommodation for the servants. They often also have secret passages that served as escape routes or hiding places for the landowner. As a boy, I loved the stories of English castles, with their towers and archways, with their arrow slits and secret passages. When I got my job here, I was quite excited. It was as if I had plunged into one of my childhood stories. As a caretaker, I had access to all the rooms, from the basement to the attic." He fell silent and looked at his folded hands. He seemed to be pondering something. Twice he opened his mouth briefly but said nothing. After a while, he looked up again and said, "Sometimes it's better if these rooms remain hidden…!"

I waited to see if he would add anything to his statement, but he said nothing more. Instead, he suddenly stood up and prevented me from further speculation. "I'm afraid I must ask you to leave now. I have quite a bit to take care of today."

"Of course!" I said, feeling uncertain, and stood up as well. I followed him to the door, and before he opened it, I asked him, "Why is it better if these rooms remain hidden?"

Mikkel's features formed a mischievous smile. He opened the door, gently nudged me over the threshold, and placed his hand on my shoulder. "I said sometimes, my dear!" He gave me a pat on the shoulder and closed the door.

Chapter 35

After dinner, I aimlessly wandered through the corridors of Fog Castle. The boarding school had grown quiet. Two buses from Tromsø had arrived in the afternoon, taking most of the students back to the city. Some parents picked up their offspring in person. My colleagues and the psychologist Kjell drove home in their own vehicles. Now only Sigrid, Runa, Mathilde, Mikkel, Lilly, and I were left in the house. It felt strange to be in such a large building.

Lilly had not shown herself all day. I assumed she had barricaded herself in her room, and I didn't want to disturb her. I hadn't heard anything from Jon Martin until now. Either he had forgotten or had not arrived at any interesting conclusions.

After a brief walk, I returned to my apartment, got ready for bed, and crawled under the covers. I had been short on sleep the last few nights, and I wanted to get a good night's rest again, although I already knew that was a vain wish. The conversation with Mikkel lingered in my mind, and I didn't know what to make of his words. He had lost his daughter on this estate, and she looked strikingly similar to the missing girls.

Was there really a connection?

I couldn't make sense of it and would have loved to bring it up with Mikkel. But I just didn't know where I stood with him. His persona was impenetrable, a presence without shadow.

I reached for my book and began to read. I wanted a distraction; it had often helped me see things more clearly afterward. Yet tonight, I could hardly get through three pages, as I woke up the next morning with a crumpled book under the blanket. Groggily, I got up and headed to the coffee machine. On the table lay a pack of cigarettes, and I was just about to grab it when I reconsidered. Jørn hated it when I smoked. In the next two days, I wouldn't be able to touch a cigarette anyway. So, I might as well forgo it now, even though it took some effort.

I got dressed, stood by the window with my coffee, and looked out at the bay. It was eight-thirty, and the first light of day streamed into the bay like liquid gold. A few lonely clouds drifted across the sky, and a bright Venus faded in the dawning day. I thought of Lilly and wondered how she was doing. I hadn't heard from her since yesterday and wondered if I should take her into town for a change of scenery. And judging by her personality, I figured she would certainly enjoy being with the Abramsens.

After my morning routine, I went straight to Lilly's room, knocked, and waited. It took almost a minute for the door to open, and Lilly stood before me, completely disheveled and with sleepy eyes.

"Man, Sondre, do you ever sleep?" She touched her face and rubbed away the impressions from her pillow.

"It's nine o'clock!" I replied, holding my watch up to her eyes.

"So what? I'm free, so nine o'clock isn't a time," she said.

I had to laugh. "Sorry. I just thought you might be interested in coming with me to see Henriette's parents. I want to talk to them. But I'd better let you sleep; we'll see each other later." I dramatically turned to leave.

"Hey, wait a minute. I'll get dressed; give me five minutes."

"No rush. We're leaving at ten. Let's meet at the parking lot."

I returned to my apartment and reviewed Henriette's file again. I read the report about the argument she had had with another student. The reason was a boy named Kristoffer, whom both girls seemed to be interested in, and neither had been willing to let the other have their respective dates. An incident that likely had nothing to do with Henriette's death, unless this Brita had pushed her over the edge over a silly argument. But I assumed the police had questioned Brita back then and ruled her out as a suspect. I couldn't find any reports from psychologists. They were most likely sealed and could only be released by order of the public prosecutor.

In Frida's file, I found a note from Sigrid. Apparently, Frida had once threatened to throw herself out the window if her teacher continued to use her as a lightning rod. After that, she stayed away from school for two days. That was all.

In Fenna Gulbrandsen's file, I found a few school reprimands, or rather, warnings. She had been caught smoking twice, once even with cannabis. She had been barred from leaving her room for a week, and her parents had been summoned for a talk.

I found no additional reports or notes for Linnea Rolvsson, which didn't mean there weren't any psychological reports about her.

All in all, one could conclude that the girls were not angels. But they hadn't been that even before entering the boarding school. Their little transgressions in Fog Castle did not lead me to any conclusions about their psyche or state of mind.

I put the files back in my hiding place and waited, reading on the sofa until it was time to leave.

Shortly after ten, I sat behind the wheel of my Nissan, Lilly silently in the passenger seat. I didn't feel entirely comfortable with the situation. A teacher going on an outing with a student at the weekend could easily be misinterpreted. However, the circumstances were exceptional, and that justified such an action. At least, that's what I told myself.

We didn't talk much during the drive. Lilly was introspective, gazing at the passing landscape. At Grøtfjord, I informed her that we would have Jørn with us on the way back.

"I'm curious if he's as restless as you are," she remarked, smiling delightfully.

"Restless?" I asked with a sideways glance. "What do you mean by that?"

"Well, you're keeping yourself up at night, getting up early, and running around the house or along the beach like a startled chicken."

"Life is too short to be lazy."

"That's true. Still, a nap during the day can't hurt."

"I don't deny that. But I'm someone who likes to do things and can't just sit around. As for Jørn, he's similar, but since he's your age, afternoons with friends have become more important than ice fishing with his father."

"I can't say I don't understand him."

We laughed.

"What do you hope to learn from the conversation with the Abramsens?" she asked.

I shrugged. "I just want to talk to them about Henriette. I want to find out what kind of person she was. If she had problems or if she was a cheerful and balanced girl. I also want to know if her farewell letter was actually written by her."

"I just hope the Abramsens are willing to talk to us about their daughter. I can imagine that such a conversation isn't easy for them."

"No, of course not. That's why we must proceed with the utmost caution."

At the end of Kaldfjord, we left the main road and turned into Bergheimvegen. The road ran along the shore of the fjord, and on both sides stood generously built houses, whose residents likely had good financial means. After about two hundred meters, the navigation device announced that we had reached house number 23. I stopped in front of the garage, and we got out. The blue-painted, two-story house stood right by the water and had a small boathouse with a jetty. The entrance of the house was covered with a porch. Two chairs flanked the front door, and a cat sat on a fur mat near the entrance. I walked to the postbox and checked the name. Jesper + Charlotte Abramsen. Lucky us, they still lived in this house.

Together, we climbed the two steps to the porch, and I rang the doorbell. Lilly looked at me with tense anticipation. I gently touched her on the forearm and nodded at her.

The door was opened by a man with a grey beard and a stern expression. He was slightly taller than I was, had weather-beaten skin, and short hair. He wore a green wool sweater and jogging trousers that were a bit too short for his long legs.

"Can I help you?" His voice was deep and friendly.

"Good day! Jesper Abramsen, I presume?"

"Yes?"

"My name is Sondre. I'm a teacher at Fog Castle, and Lilly here is a student. We have a matter we would like to discuss with you and your wife."

Jesper furrowed his brow. "What matter?"

I exchanged a glance with Lilly. "Well, the matter is a bit delicate. A student was found dead near the boarding school yesterday."

Jesper's expression changed instantly. His forehead became even more wrinkled, his eyes widened, and he looked back and forth between me and Lilly. However, he remained silent.

"I can imagine," I continued, "that this news brings painful memories for you, and I am truly sorry to burden you with our visit here. However, the matter is of the utmost importance to us, and we hope that you can help us shed light on these strange occurrences."

"I see no reason to do that." He was about to slam the door in our faces when a woman's voice could be heard from behind.

"Honey, who is at the door?" A woman with grey, shoulder-length hair appeared behind Jesper and wrapped her arms around him. I recognized a slight French accent in her speech. She had a pointed face and, due to the heavy makeup, looked like a porcelain doll.

I introduced ourselves again, and when I mentioned the boarding school, I noticed a change in Charlotte's demeanor as well. Her smile vanished instantly, and her hand, which was around her husband's arm, twitched briefly.

"As I just told your husband, a girl was found dead near the boarding school yesterday. I would like to talk to you about Henriette and find out how this tragic event occurred."

"What does that matter to you?" Jesper exploded. Charlotte placed her hand on her husband's shoulder. "Jesper, please calm down." Turning to us, she said, "Why do you want to talk about Henriette? This happened two decades ago."

I was glad Charlotte was holding her husband back a little. "I may need to elaborate a bit. Before I became a teacher, I worked for the police in Tromsø. Due to an accident, I could no longer continue in that profession, and I recently switched to teaching at the boarding school. During my time with the police, I developed certain instincts that often helped me in my personal life. You start to notice things that others overlook. From the moment I took my position at Fog Castle, I had a strange feeling. I can't quite describe it, but the atmosphere there is very peculiar, as you may have noticed back then."

Charlotte sighed, but said nothing in response. "The reason we are here is as follows: Since Henriette's death, four more young girls have died at the boarding school."

Charlotte held her left hand over her mouth. "Four more girls?" she whispered.

"Yes, four! And each of these cases has been declared a suicide by the school administration and the police. Lilly and I have difficulty accepting this conclusion and doubt its accuracy. Therefore, we have begun to investigate these cases to get to the bottom of the inconsistencies and to bring justice to the deceased, even if it may be a bit too late."

Charlotte looked up at her husband, who was still scrutinizing us suspiciously. After a while, however, his facial features relaxed, and he stepped aside. "Come in!" Lilly and I entered the house with relief and followed Charlotte into the living room.

"Please, have a seat," she said.

The sofa was positioned near the window, from which one could overlook the fjord and the mountains behind it. On the windowsill, I noticed a framed photo of Henriette. Right next to it, a candle was burning.

Jesper and Charlotte sat down, both looking at us with tense anticipation.

"I'm truly sorry to trouble you with this tragic incident..." I began the conversation, but was immediately interrupted by Charlotte.

"You said that four more girls have died at the boarding school since Henriette?" It sounded more like a question than a statement.

"That's correct."

"But that was never reported in the newspapers!"

"Also true."

She looked at us, confused.

"Suicides aren't something that gets reported up here. There's a fear that others might take the method as an example and follow suit. Therefore, the public rarely learns about such occurrences."

Charlotte nodded, embarrassed.

"As I mentioned earlier, I do not share the views of the school administration. Unfortunately, I don't know what the police found in the death investigations. I wasn't involved in the investigations at the time. However, I think something must be off about the whole situation. Henriette was one of the first victims at Fog Castle, and I want to understand what happened to her. For that, I would need to learn something about her character and moments in her life. Only you can help me with that, as you knew your daughter best."

Charlotte exchanged a glance with her husband. However, he did not seem inclined to say anything. Charlotte sighed and lowered her gaze. I was already fearing that we wouldn't get anywhere. "I can understand what the loss meant for both of you. I have lost a child myself."

Jesper flinched almost imperceptibly. His gaze fixed on me, and I was sure he was trying to read me. I felt Lilly's horrified gaze on me but did not react.

"I'm sorry to hear that, Sondre," said Charlotte.

"Thank you. You see, I know what I'm talking about, and I also know how much such a conversation can take out of you. Nevertheless, I want to bring light to the darkness, even if it no longer helps your daughter. The bereaved could live on with the knowledge that their child did not leap to her death of her own accord."

Charlotte tilted her head. "But that was unfortunately the case with Henriette."

I nodded. "The farewell letter?"

Charlotte took a deep breath. "The worst lines I have ever had to read in my life. Each of her words felt like a dagger blow. After each sentence, you wonder where I, as a mother, failed. Why didn't we see this coming?" She wiped her nose.

"I can understand why one would ask those questions. As parents, you want only the best for your child. But one thing I have learned as a father: being a parent is one of the most demanding, yet also one of the most beautiful jobs in the world. Sometimes fate strikes without you having contributed to it at all."

Charlotte nodded sadly.

I waited a moment before continuing. "In my investigations, I found that no farewell letter was found with the other deceased students. Nevertheless, suicide was assumed in the investigations. I — or rather we," I gestured to Lilly, "believe that something else must have happened to the students. Among other things, we discovered that the police, in all death cases except Henriette's, initially questioned the possibility of suicide, but could not prove anything to the contrary despite investigations, which is why suicide was considered the only option. Since a suicide was indeed at the forefront in Henriette's case, the other death cases pointed in the same direction. The school administration had supported the suicide theory in all cases."

Charlotte exchanged a brief glance with her husband but said nothing.

"That was not the only thing that caught our attention," I continued. "I looked at the files of the deceased students and found hints that made me suspicious. For a moment, I even thought that Henriette's farewell letter might have been forged to distract from a crime. However, this seems, as you confirmed earlier, not to be the case." Jesper leaned forward, elbows resting on his thighs, hands shaped into a funnel. I was almost afraid he would send us straight to hell. But when he began to speak, his voice sounded very gentle. "I wish the investigations back then had painted a picture other than suicide. If a murderer were responsible for my daughter's death, then I wouldn't have had to bear the blame for her death for years. It wouldn't make her death any less painful, but my conscience wouldn't be so burdened." He lowered his gaze, and Charlotte squeezed his hand.

"May I ask why Henriette had to attend the boarding school?" I inquired.

Jesper swallowed awkwardly. "Henriette had always been an upbeat girl, even as a child. She was rarely in a bad mood, had many friends, hobbies, and did well in school. When she reached her teenage years, there were of course a few arguments, as is typical with young adults. However, Henriette remained true to her nature. She didn't change much. I could still go hiking with her, have great deep conversations—conversations that I could never have had with my parents. Henriette knew that she could talk to me and her mother about anything. We had shown her this since she was a child, and she appreciated it. At seventeen, she met this Morten, a somewhat disheveled boy with long hair and piercings. Shortly thereafter, they became a couple, much to our dismay. I never liked him from the beginning. I couldn't see in him what my daughter seemed to see, no matter how hard I tried. But that's just how it is. Daughters' friends don't have it easy with their fathers!" A hint of a smile flickered briefly. "Morten already had a rather unsavoury past. He was even known to the police. He had stolen cars, graffitied walls, committed shoplifting — the whole range. My wife and I tried to make Henriette understand that being around him was not good for her. But Henriette would not be dissuaded. Morten could do whatever he wanted with her, and she went along with it. Suddenly, her grades began to suffer, and we had to meet with her teachers several times. But nothing helped. She showed no insight; she was so blinded by Morten that she didn't seem to recognize the seriousness of the situation. Not long after, what Charlotte and I had long feared, happened. Morten and Henriette were caught stealing a car and taken away by the police. Fortunately, our lawyer managed to ensure that Henriette only received a fine. However, the matter was not resolved for us. After this incident, we tried to talk to Henriette, to teach her that Morten was destroying her life. We grounded her more often in an attempt to keep her away from Morten. You can imagine the discussions that ensued. The grounding was useful for keeping her away from him in her free time, but she still had to go to school, and there was Morten. And so it happened as it had to. A few weeks later, she was caught on a security camera stealing clothes at the Nerstranda shopping center. This finally sealed our decision to shield Henriette from Morten for good and send her to the boarding school, even though it took a lot of courage for us. At that time, we saw no other solution." He paused and swallowed awkwardly again. Charlotte wiped a tear from her eye.

"Of course, Henriette did not want to accept our decision," he continued after a while. "She didn't speak to us for a whole week, not even coming out of her room to eat. One afternoon, while Charlotte was in the kitchen reading the newspaper, she heard a scream from Henriette's room. She ran upstairs and found our daughter on the floor. A knife lay next to her, and her right wrist was bleeding. My wife immediately called for an ambulance, and she was taken to the hospital. Fortunately, the wound was only superficial, and it was obvious that she had only wanted to get attention with her act. At least, that's what we thought at the time. Nevertheless, her act left an uneasy feeling, and we did not know if Henriette would seriously injure herself the next time. As the admission to the boarding school was imminent, we informed the administration about the incident. Sigrid promised us that the internal psychologist would take care of her as soon as she entered.

Two weeks after the knife incident, we noticed a change in Henriette. She began to talk to us again. She came out of her room, ate with us, watched TV with us. Apparently, she had recognized the seriousness of the situation. She tried to convince us that she would improve, make an effort in school again, and break up with Morten. She begged us to give her another chance." Jesper sighed and rubbed his hand across his face. "When your child begs you through tears not to send them away from home, you have to be really strong inside to endure it. But we held firm to our decision and did not back down, even when we heard Henriette crying in her room, utterly unhappy. The fear that she would return to Morten was too great.

The day before we took Henriette to the boarding school, I went hiking in the mountains near Breivikeidet with her. When we reached the summit, we sat down and ate our provisions. We didn't speak; both of us were lost in thought. As we sat there, she suddenly laid her head on my shoulder and apologized for the worries she had caused us. She began to talk about her future plans. She wanted to go to university to study architecture. It sounded so contradictory to her escapades with Morten that I wasn't sure at that moment if she was just telling me this to change my mind." He shrugged sadly. "I hugged her, kissed her forehead, and told her that I loved her and would always be there for her, but that we would stick to our decision. She cried in my arms, and I cried with her." He cleared his throat awkwardly.

"When the day of the farewell finally came, she was sadder than ever before. On the way to the boarding school, she didn't say a word to us. From the parking lot to the front door of Fog House, she trudged ten meters behind us, and when she was led upstairs to her future room by Sigrid half an hour later, she didn't even look over her shoulder." Jesper's voice broke, and he sobbed. Next to me, I could hear Lilly's deep breath. I swallowed hard and internally scolded myself for bringing the couple back to one of their darkest hours.

"That was the last time we saw our daughter alive," Jesper said after he had recovered. I lowered my gaze, and for an agonizingly long moment, no one said anything. Somewhere, a tap dripped, outside children were shouting, and a fishing boat chugged toward the open sea.

I was the first to break the silence in the house. "I'm so terribly sorry. I...I can sympathize with your pain. I've been carrying the same burden with me for years." Jesper and Charlotte nodded, both with tears in their eyes. "And then the police brought us her farewell letter," Charlotte said. "At first, I didn't know if I should even read it. But of course, I did. Her words didn't come out of nowhere. Jesper and I suspected the reason. Henriette didn't want to live without her Morten, and she felt like a prisoner at the boarding school. She couldn't stay locked up for three years. Apparently, she had also had a confrontation with Sigrid. Sigrid had caught her talking to Morten in front of the house at night. As a result, she was not allowed to leave her room for three days, which only worsened her condition."

Jesper leaned forward.

"Were no farewell letters found with the other students?"

"No, not that I know of. But I don't know all the details either. Perhaps Sigrid could help me further, but I don't think she would provide information. After all, she also has a kind of confidentiality."

"Did you know that Sigrid also lost a child?"

I stared at Jesper unblinkingly. "No, I didn't know that." I looked at Lilly, who just shrugged her shoulders. "What happened to the child?" I asked.

"I don't know exactly. We only know it from a third party."

"From whom?" Jesper turned to his wife: "Do you remember the name of the police officer who told us?"

Charlotte squinted thoughtfully out the window but shook her head. "I'm sorry, I don't remember. I just know that he told us this years later when we happened to run into each other in town and talked about Henriette's case. I believe he hadn't been with the police for long at the time of Henriette's death."

"A police officer told you this?" I asked in astonishment. Jesper nodded.

"Was his name by any chance Jon Martin?"

Jesper's eyes widened. "That's the name. How do you know that?"

"I know him from my time with the police. He is the investigator in these death cases."

"Oh!" "Is there a reason why Jon Martin told you this?"

Jesper shrugged. "I can't remember exactly. I think I mentioned to him that this Sigrid was quite an unemotional personality. He must have then told us about her loss. But I don't remember the details."

I touched Lilly's back to signal that it was time to leave. I had learned what I wanted to know. Whether it would help me remained to be seen. I thanked Charlotte and

Jesper and apologized once again for reopening old wounds.

At the door, Jesper held me by the arm. "I'm sorry for my initially rough tone. The wound that Henriette's act left will never heal. I know you can understand."

"More than anyone else." I placed my hand on his shoulder and nodded at him. He nodded back and closed the door.

Chapter 36

As I drove the car out of the driveway, I felt Lilly's demanding gaze. I glanced over at her. "My deceased son?"

She nodded.

"Just a moment. First, I want to know what you think of the Abramsens."

She pursed her lips. "An incredibly sad story. Unimaginable what parents must go through in such a situation."

I nodded. "Indeed. In the blink of an eye, life is turned upside down. Nothing is as it was before. What was important is now insignificant. The Abramsens still suffer from the loss, and they will until the end of their days. That much is certain. And the knowledge that their own daughter actually committed suicide makes the whole situation even more painful."

"But this news dampens our investigations, doesn't it?"

"Not necessarily. Just because Henriette committed suicide doesn't mean the same was true for the others."

Lilly nodded.

"Did you know that Sigrid had children?" I asked her.

"I only know that there's a photo of a girl on her desk. But I never thought much about it."

We drove along the Fylkesvei, and soon the city appeared in the distance. The meteorological service had once again forecast a severe storm, and I hoped we would be back at the boarding school before it arrived. "Is there anyone at the boarding school who knows about Sigrid's private life?"

Lilly thought for a moment. "Maybe Runa."

"Right. They must have known each other for a long time. We should talk to her."

She looked at me suspiciously. "Not me. You can forget that right away."

"I figured as much." I sighed. "Let's think about something for a moment: The students were usually found two days after they disappeared. Correct?"

"I believe so," Lilly confirmed.

"They were found not far from the school. Once at the beach, another time a bit further north or south. So they couldn't have just been lying there for two days without someone noticing. Also correct?"

"I guess so."

"This means the girls must have been held somewhere before their deaths."

"Possible."

"Good. It stands to reason that they were held somewhere in the house since there are no other houses within several kilometers."

"They could have been held in any of the apartments or in a kitchen pantry where only the cook has access. I don't know of any other rooms that would be inaccessible."

"What about the cellar? Have you ever been down there?"

"No. I don't know that part at all. As far as I know, all access to the cellar is locked."

"A good place, then, to make girls disappear?"

Lilly looked at me. "In the cellar? Do you really think so?"

"Right now, it seems to be the only logical explanation. If the girls were indeed held in the house, then it would be there."

Lilly nodded. "And what do you plan to do now? Are we breaking into the cellar?"

I nodded as well, but my mind was already a step ahead. I needed to call Jon Martin before Jørn joined us. I didn't want my son to be involved in this matter. "I'm going to call Jon Martin now. But you have to be very quiet. If he realizes someone else is listening, he definitely won't tell me anything."

"Fine, I'll keep quiet." She zipped her lips with her thumb and index finger.

"Please look for Jon Martin in my phone."

Lilly scrolled through my contacts and finally pressed the green phone symbol.

"I know why you're calling," Jon Martin said before I could even say a greeting. "But I can't tell you anything more yet. The victim is now with forensic medicine. I'm awaiting their report."

"Do you have any suspicions yet?"

"No. However, the victim showed no signs of violence. The body was found in the water, making it difficult to determine the time of death."

"I understand. Thanks for that info. The reason I'm calling, though, is different. I just spoke with the Abramsen family. Do you remember them?"

"Of course. Henrietta's parents. What did you want from them?"

"I wanted to talk to them about their daughter. I wanted to understand what drove her to such an act."

"And what did they tell you?"

"Primarily, they spoke about Henriette's character, the problems she had at school, and her then-boyfriend. They also told me about her half-hearted suicide attempt. Henriette was certainly not an unmarked page, but they also said that their daughter seemed to have come back to herself shortly before her admission to Fog Castle, that she seemed to understand what she had done. But her emotional turnaround evidently didn't last long. You know the tragic outcome of the story."

"Yes, I know. Unfortunately."

"During the conversation, Jesper also mentioned the vice principal of the boarding school, Sigrid." I paused briefly to give Jon Martin a chance to say something. But he remained silent, so I continued. "You once told the Abramsens that Sigrid lost her child."

Jon Martin let out a soft laugh. "You seem to know everything!"

"You said it yourself: Once a policeman, always a policeman!"

He laughed. "My goodness, Sondre, you're putting me in a tight spot."

"That's not my intention," I replied, gritting my teeth.

A long pause ensued, and I feared he wouldn't divulge any more details. Finally, he said, "Yes, Sigrid lost her girl."

"Do you know how that happened?"

"No, unfortunately not. It was too long ago. I learned this information from a resident of Tromvik. I would certainly find out more about it in the investigation files, but I can't tell you anything about that."

"I understand!" I said briefly, already having the next question on my tongue. "Did you focus on certain individuals at the boarding school during your investigations into the other deaths?"

Jon Martin made a long humming sound. "Not really. We primarily questioned the close circles of the victims, meaning the girls' teachers, the psychologist, friends, and classmates. But we couldn't prove anything against anyone; no one had a motive or could provide us with any other clues that would have brought a crime to the forefront."

"So you never had a main suspect?"

"I wouldn't say that. A teacher repeatedly came into our focus."

I waited for him to name her, but he remained quiet. "Could you tell me her name?"

"You're making me laugh, Sondre." He sighed loudly, and it took almost ten seconds before he spoke up. "Runa."

"Runa?"

"Yes, Runa. She couldn't verify her alibi through anyone, and — she has been there since the establishment of the boarding school. Those were two reasons to take a closer look at her. But first, we found no plausible motive for her, and second, you all sleep alone in your apartments there. So it's difficult to verify alibis. The only exception was Sigrid. For the first incident, which was many years ago, she had an airtight alibi. I wasn't involved as the lead investigator back then; that was before my time."

"Where was she that night?" I asked him, surprised.

"Sondre, I can't and shouldn't tell you more."

"Yeah, I know!" I said somewhat resigned. "Can I ask you one more question?"

"Go ahead, you pest!"

"Could you tell me the name of the person who passed you the information about Sigrid's child?"

"I would need to check the old files for that, and I don't have time right now. But I still remember the house in Tromvik. It was a bright yellow house on the main road, just before the street ends. As far as I know, the guy used to be a teacher at Fog Castle. I can't tell you if he still lives there."

"That helps me. Thank you, Jon Martin."

"You're welcome. And Sondre, I don't need to explain that you have to pass on important information to us."

I assured him of my cooperation and said goodbye.

"You have quite a bit to do!" Lilly said, half-joking, half-serious.

"Indeed!" I replied thoughtfully.

"Why did Jon Martin mention the alibis of the very first death at the boarding school? That was Henriette, right? No one needed an alibi then."

"Yes, that's true. I haven't told you yet. The very first case wasn't Henriette, but Malin. The daughter of the then caretaker."

"Ah! That's new to me."

"I'm sorry. I have so many thoughts in my head that this information must have slipped my mind."

We approached Sandnessund Bridge. I had to think. The next two days would have been perfect for further investigations. However, with Jørn by my side, this would be a difficult endeavor. I had no choice but to postpone the plan until Monday, even though it almost consumed me inside.

For the next five minutes, neither Lilly nor I said a word. Too much hung in the air that needed contemplation. Jesper and Charlotte kept surfacing in my mind, and I could see the pain still smoldering within them, like the embers of an old fire. I thought of Raik and remembered that I had promised Lilly earlier to tell her about him. "Should I tell you about Raik? My second son."

"If you want to, sure," she replied.

So I began to tell her about Raik, his illness, his suffering, his fight, and his laughter when I played the clown in the hospital. I recounted the sleepless nights, the never-ending workdays, the arguments between Marit and me, and the difficulties of being the perfect father and mother for our first son at the same time. I told her how the hours by Raik's bedside dragged on painfully slowly. Hours spent pacing the room, plagued by dark thoughts of the future, fear, hope, and disappointment. The days would rush past the hospital window in fast motion, but inside, time stood still, as if one were in a vacuum. You knew every cable in the room, every stain on the walls and floors, and could recognize the beeping of every machine. You would sit down crying, stand up again, hold Raik's hand, walk to the window where the last rays of sunlight fell, but still only see your own dull reflection. You became a shadow of yourself. The day turned into a series of mechanical routines, the night into an odyssey. I described how difficult it was to give your child an encouraging smile when minutes before, you had received bad news from the doctors. You lived the whole day like it was a play. You couldn't be yourself; you had to be strong, brave; inside, everything was falling apart.

And finally, I told her about Raik's last moments, when Marit and I held his hands, listened to his breathing, and he looked at us one last time before forever closing his eyes.

Lilly wiped a tear from her eye and looked at me, unsure. She stayed silent for a while, opened her mouth a few times as if she wanted to say something, but the words withered on her tongue. After a painfully long minute, she finally said, "I'm so sorry, Sondre. I - I can't even imagine what you must have gone through."

"Thank you," I replied. I looked south, where the sun dipped between two clouds, bathing the strait in brilliant light. "You know, that's why I can understand the Abramsens so well. I know what it's like for them. The pain doesn't get better with the years; you just get used to it. And that's pretty hard to accept!"

Lilly nodded and wiped her nose.

The last few meters to my ex-wife's house passed in silence. A few minutes later, I turned into Krillvegen and stopped in front of my old house. Fredrik's car was parked in front of the garage, and my throat felt as if a mouse were stuck in it. Lilly was about to get out of the car when I held her back by the arm. "Wait!" She looked at me in surprise.

"I don't feel like ringing the doorbell. That car belongs to Marit's partner."

I tooted twice, and shortly after, the door opened. Jørn's face appeared in the doorway. He called a goodbye to his mother and then got in the car with us. Lilly turned around and extended her hand to him. "I'm Lilly. I've heard a lot about you!" She winked at him.

Jørn shook her hand but said nothing.

"Lilly is one of my students," I explained to him.

"All good?" Lilly asked him.

"All good!" he replied, putting on the silly grin of a hormone-driven teenager.

I started the engine and drove toward Kaldfjord. The weather was deteriorating rapidly. Leaden clouds rolled in, and it grew dark. As we approached Kaldfjord, Lilly and Jørn were engrossed in an animated conversation about TV series and music genres, and I could tell from my son's tone that he seemed to enjoy the female company in the car. Unable to keep up with their topics, I directed my thoughts back to the deaths and the conversation with Jon Martin. I wondered if there was more behind the investigations than he was willing to admit. In any case, I couldn't meddle further in police matters and had to try on my own.

Jon Martin hadn't mentioned Mikkel, and I had forgotten to ask him about the caretaker. But it didn't matter; I didn't want to call him again, and now I had to make do with what I knew. I thought about the rooms Mikkel had mentioned and wondered again what he meant by that. If he truly had something to do with the incidents, why was he giving me a hidden clue? Did he want to lure me into a trap? Did he want to get caught? There are criminals who want to be caught! They know they are doing something wrong but can't stop themselves and rely on the authorities to stop them. However, I deemed this possibility to be unlikely. Still, Mikkel remained a mysterious figure to me.

Jon Martin had also spoken about Runa and Sigrid, and I would have liked to know what alibi Sigrid could provide. Apparently, though, she was definitely ruled out for these crimes. I kept the fact that she had lost a child in mind and resolved to find out as soon as possible with whom Jon Martin had spoken in Tromvik. For now, this seemed to be the only lead that could somehow help me.

At least I hoped so!

I glanced in the rearview mirror and noticed Jørn's blissful smile. He seemed to be warm-hearted.

As Tåkevik came into view, the weather had deteriorated so much that the cliffs north and south of the bay were no longer visible. A curtain of snow was drifting toward us from the sea, promising a cozy evening in the warm living room. Fog Castle loomed like a threatening backdrop from a Hollywood production, nestled in the bay. Only a few lights were on, adding to the somber atmosphere. I steered my car into the parking lot, and we got out. Lilly walked ahead, and Jørn trailed after her.

"Welcome to Fog Castle!" I announced solemnly as we entered the building.

Jørn stopped and spun around with his mouth agape. "Not bad, this place!" he exclaimed, looking at Lilly.

"Come on, I'll show you the house and my room." Lilly took Jørn's hand. "Is that okay with you?" She looked at me questioningly.

I actually wanted to take charge of that, but the two seemed to be having fun, so I let them go. Maybe I could use the break to visit the person Jon Martin mentioned in Tromvik, even though the weather was making me less than enthusiastic about another drive.

"Here's the key to my apartment." I tossed Jørn the apartment key. "I need to step out for a moment."

Lilly looked at me questioningly. "Where are you going now?"

"To Tromvik," I replied. "I want to have a quick chat with a former teacher there."

Lilly nodded.

"I'll be back in no more than two hours. Then we can have dinner together."

"Sounds good. See you later," Lilly said, and both of them disappeared up the stairs.

I walked back to my car. The snow front sent the first timid flakes into the bay, and I drove back on the mountain road toward Tromvik. When I reached the main road, I kept to the left and scanned the street for a yellow house. People seemed to have retreated into their homes. The road was deserted, my car the only one creeping through the town.

After about five hundred meters, a yellow house appeared on the left side. The driveway was completely snowed in. Apparently, no one had come in or out for a while. I parked my car at the roadside and observed the house for a moment. Behind one of the windows on the ground floor, I noticed a bluish glow. Someone was apparently watching TV. I got out and walked to the front door. The name on the doorbell read Gustav Haraldsson. Was this the right man?

I rang the bell. The blue flicker disappeared, and a few seconds later, the door opened. A man, approximately to be in his mid-sixties, stood before me in shorts and a T-shirt stained with food. He had only a few tufts of hair above his ears, which looked greasy. His belly hung over his trousers, and he wore neither slippers nor socks. Along with his appearance, the smell of stale food and beer hit me. I would have preferred to get back into my car immediately.

"Good day," I greeted him instead.

He swallowed a mouthful and returned my greeting.

"My name is Sondre. I'm a teacher at the boarding school up top. Am I correct in assuming that you used to work there as well?"

He nodded, frowning as he added, "Yes, that's correct."

"I'd like to explain briefly why I'm here. The thing is…"

"Don't you want to come in?" he interrupted me. "It's freezing out here."

I would have preferred to decline. The smell was simply too repulsive. However, since he was only lightly dressed in the cold, I had no choice but to enter his cave.

The mess inside the house was overwhelming. Crumpled fishing magazines and old newspapers piled up on the floor, dirty socks lay among other filthy clothes, and the coffee table was barely recognizable beneath junk food wrappers. There were two sofas, each with two seats. He pointed to the left one.

Reluctantly, I took a seat.

"I'm sorry to just drop in on you like this," I started. "As I was about to explain, I recently became a teacher at the boarding school. Unfortunately, my start at the school has been rather bumpy, to put it mildly."

"Oh?" Gustav raised his eyebrows. "Why is that?"

"A student was found dead yesterday."

Gustav's eyes widened. He opened his mouth, and I felt he wanted to respond, but he held back.

A bit uncertain, I continued, "I wanted to ask if anything similar happened during your time there?"

Gustav's jaw dropped again, and he shook his head. "No. Not during that time. But a year before I started, a student was found dead. I think her name was Frida…!"

That would match the records from Sigrid's office.

"Was there any discussion about this incident? During your time there, I mean?"

Gustav grunted. "Not much. At least not among the staff. But I can't say how it was before my time."

I nodded. "Does the name Mikkel ring a bell?"

His face brightened. "Mikkel? Of course. The caretaker. A real handyman. He could do anything, from cleaning up vomit to renovating apartments. The born craftsman."

"Did you have frequent contact with him?"

Gustav shrugged. "Now and then, yes. But everyone did. He was a nice guy."

"Didn't he seem in any way—how should I put it—mysterious to you?"

He raised his eyebrows. "Mysterious? No, not really. Why do you think so?"

"Just wondering." I didn't want to disclose the reasons for my thoughts, especially that I considered him one of the suspects.

"He always had a kind word," Gustav continued. "That was more than you could say about certain other people

296

there. Unfortunately, I haven't seen Mikkel since my last day at the school."

I didn't pursue that topic but asked the next question, hoping he wouldn't mind being put through the wringer. "What do you think of Sigrid?"

Gustav curled his right lip. "Sigrid? She was a strange bird, or rather a strange woman." He laughed heartily. "No, seriously. She was as cold as a January morning. But don't tell her I said that."

I shook my head. "Of course not."

"In my eight years at the boarding school, I never spoke more than ten sentences in a row with her. She was someone you just couldn't get through to. Her expression never revealed what was going on behind her facade. It was pure guesswork. I avoided her as much as possible."

"I wonder why someone like Sigrid, who has to communicate with so many people every day, can show such emotional coldness," I interjected, hoping he would catch on.

"Some people are just like that." He shrugged. "I think she's had a tough life."

I feigned ignorance. "What do you mean by that?"

"She lost a child, a girl. That loss must have affected her."

I nodded as if I understood, which I did, even though this explanation was still unsatisfactory. "What did she die from?"

"Pneumonia, I believe. But I can't swear to it. I only know it from a former colleague at the boarding school. His name was William. Unfortunately, he's no longer with us. He had a heart attack. I wasn't surprised, though. He ate like a bear, even during class. A miracle Mikkel didn't have to widen the doorframe of his apartment." He laughed again, like a boat engine that wouldn't start. Once he had regained his composure, he continued, "Where was I? Oh yes, right. Sigrid's child. William told me that the girl didn't recover from a severe case of pneumonia. I can't tell you when exactly that was."

"That's okay," I said, even though it bothered me.

"Say, Sondre, why do you even want to know all this?" he asked, putting his calloused feet on the table.

"I'm just trying to understand why there are so many deaths at the boarding school."

Gustav looked at me silently for a while. After a sigh, he shrugged indifferently. "Well, for me, it's really not a mystery. I dealt with students who were really struggling psychologically. Some of them had a very troubled past. I remember one student whose wrists bore several healed scars. Others had scars from fights. There was a whole spectrum of backgrounds, and that made teaching no easier. You'll get used to it, though. At first, I also struggled to get into the minds of those teenagers. But after a while, you understand how they tick. Such acts don't happen for no reason."

I didn't share his opinion but didn't want to express that. So, I just said, "You're probably right. I'll surely get used to the circumstances over time." I theatrically glanced at my watch. "Well, I need to go. Thank you for the interesting conversation."

"Don't mention it, colleague." He patted his thighs and walked me to the door. We shook hands, and I stepped out into the fresh air.

***

At the same time that Sondre was walking back to his car in the falling snow, Mikkel was shuffling through the deserted hallways of Fog Castle, enjoying the silence he had almost forgotten. The few people still within the walls did not show themselves. As so often in such hours, he listened for the voice of his daughter, who always sang her way up the stairs to their apartment after school. And he heard her voice every time. But he knew she only sang in his thoughts. It was an echo from long ago. He missed those days, just as he missed her.

He carried an envelope in his hands, and on the envelope, it read in swirling letters — *For Sondre from M.*

Chapter 37

After Lilly had shown Jørn her father's apartment, she led him through the hallways of the boarding school. She noticed that while Jørn appeared interested, he wasn't fully engaged in the tour. She sensed that he was more interested in her than in the building itself. Although she was a year older than him, which felt like a decade in the teenage years, she couldn't deny a certain interest on her part. He seemed bright and good-looking. With his white sneakers, tight black jeans, and olive-green hoodie, he was also stylishly dressed. She liked his wavy brown hair and angular face. He had his father's eyes, a mix of green and golden brown, like a leaf in autumn.

They reached the lounge and sat down in armchairs. Jørn leaned back, clasped his hands behind his head, and looked around the hall. Lilly watched him for a while and noticed the similarities between him and his father, particularly the way he ran his hands through his hair, something she had also noticed with Sondre.

"Your place here is pretty impressive!" Jørn suddenly exclaimed.

"Yeah, it is. Quite something, isn't it?"

"Who builds something like this?"

"An Englishman. Blake Hargrave, he was called."

"And where is he now?"

"No idea. The house now belongs to a John Birch. He's the director. Rarely around, though."

"Do you have many friends here?"

Lilly shrugged. "It's okay. There are a lot of oddballs at the boarding school. You wouldn't want to be friends with them. But there are also interesting people that I get along with really well. But I don't actually have a best friend. Or rather, not anymore."

"Did she finish school?"

"She died."

He looked at her in shock. "Died?"

"She took her own life."

"How terrible. Were you close?"

Lilly nodded. "Very much so. We were like sisters. That's why I don't really believe she would have killed herself."

Jørn looked at her, furrowing his brow.

"Long story," Lilly said, waving her hands dismissively.

"No worries, I don't have much going on right now." He winked at her.

She laughed. "I'll tell you later, I promise."

"Whatever you want."

For a moment, neither of them spoke. Then Lilly said, "Can I ask you something?"

"Sure!"

"But it's personal."

"That's fine."

"Your father told me about your brother. That must be really hard for you."

Jørn's smile vanished. His gaze dropped to the floor and lingered there for a while. "Yeah, it is," he replied, nodding sadly.

"Unfortunately, I never had a sibling. But I can imagine he is sorely missed."

"He is. Especially when I sit alone in my room with nothing to do. Those are the toughest moments."

"At our age, we shouldn't have to go through such things. Can you talk to someone about it?"

"I don't like to talk about it."

"Sometimes that helps, though."

He shrugged. "I know. Still, I'd rather talk about happier things."

"I can understand that."

An oppressive silence settled in, and Lilly wished she hadn't brought up the topic. But it was too late now. She tried to steer the conversation in a different direction. "By the way, I think your dad is pretty cool."

"Cool?"

"Yeah. He's very popular here. And you can't say that about every teacher."

"Maybe," he said with a shrug. "I just don't understand why he wants to teach out here. It's so desolate."

Lilly shook her head slowly. "Desolate, as you put it, it's certainly not. I thought so at first too, but there's always something happening here."

"Like what?"

A smile formed on Lilly's lips. "We have a whole house full of teenagers, and at least one of them comes up with a stupid idea every day."

"For example?"

"There's the gender segregation of the rooms. Male students aren't allowed in female rooms and vice versa. Of course, not everyone follows that rule and gets caught. And that causes quite a bit of trouble. Some also get caught smoking or doing drugs from time to time. Such incidents provide plenty of gossip. And you should see the fights. Sometimes it gets pretty intense."

"Sounds like conditions in Shawshank prison!" Jørn's lips curled into a smile. "Do you know the movie?"

"I do. But it's not that bad."

Lilly laughed as well.

"So, what trouble have you gotten into?" Jørn asked.

"Smoking on school grounds!"

"That's nothing serious."

"No, it's not. But it still had consequences. Besides, I was outside after ten p.m. and got caught." She shrugged. "You learn from your mistakes. Most of the time, anyway." For a moment, she looked at Jørn thoughtfully. Should she tell him about Tiril? Sondre had remained silent about her, probably for a good reason.

Would he be angry with her if she told his son? Jørn should figure out on his own that something was off. A boarding school without students? "Haven't you wondered why the boarding school is so empty?" she finally asked him.

"Honestly, yes. But I assumed the students went home on Fridays."

"That's unfortunately not the only reason." She straightened up. "The day before yesterday, a student was found dead down by the beach."

Jørn froze and looked at her with a furrowed brow. "Come on, really?"

"I'm not kidding. Her name was Tiril. She disappeared a few days ago. No one knew where she was. Until the day before yesterday."

"Dad didn't tell me anything about that."

"Maybe he was worried you wouldn't want to come here under those circumstances."

Jørn shrugged. "I would have come anyway. My buddies would have been all ears if I could have told them a story like that."

Lilly laughed. "They might not have believed you."

"Quite possible. Do they know how she died?"

"We're not sure. Accident, suicide, murder. I don't know."

"Did you know her?"

She nodded.

"Where was she found?"

"Shall I show you?"

"Now?"

"Why not?"

Jørn pointed to the window.

"Because of a few snowflakes?" she asked, grinning, and got up. "Come on, you wimp. Get your jacket, and we'll meet at the front door."

Five minutes later, they trudged through the snow toward the beach. Lilly felt a bit uneasy about it. The fright from the previous evening still lingered in her bones. Since then, she had repeatedly wondered if it might have been another student trying to scare her. However, it would have been a rather morbid joke.

The snowfall had intensified, the sun had set, and the remaining light of the day was swallowed by the clouds.

"It's a bit creepier out here than in town," Jørn commented.

"Indeed. Sometimes it's almost too eerie. I grew up in the countryside, but this oppressive silence takes getting used to. But it also has its beautiful sides. The peace out here has something meditative about it. It gives one a reason to reflect. And many people here need that."

"Isn't it too quiet or too remote for some?"

"Yes, of course. But when you're here, you're here. There's not much you can do about it."

They reached the rock formation at the southern end of the beach and stopped. "This is the spot," Lilly said, pointing to the rocks.

Jørn tilted his head back and stared up at the cliff. "Do you think she jumped?"

Lilly shrugged. "I didn't know Tiril as well as Linnea. But I doubt she took her own life. Just like the four before her!"

Jørn raised his eyebrows and looked at her: "Four?"

Lilly nodded. "Tiril is victim number five. Four girls have already died in this bay before her."

Jørn looked up at the cliff again. "That's creepy. And they all died here?"

"I'm not entirely sure. It's possible that one or two of the girls were found a bit further north or south along the coast. But even if they were, it doesn't make the situation any less complicated. Your father and I have been doing some research in the last few days and have found out quite a bit. We're convinced that something is amiss with these deaths. Someone must be responsible."

"You mean someone killed the girls?"

"That's what I mean. The students each went missing for a few days before they were found dead. During that time, they must have been held somewhere. And I'm sure they were kept captive at the boarding school."

"Aren't the rooms in the house generally accessible? That should have been noticed by now."

"Actually, yes. The only place that isn't accessible to everyone is the basement. I've never been down there."

"What do you mean by not accessible?"

"The doors to the basement are locked. I've never seen anyone go in or out."

"Is there only one access point?"

"No. There's a door on the side facing the bay that also leads to the basement. I wanted to check it out with Linnea once, but it was locked."

"Should we try again?"

"If you want to, sure. It's getting uncomfortable down here anyway."

The wind picked up speed, driving the snowflakes horizontally across the beach. Lilly led the way, and Jørn followed closely behind.

"Why are you going to school here, anyway?" Jørn asked.

"I was naughty!" she replied shortly.

Jørn laughed. "What does that mean?"

"I messed up back home. We burned down a barn!"

Jørn hesitated for a moment before responding. "Really?"

"Yes, unfortunately."

"How did you manage that?"

Lilly briefly recounted how the tragedy occurred and how it changed her life in an instant. Jørn listened to her story, and in the end, he said, "That's terrible. But at least you weren't the ringleader."

"No, that's true. But that doesn't help the poor horses anymore."

They continued walking in silence. It had become so dark that Lilly had to take out her flashlight and illuminate the path ahead. Suddenly, she stopped, and Jørn almost collided with her.

"Hey, what is -?"

Lilly pressed her hand over his mouth. "Shh!"

Jørn tried to respond, but all that came out was a muffled mumble.

"Shh!" Lilly swung her flashlight back and forth.

"What's wrong?" he asked when she removed her hand.

"I just felt like I saw someone."

"Where?"

"Right there!" She pointed the beam of light to the left. "I could swear something fled from the light. I just saw a shadow dart away."

Maybe it's an animal?" Jørn speculated.

"It was too big for a fox or a ptarmigan."

"Reindeer?"

"I've never seen one here. They're all up on the pass."

She felt her knees weaken. The memories from the last time made her hold her breath. Fear spread through her. "Stop with that nonsense, damn it!" Jørn cursed and gave her a light slap on the upper arm. "You're freaking me out." "I'm not joking." Lilly swung the flashlight in all directions, but the snowfall was too thick to see more than a few meters ahead. "Maybe we'll find footprints."

"You must have been mistaken," Jørn countered, and she hoped he was right.

After a while, they continued, alert, muscles tensed, eyes wide open. Lilly quickened her pace, and after two minutes, they reached the west side of the building. "Did you find any tracks?" Jørn asked.

"Yes, here." She shone the flashlight a few meters to the side, and indeed, there were footprints.

"Who could they belong to?"

"Ask me something else. No idea. There's hardly anyone in the building."

"Maybe just someone stretching their legs."

Lilly sighed. "Let's hope so."

They walked along the wall until they finally reached a wooden door. They stopped there.

"Here's the entrance to the basement," Lilly said. "Do you see the footprints? They lead away from the door and disappear into the darkness."

"Someone must have come out of the basement." Jørn squeezed past her and pressed the doorknob. A creak sounded, and the door opened a tiny crack. Startled, he let go of the doorknob and stared at Lilly's horrified face.

***

He knew this feeling all too well—the emptiness left behind when his beloved princess was no longer there, when she left him alone, without a word of farewell, without hope of return…! It felt like hunger that could not be satisfied, like a longing for affection that one never receives. And the uncertainty of when he would see her again was the worst part of it all.

He left his room and stepped outside the building, stretching his face into the wind and letting the snowflakes fall on his skin. He opened his mouth and caught the white tufts with his tongue. When his face was already completely white, he trudged on towards the beach.

Halfway there, he suddenly stopped, listening to the silence like an animal when danger lurks. He had heard voices, very close. For a moment, he stood hesitantly, anxious yet curious. He heard them clearly between the gusts of wind. Now he even saw a faint glimmer of light, just weak, but sufficient. The voices were getting closer. They belonged to a girl and a boy. He recognized one of the voices and became very excited.

Was it his princess? Had she returned?

He followed the sound of their voices, their footsteps; the deep voice puzzled him, but he ignored it. Striding through the snow, he wanted to block their path, to see if his princess had come back. The wind carried the voices away and then brought them back. He was now very close; any moment he would see them. In her dress, white with pink flowers, her hair pinned up, the silver crown sparkling in the snow.

A sudden bright light blinded him. He raised his arms to shield his face and jumped to the side.

The voices ceased. He could only hear the wind. With a pounding heart, he crouched down in the snow, waiting, listening. Soft murmurs reached his ears. Snow hit his face directly, and he tried to make himself even smaller. The beam of light started moving again, and he followed it from a distance. Now he could make out the pair just a few meters ahead of him. They had stopped, close to the wall of the building. They were talking to each other. What about, he couldn't understand. He saw them start moving again, walking along the building wall, and finally stopping in front of the basement door.

Like a thunderclap, he suddenly realized that he had made a mistake. A mistake that should not have happened. Terror shot through his limbs as he watched the boy press the doorknob and swing the door open.

Chapter 38

I steered my car onto the mountain road towards Tåkevik, cracked the side window open, and blew cigarette smoke into the night air. The storm that had been predicted was whipping its first gusts over the mountain, and the snowflakes were blowing sideways across my car and the road, so that the road could only be discerned by the colored markers.

I thought about the conversation with Gustav and his suspicion that Sigrid's daughter had succumbed to pneumonia. Whether that was true or not would not be easy to verify. I couldn't exactly ask her about it. On the other hand, the cause of death might not even be relevant. I found it more important to consider whether the loss of her daughter might give her a motive to abduct students here at the boarding school and kill them. The same question applied to Mikkel. Physically speaking, Mikkel would certainly be better able to abduct someone from a room. Moreover, he knew every corner of the house, which also applied to Sigrid.

As I reached the other side of the mountain past the barrier, the condition of the road became increasingly difficult. The storm had already dumped a considerable amount of snow on the slopes of the bay, and there didn't seem to be any snowplows around. In a sharp left turn, the car slid a bit to the right and buried its front wheels in the snow. I put it in reverse and pressed the pedal, but the wheels just spun in place. I tried again a second and third time, with the same result. The right headlight was buried in the snow, and I couldn't see how far I was from the edge. Moving forward was not an option. Cursing, I got out and examined the wheel. It was completely buried in snow. I went to the trunk, pulled out a small snow shovel, and began to clear the snow away. The strong wind swept the top layer of snow across the road and blew snow crystals into my face like a sandblaster. I had no gloves on, and my fingers were ice-cold within seconds, making it hard to move them. After five minutes, the wheel was cleared, and I sat back behind the steering wheel. I thawed my fingers on the heater, which hurt like hell. Then I shifted into reverse, and on my second attempt, the wheel slid back onto the road.

After another arduous twenty minutes, the first lights of the parking lot shone through the snowstorm, and I parked my car next to a pickup truck. When I stepped through the entrance door, the dull silence of the house enveloped me, as if I had cottonwool in my ears. The lounge was empty, as was the dining room and the staircase. I called out for

Lilly and Jørn. But their names echoed in the long, dark corridors of the ground floor.

They might be in my apartment.

As I stepped through the door, I almost stepped on a brown envelope. Puzzled, I picked it up and examined it from all sides. It wasn't sealed, but on the front, in flowing handwriting, it said: For Sondre from M!

M?

Mikkel?

On the dining table, I noticed Jørn's backpack, but his jacket was missing. It wasn't hanging on the coat rack either.

Were they outside in this weather?

With the envelope in hand, I sat down at the dining table and took out an A4-sized sheet of paper. It was a copy of a newspaper article from 1985, clearly reporting a house fire.

Tåkevik

On the night of January 23, a residential house in Tåkevik burned down to its foundations. The house had been built not long ago by Blake Hargrave, on his property near Fog Castle.

Ailin Fosnes with her two children, Elida and Bjørk lived in the house. When the rescue services arrived after hours, it was too late for nine-year-old Elida. Ailin's son, Bjørk, survived the inferno with severe burns. He was found by rescuers on the beach, holding a clump of his sister's hair.

According to initial findings, the fire was caused by a burning candle.

Above the article were two black-and-white photos. One showed a fire ruin, and the other featured a woman with two children. All three smiled at the camera. The boy was slightly taller than the girl, had a moon-shaped face, and short, wavy hair. The girl had delicate features, a round face, and long, curly hair. Both wore similarly knitted wool sweaters. The boy also wore jeans, and the girl had a skirt with stockings.

The woman, presumably the mother of the two, also had a round face, short hair, and…!

I paused. Something about the photo disturbed me, but I couldn't immediately pinpoint what it was. I held the photo a little closer to my eyes and examined the people more closely. The children resembled each other. The girl had the fine features of the mother, while the boy seemed more coarsely chiseled. I recognized the bay in the background. It was Tåkevik, taken in late summer or autumn. Otherwise, I found nothing unusual.

Yet something caught my attention. And this something became clearer and clearer. Suddenly, I saw it in all its clarity before me. Just a nondescript detail, but it stood out from the photo as if the photographer had deliberately focused on this one detail.

A sensation, like an electric shock, coursed through my body. I looked up, swallowed hard, and studied the photo again. My hands were trembling.

It was them!

It had to be them. The woman's lips, the long, dark hair of the girl, unmistakable! In the photo, the woman had a short haircut. Today, she wore long hair, and the hard, authoritative look had not changed over the years. And her eyes were just as piercing as at the time the photo was taken.

Shocked, I set the picture aside. A thousand thoughts rolled through my mind, like a thousand marbles released all at once.

What did the photo mean? What was the woman hiding? What secrets had she guarded all these years, and what role did she play in this house? Gradually, the mystery of Fog Castle began to visualize itself before my eyes. Speculations and conjectures lost their foundation. The truth came into the right light, frame by frame, shaking me to my core.

I could see it before me. The fire, the fear, the children exposed to all of it. The death of their daughter and the helplessness of their son. I understood the pain of the mother who had abandoned her children. The lies that had arisen from it and caused so much suffering.

It was like the famous quote from Sherlock Holmes: *When you have eliminated the impossible, whatever remains, no matter how improbable, must be the truth.*

Mikkel was ruled out as a suspect. His daughter was just as much a victim as the other girls. Yet I couldn't shake the feeling that he knew the secret of Fog Castle. Why he hadn't revealed it to me remained a mystery.

Chapter 39

Lilly and Jørn tiptoed into the basement. Both were as tense as guitar strings. No one spoke a word. Lilly felt Jørn just a few centimeters behind her; he was breathing down her neck, and he seemed nervous. The hallway before them was only dimly lit and faded away into darkness far behind.

"Do you really want to continue?" Jørn asked without warning, and Lilly jumped.

"Are you crazy to scare me like that!" she hissed, coming to a stop. "Of course I want to continue. I'm not turning back now. Are you scared?"

"No, of course not." Jørn tried to sound cool.

"Yeah, right." Lilly nudged him in the side. "You look very relaxed."

"Who just got scared a moment ago?"

Lilly nudged him again. "There's a door here. Let's open it." She carefully pressed the handle down. A squeak echoed through the hallway, and she paused. Holding her breath, they looked at each other. No one moved a muscle.

But nothing happened!

Gently, Lilly pushed the door open and aimed her flashlight into the room. It presented a chaotic sight.

"Did a bomb go off here?" Jørn whispered, entering the room and pulling her along by the arm. He rummaged in his pocket for his phone, turned on the display, and shone it on the pile of junk. Meanwhile, Lilly inspected an old sled. The runners were partly splintered, and the handle was broken. Right next to it lay a wooden ladder, its rungs, like the sled, splintered and no longer usable.

"Look at the old school desks." She stood in a corner, lifting the wooden top of a school desk. "You hardly find stuff like this anymore."

They examined a few more items but found nothing of significance.

"No signs that anyone was held here against their will," Lilly said. "No ropes, no chains, nothing. Let's move on."

The next door was ajar. Lilly pushed it open and shone her light into the room.

It was empty.

Jørn went inside and illuminated the walls and corners with his phone. "Nothing!" he said, disappointed.

"Look...!" Lilly whispered from the other side of the room.

"What is it?"

"Here, the iron ring in the wall. You could tie someone to that. And here, on the floor, a dark liquid. Not fully dried yet."

At that moment, they heard a noise above their heads. Lilly instantly turned off the flashlight. Jørn put his phone away in his pocket. They were enveloped in complete darkness. The dim light from the wall lamp in the basement hallway did not reach into the room.

"What was that?" Jørn whispered, anxious.

"Sounded like footsteps," Lilly replied.

"Where did they come from?"

"Above us. It could have been Sigrid. She always wears high heels. On the stone floor, it sounds like gunshots."

"Who is Sigrid?"

"The vice principal."

"And what if she comes down here?"

"I don't think so. What would she be doing down here? There's nothing here."

"If there were nothing important, it wouldn't be all locked up, would it?"

The footsteps faded, and it became quiet again.

Lilly turned the flashlight back on. "What could that liquid be?"

Jørn knelt down and smelled it. "Smells like... like urine!"

Lilly looked at him in horror. "Urine?"

"It could also be from an animal," Jørn suggested.

"I don't think so. Where would that come from?"

"Through the door, if it's open."

"Very unlikely."

For a moment, they stood indecisively. Lilly felt her heart pounding against her chest from the inside. She was sure they had just found a killer's hideout. She wished Sondre there, but she had no idea if he was back from

Tromvik yet. She fumbled for her phone, hoping she had reception.

No signal!

She glanced at the door. "Let's go to the next room. But quietly. Then we'll go upstairs and call your dad."

The last door was just before a staircase that led into darkness. In this room, they found a multitude of shovels, pickaxes, wheelbarrows, a workbench, and a shelf full of lanterns and ropes. Everything was covered in a layer of dust an inch thick.

"The ropes look unused." Jørn lifted one and examined it from all sides.

Lilly nodded.

"What do we do now?" Jørn asked.

"We go upstairs," Lilly replied.

"Up the stairs?"

"No. There's a risk we might run into Sigrid. Besides, I doubt there's a key in the door lock."

She had barely finished the sentence when they heard a door slam nearby.

They flinched, and Lilly dropped her flashlight in shock. It clattered to the ground, sounding in that room like a landslide of gravel. A loud snort echoed through the basement hallway, and they looked at each other, startled. Lilly picked up the flashlight, turned it off, and stepped out into the hallway with Jørn. In the dim light, they noticed a shadowy figure standing motionless at the basement exit, staring in their direction. Lilly grabbed Jørn's hand and squeezed it tightly. Jørn himself stared wide-eyed at the enormous figure, which suddenly began to move and ran rapidly toward them.

Chapter 40

Sigrid sat at her desk in her office, working on a report for the headmaster of the boarding school. He was currently in England and wanted to be informed about the latest events. She wrote what was necessary, no more, no less.

After ten minutes, she finished the report and sent it via email. She was about to get up from her chair when there was a knock at the door.

"Yes?" she called.

The door opened, and Runa stepped in. "Good evening, Sigrid."

"Good evening, Runa."

She approached the desk. "Have the police said anything regarding Tiril?"

Sigrid shook her head. "No. I don't think we'll get any new information until next week. But I assume that Tiril committed suicide. She had problems, and I knew that, as did Kjell. We informed the police about it. What they make of it now is their business."

"I hope we can return to normal soon," Runa said, crossing her arms.

"The school must go on. Parents are paying a fortune for their children, and they expect classes to resume soon."
"Of course," Runa said, nervously scraping her feet on the floor. "I wanted to talk to you about something." She stepped a little closer. "I've noticed recently that this Sondre hangs out with Lilly a lot. I find that a bit—how shall I put it—strange. I even wondered if something is going on between them?"

Sigrid raised her eyebrows knowingly. "I've noticed that too. I'll look into it next week."

"I find his behavior quite inappropriate," Runa added to her opinion. "Did you know that they are both staying here over the weekend?"

Sigrid looked at her in surprise. "No, I didn't know that."

"It's true. I saw his car, and this morning, I happened to overhear Lilly telling a classmate that she was staying here for the weekend."

Sigrid raised her eyebrows again, but only remarked, "Interesting."

"Shouldn't we confront them about this?"

"As I said, Runa, I'll take care of it. I have something else to deal with now, and I don't have time for that." Sigrid gave her an annoyed look, stood up from her chair, and walked past her to the door.

Runa followed her uncertainly and stopped in the hallway. "Shall we have coffee together tomorrow?"

"Yes, why not," Sigrid replied, lacking enthusiasm, as she stepped into the hallway.

Runa put on a forced smile. "Great, see you tomorrow then."

Sigrid nodded at her, and Runa left. She locked her office and went to the kitchen to brew herself some tea. As the water began to boil, she looked out at the storm. Snowflakes flew horizontally past the building, and the wind howled like a trapped dog. She thought about Runa's words, about the suspicion she had voiced. Was there really some truth to it?

If so, she would put an end to it quickly next week. Relationships between teachers and students were unacceptable.

At the edge of her vision, she suddenly noticed a movement in the darkness. At first, she thought it was a light reflection from the kitchen. But then she realized it was the dancing beam of a flashlight.

Who the hell was wandering around in this storm?

The light moved away from the house, swallowed by the snow and darkness. She moved closer to the window, waiting a minute. But the glimmer didn't return. Frowning, she turned away, switched off the kettle, and left the kitchen without her tea. In the entrance hall, she looked out a window to confirm whether Sondre's car was actually there.

It was!

For a while, she stared at the illuminated parking lot, deep in thought and squinting her eyes. Finally, she turned around and headed straight up to the second floor, stopping in front of Lilly's room.

Chapter 41

Lilly had already experienced several adrenaline-pumping moments in her life, but none could compare to her current situation. Just seconds ago, the only sound in the basement had been dripping water. Now, loud snorting and pounding footsteps mingled. In the light of the wall lamp, she recognized the outline of a giant lumbering down the corridor toward her like a steam locomotive. Jørn instinctively stepped backward and slammed his back against the wall. Lilly had only about three seconds to come up with an escape plan.

The stairs!

She grabbed Jørn by the arm and pulled him with her. "Run!" She took off, with Jørn following, but he stumbled over a protruding stone and fell flat on his face.

"GET UP!" Lilly screamed, running over to help him to his feet.

"RUN!" she shouted, seeing the man had closed in to just a few meters away. Jørn ran after her, and they reached the stairs. They raced up as fast as they could and soon stood in front of a closed door. Lilly twisted the doorknob, but it wouldn't budge.

Jørn shoved her aside and panicked, shaking the door. "Open, you damn thing!" He pounded against the wood and shouted for help. "Help us, hellooooo! Heeeelp!"

Lilly grabbed Jørn by the upper arm. However, he was so overwhelmed with panic that he didn't feel her touch.

"Jøøørn...!" she finally shouted and spun him around.

"What?"

But Lilly didn't answer. She was staring at a huge man who stood just two steps below them, snorting and glaring at them. She recognized that snorting from the night when she had been chased outside the building. A horrible stench spread through the air, and she fought against a wave of nausea. Jørn stepped in front of her, trying to shield her. The figure stepped into the light of a wall lamp, and Lilly gasped. Jørn also stepped back as the man approached them, his grotesquely disfigured face coming closer. The left half of his face was marked with scars, and he had growths and creases, as if he had been mutilated with a knife. His eyes were clear and sparkled like two rubies. His gaze flickered back and forth between Lilly and Jørn. Drool dripped from his mouth onto his frayed sweater.

Suddenly, he grabbed a handful of Lilly's hair, catching a bunch before she could pull her head back. Paralyzed, she watched as he brought the hair to his nose and sniffed it. His eyes were closed, and he let out a soft grunt.

Jørn suddenly lunged forward and pushed the man with all his might against the chest. However, the impact with the massive body didn't have the desired effect. The man grabbed Jørn by the throat and squeezed. Jørn gasped for air, his face contorted in pain.

"Let him go, you monster!" Lilly screamed, trying to punch him in the face, but he deftly dodged. She was about to lunge at him when the door behind them swung open, and all three froze in their movements.

A woman looked down at them, her expression one of confusion. "What's going on here?" she bellowed.

"Help us!" Lilly held onto the man's hand, trying to push him away from her.

"What's going on?" the woman asked, her gaze fixed on the man.

"They were in the basement, Mom!" he said quietly, loosening his grip on Jørn's throat. He still clutched Lilly's hair tightly between his fingers.

Lilly looked up at the woman in astonishment. Had the man just called her "Mom"?

The woman pushed through the door and locked it from the inside. Then she ordered the man to take them downstairs. Lilly felt him grab her arm, and he did the same to Jørn. Then he roughly shoved them down the stairs. To Lilly and Jørn's astonishment, he began to sob.

"Stop crying, that doesn't help," the woman said brusquely.

"What do you want from us, you stupid cow? Let us go!" Lilly tried to break free but quickly realized she had no chance against his immense strength.

"Be quiet!" the woman hissed behind them, hitting Lilly on the back of the head. "Or you'll regret it."

Despite the warning, Lilly screamed for help again. A flash of light exploded before her eyes, and she felt her legs give way. The walls began to spin, and she felt nauseous, her head pounding. She sensed herself being lifted and dragged along. She barely managed to put one foot in front of the other.

They finally reached the bottom of the stairs. Still slightly dazed, Lilly watched as the woman stepped up to the cellar wall and put her hand into a wall niche. Shortly after, there was a rumbling, and the wall moved back a bit before disappearing to the left behind the masonry. A space the size of a phone booth opened up. A wooden door led into another room. The woman stepped through the wall opening, unlocked the door, and nodded for the man to come over. Lilly and Jørn were pushed through the entrance, and the wall closed behind them. They were trapped. The room was enveloped in complete darkness. A match was struck, and soon three candles burned on a nightstand.

Lilly noticed two beds, a wardrobe, and a chair. It smelled of old, unwashed clothes and dampness.

The woman approached Lilly and Jørn with her arms crossed. "What are you doing down here?"

Neither Lilly nor Jørn answered the question.

"Answer me!" she said more forcefully.

"I just wanted to show Jørn the basement," Lilly said quietly.

"Didn't you learn on your first day that the basement is a private area? Wasn't that clear enough?" The woman's lips became so pointed that she almost spat the last words.

Lilly's gaze fell to the ground.

"Answer me!" The woman grabbed Lilly's jaw and glared at her angrily.

"Yes, it was clear enough," Lilly replied sharply.

"Leave her alone!" Jørn hit her on the forearm. No sooner had he done this than the man's plate-sized hands were squeezing his throat. "Leave Mom alone!" he bellowed right next to Jørn's ear, throwing him forward. Jørn lost his balance, fell onto the bed, and hit his head hard against the wall. He let out a cry of pain and thrashed around on the bed.

"Who are you?" the woman asked, stepping closer to him.

Jørn didn't answer but held his head in pain. Blood seeped between his fingers.

"Who are you?" she asked again, hitting him on the thigh.

"This is Jørn, Sondre's son," Lilly replied in his place.

"Oh really!" The woman stepped back a bit and looked at Jørn suspiciously. "Where is your father?"

Jørn sat up, leaning against the wall. He shrugged. "I don't know. He just went out for a bit."

"Don't talk nonsense. His car is parked up there."

"Then he's just come back," Jørn retorted defiantly.

In that moment, Lilly realized she had to somehow attract Sondre's attention. Screaming wouldn't work; the walls were too thick. And her phone wouldn't help down here either.

Dumbfounded, she looked at the woman, the person she had seen every day since entering the boarding school. What did she have to do with all of this? Did she actually have something to do with the dead students? And this giant baby was supposed to be her son? Had she kept him trapped down here his entire life? And why did he look like a character from a horror movie?

She scanned the room and noticed two iron chains embedded in the wall behind one of the beds. At each end of the iron chain was a leather strap lined with fabric.

"How did they get in here?" the woman asked, turning to her son.

His expression, which had just resembled that of a snarling dog, suddenly looked as meek as a hamster's. Embarrassed, he looked down, his lips trembling. "I... I left the door open," he stammered in a whiny voice.

The woman grimaced in annoyance. "Haven't I told you a thousand times that you must always lock the door when you go out?"

He nodded ashamed.

His mother sighed loudly and turned away. Nervously, she paced back and forth in the room, seemingly deep in thought. Occasionally, she glanced at the trio and shook her head continuously.

"What are we going to do with them, Mom?" her son suddenly asked.

She didn't answer right away but rubbed her face with both hands. After another lap around the room, she approached him with a determined expression. "Well, my boy, there's only one solution for the two of them. Hold them tight; I'll get the chloroform."

"But Mom…"

A look from his mother was enough, and he crouched down like a dog expecting to be beaten. She turned on her heel and left the room. Lilly seized the opportunity and screamed at the top of her lungs for Sondre.

The woman paused in the doorway and threw Lilly a pitying glance. "You can scream as loud as you want. No one can hear you down here." With a mocking laugh, she turned and disappeared around the corner of the wall.

Chapter 42

I placed the newspaper article back in the envelope and tried to organize my thoughts. All the stories I had heard about the dead students were swirling in my mind. I traveled back to the past of Fog Castle, thinking of Mikkel. I imagined various scenarios, speculating about their outcomes, their protagonists, their motives and reasons. I now knew that someone at the boarding school was definitely up to something sinister. And this someone was now suspect number one.

I picked up the photo again, and slowly the puzzle pieces began to fit together, even though I wasn't entirely sure if I was right in my conclusions. A slight dizziness came over me, and I closed my eyes.

If only I knew where Lilly and Jørn were right now!

I reached for my phone and dialed Jørn's number. The call went straight to voicemail. I didn't have Lilly's number. Worried, I put my phone away, grabbed a flashlight, and left the apartment. At the stairs, I called out for the two of them again, but received no answer. So, I headed straight to Lilly's room and entered without knocking.

No one was there. I couldn't see her jacket anywhere, so it was likely that they were outside the building. However, my call shouldn't have gone straight to voicemail if that were the case. Suddenly, the basement came to mind. The reception down there might be limited, if not completely blocked.

If I catch them down there, they'll get a lifetime being grounded!

I left Lilly's room and ran to the ground floor. The basement door was locked as expected. Should I break it open? The option seemed a bit too extreme. I needed a key, and the only person who could give me one was Mikkel. I ran back upstairs and knocked breathlessly on Mikkel's apartment door.

No reaction! After a minute, I knocked again, but Mikkel didn't appear. "Mikkel! Are you there? It's me, Sondre!" Silence. I pressed down the handle, and the door opened. Light flooded the room, and I immediately sensed something was wrong. I searched for the light switch, found it, and turned on the ceiling light. At first, I thought I must be in the wrong room. It was empty - completely empty! No table, no bed, no shelf, no locket at the window - nothing at all. The room looked as if it hadn't been used for years. A thick layer of dust covered the floor. Old and new cobwebs hung in the corners, and the window was grimy. With shaky knees, I stepped into the room and looked around.

Was I on the wrong floor?

I went back into the hallway, saw the chapel across the way, and felt even more confused. This couldn't be true! Where was Mikkel's furniture? Where was Mikkel? Why did it look like no one had lived in this apartment for decades?

I went to the window and looked out into the darkness. What was going on here? Was I dreaming? I opened the window and took a deep breath. Snowflakes whirled into the room, and I closed the window again. On shaky legs, I staggered to the door, paused in the frame, and took one last look at the incomprehensible scene. Then, like a drunken person, I made my way back to my apartment, threw on a jacket, and trudged down the stairs to the outside. Snow whipped into my face, and within seconds I was covered in white from head to toe. Not far from the entrance, I found footprints that were already almost covered with snow. With more secure and swift steps, I followed the trail to the west side of the building, where the wind blew even stronger. The snowflakes hit me like little arrows in the face, and I could barely keep my eyes open. I usually loved this weather, but in this situation, I wished for a calm, clear moonlit night.

I couldn't make out the beach, but I knew which direction it was in. I directed the beam of my flashlight back to the ground and saw that the footprints led towards the beach. Just a few meters away, there was another trail, but it went in the opposite direction. Apparently, the two had turned around and returned to the house, which seemed strange to me because I should have encountered them. Still, I decided to follow the tracks to the beach, even though I had little hope of finding them there. When I stopped a few minutes later near the beach, I shouted Lilly and Jørn's names into the storm. But it was as if the wind carried my voice away and mocked me with a derisive howl.

"What a mess!" I cursed. I tried again to reach Jørn on my phone, but once again I only got voicemail. Anxiously, I followed the footprints back to the house. The wind at my back urged me on, and before long I reached the west facade. The footprints ended before a door that seemed to lead into the basement.

So those brats were actually in the basement! I turned off my lamp, gently pressed the handle down, and had to hold the door to keep the wind from tearing it from my hands. A gust of snow whirled with me into the dimly lit hallway, and I closed the door again. The floor was covered in wet shoe prints. I listened to the silence of the basement but only heard the dull roar of the wind. From where I stood, I noticed three doors on either side. The end of the hallway faded into darkness. I walked toward the first door and stopped before it. My heart raced faster with every minute, and I took a deep breath. With trembling hands, I opened the door, turned on my flashlight, and surveyed the pile of junk that was stacked almost to the ceiling. The floor was littered with wet footprints. So they must have been in here as well.

I switched off the lamp and turned it back on only when I was in the next room. Here too, there were numerous shoe prints. Otherwise, the room was empty, except for a metal ring set into the wall. The floor around the ring was wet—much wetter than could be caused by shoes. I shone the light on the ceiling, but it was dry. I knelt down, dipped a finger into the liquid, and smelled it.

Urine!

With a racing pulse, I stood up, and at that moment, I thought I heard a distant scream.

Chapter 43

Startled, I listened into the silence, my heart pounding in my throat. The scream had faded, and I couldn't say for certain whether it had come from the cellar or upstairs.

What the hell was going on here!

I left my position and walked to the door. Just as I was about to step into the hallway, I heard a deep, mechanical growl, as if a boulder was being dragged over a stone floor. At the same time, indistinct murmuring echoed through the cellar, followed by another scream. And this time I was sure it was Lilly. Next, I heard footsteps, followed by the same growl as before. Cautiously, I peered into the hallway but couldn't see anyone.

What had that growl been?

Hidden rooms!

Mikkel's hidden rooms.

At the end of the hallway, I could now make out two steps of a staircase. Right in front of it, on the left side, a door stood open, and the footprints led inside there too. I switched on my flashlight and approached the room. I stopped at the door, leaned around the corner with the caution of a watchmaker, and looked inside. All I could see were old tools. I entered the room and inspected the ancient work equipment. Some were almost museum-worthy. Next to the door, I spotted a pickaxe and took it as a weapon.

Suddenly, I heard a scream again, though muffled, it was unmistakable. It came from Lilly! I stepped out into the hallway and looked around in confusion. There had to be a hidden door somewhere. The question was, where? I examined the opposite wall. The stacked stone blocks were joined with cement and looked quite stable. I couldn't imagine there being a hidden opening here. Near the staircase, I began to inspect the wall inch by inch. After a while, I discovered a crack in the wall that ran from the floor to the ceiling. Close to this line was a small indentation, just big enough for three fingers or a small fist. I reached in and felt a metal handle. With my index and middle fingers, I pulled it upward, and at that moment, the wall receded backward, slid to the left, and soon disappeared behind the cellar wall.

Hidden rooms!

Behind the cellar wall appeared a wooden door. I was sure Lilly and Jørn were behind it. I stepped up to the door and listened, holding my breath. Indeed, I could hear Lilly's voice.

I readied the pickaxe, took a deep breath, and charged through the door.

Chapter 44

It was an unreal scene unfolding before Lilly's eyes. Still slightly dazed, she watched as the figure approached her and grabbed her by the wrists.

"SONDREEE!" Lilly screamed as loud as she could.

The man slapped her and pushed her onto the bed.

Lilly looked to Jørn for help, but he was still holding the back of his head and seemed only partially aware of what was happening. She saw the man bend down towards her and press one of her wrists into a leather cuff. Furiously, she struck at him with her free hand. But it was as if she were hitting a concrete wall. He grabbed her other hand, and soon she was bound at both wrists.

"Leave her alone!" Jørn suddenly shouted and lunged at the man. However, the man reacted too quickly for Jørn and dealt him such a heavy blow to the face that he fell to the ground and lay motionless. For a moment, the man stared down at Jørn, holding his hand to his mouth as if he were horrified by his own reaction. He stood there hesitantly, then returned to his bed and sat on the mattress.

Lilly leaned over the edge of the bed and began pleading with Jørn. "Jørn, say something! Jørn, please!" She started to cry. She saw the gash on the back of his head, the blood soaking his hair and dripping onto the cellar floor. "You bastard!" she screamed at the man. He merely stared blankly ahead, as if he were an museum wax figure. At that moment, the door flew open! Lilly flinched, and when she saw who burst through the door, she wanted to scream. But in her astonishment, she couldn't make a sound. She looked incredulously at Sondre, who stood in the doorway with a pickaxe in his left hand and seemed determined to confront whatever lay ahead.

The giant awoke from his lethargy, straightened up, and glared at the intruder with a flushed face. A moment later, he charged at Sondre in a furious rage.

***

I was prepared for anything as I kicked in the door. But what I found simply took my breath away. Lilly was shackled, and my son lay motionless on the floor. Next to him stood a hulking man. It took a few seconds for my brain to process the information correctly. Before I could fully comprehend what was happening, I saw the giant rushing at me, wildly gesturing and shouting. Instinctively, I swung the pickaxe. But the distance to him was already too short, and in the next moment, I felt a heavy blow, stumbled backward, and fell to the ground. The pickaxe flew from my hands and landed somewhere against the wall behind me. A weight, like that of a small car, pressed me to the ground, and at the same time, I detected a putrid smell that made me gag. I stared into the red face of a man whose mouth dripped with saliva, pressing both of my arms down to the ground with his knees. I tried to throw him off me with my hips, but his weight was overwhelming. In the background, I could hear Lilly's shrill screams as if they were muffled by cotton. I began bucking like a horse, but nothing worked. The pain in my arms escalated to unbearable levels. My hands felt numb.

At that moment, the colossus leaned forward, and I seized the opportunity. I thrust my head forward and hit him above the nose. A flash of light burst before my eyes, and at the same time, I heard a crack followed by a guttural scream. My forehead throbbed as if someone had hit me with a hammer. But the pressure on my arms lessened. My opponent fell back, holding his nose with both hands. Blood oozed between his fingers, and he made loud, snorting noises.

Dazed, I struggled to my feet and tried to grasp the scene before me. Jørn lay unconscious next to the giant. Lilly was desperately tugging at her restraints, and I gasped for air. I searched for the pickaxe and finally found it lying on the floor a few meters away. Just as I was about to pick it up, I noticed movement at the edge of my vision. The giant had recovered from my blow and was charging at me, roaring loudly. This time, however, I was prepared for his attack and leapt to the side, causing him to stumble past me and crash into the opposite wall. He screamed and fell to the ground, shielding his head with his hands. With bloodshot eyes, he glared at me. His face and hands were smeared with blood, and he breathed in harsh gasps. The pickaxe lay now exactly between him and me. Seconds passed in which neither of us dared to move. Each seemed to be waiting for the other to react, just as if we were engaged in a Western-style duel.

I could hear Lilly's deep breaths, I heard the blood rushing in my ears, but I heard nothing from Jørn. We both ran at the same moment, blindly and determinedly. In the middle, we collided violently, entangled, hitting and kicking each other without regard for pain or loss. I forgot all the combat techniques from my police training. I just pounded him, beating him like a punching bag. All the years of pent-up rage and grief over Raik's death, over my failed marriage, over my distancing from Jørn channeled into my fists at that moment. My body functioned like a robot, devoid of pain, sensitivity and rational thought.

Tangled together, we rolled across the cellar floor and finally slammed against a bedpost. My opponent hit his head first, and for a brief moment, he released me from his iron grip. I seized the opportunity and crawled backward toward the pickaxe. My stiff wrist sent pain surges through my body with each heartbeat, but I ignored them, grabbed the garden tool, pulled myself to my feet, and charged at the man with the weapon raised.

"NOT ANOTHER STEP, OR YOU'LL DIE!" a female voice screamed through the room.

I stopped abruptly and turned around, the pickaxe still ready to strike. She stood in the doorway, armed with a nail gun, aiming directly at my head.

Chapter 45

Mikkel stood at *the* place where he had lost his daughter many years ago. He could not remember how many times he had stood here, desperate, sad, and lost. He no longer knew how many times he had wanted to jump off the cliff into the darkness. The memories withered like a summer meadow in autumn. Time took everything away; images, scents, desires, and hopes. Everything was fleeting if only enough time passed.

For so many years, he had followed Malin here, always hoping that he could catch up with her today. But every time he arrived, she would glance back over her shoulder and disappear into the impenetrable darkness before him, leaving only the wailing of the sea behind.

However, everything was different this night. Malin was there, standing just a few meters in front of him, half hidden in the darkness, yet he could see her clearly. And she stood still. She did not disappear but smiled at him. He smiled back. He wanted to go to her, but she shook her head, and he paused, wiped away a tear, and nodded. She formed a word with her lips, and he was sure she had said "soon." He nodded again, then looked at the box in his hand. Carefully, he placed it back between the rocks, and when he looked up, Malin had vanished. With a smile on his face, he turned around, and as he walked back over the beach to Fog Castle, he felt that his stride was lighter than in previous years. His steps were weightless, and he no longer had to struggle. The time of uncertainty and unrequited hope was over. The endless nights and even longer days were counted. The end of a long journey was within reach. Now, only the finale was missing, and everything would be alright.

Relieved, he entered Fog Castle, and behind him, the wind blurred his traces, as if he had never been there at all.

Chapter 46

I stopped mid-motion, turned around, and looked down the barrel of a nail gun. Behind it was the cold laughter of a woman who had lost everything in her life.

"Drop the pickaxe!" she said sharply.

Slowly, I let the tool slide to the ground. The man moved away from me and leaned against a bed. An infinitely long silence fell, during which I could only hear my pounding heartbeat and the man's heavy breathing. I looked into the icy eyes of a woman I had just recognized from a newspaper article a few minutes ago. Now she stood before me, and I was afraid of what would come next. This person was capable of anything. Still, I challenged her. "This is where the journey ends — Ailin Fosnes!" I said to her.

At first, she showed no reaction. Whether out of astonishment or fear, I couldn't tell. After a while, her thin lips twisted into a smile. "You're right, the journey does indeed end here, Sondre, but not for me and my son. For the three of you, however, things look less promising."

And that statement frightened me. I was about to reply when Lilly interjected.

"Ailin Fosnes? Sondre, what nonsense are you talking about?"

"This isn't nonsense," I replied. "This is indeed — Ailin Fosnes."

"I don't understand a word. That's Sigrid, right?"

"On paper, that's true. But she was born under a different name."

Lilly looked at me as if I had lost my mind. At that moment, Sigrid moved, walked past me, and stood next to her son. She had kept the weapon trained on me the whole time.

"Are you okay, my boy?" she asked him.

"He hurt me," he replied, tearfully.

"I know. But he will regret it." She looked at me intently. "He will wish he had never interfered in our affairs."

"Do they have to go too?" he asked, looking at her with a pleading expression.

"I don't know yet." She detached herself from her son, moved a few steps away, the weapon still aimed at me. "Why couldn't you just stay out of it?" She looked at me, shaking her head. "Why did you have to snoop around and reopen old wounds? It could have all been so much easier!"

For a moment, I didn't know how to respond. But Jørn didn't give me time to think of a suitable answer, as he suddenly groaned and clutched his head in pain. I took a step towards him when Sigrid aimed the nail gun directly at my head.

"Not another step, or it will be your last," she barked. "And your son will share the same fate."

I glared at her fiercely, and her eyes met mine with a cold indifference.

"Can someone explain to me what's going on here?" Lilly demanded.

Sigrid and I exchanged uncertain glances, and since she made no effort to answer Lilly's question, I began to speak. "Do you want to explain it to her, Ailin, or should I take over?"

She shrugged. "You seem to know everything."

Jørn groaned again.

"First, I need to take care of my son," I replied, taking a step forward.

"Now, now…! Stay where you are."

"I can't just leave him lying there, you bitch! He's my son."

She looked at me hesitantly. "Fine, help him up and sit him on the bed. But that's it. One wrong move, and I'll pull the trigger."

I helped Jørn to his feet, carefully placed him on the bed, and examined his wound. "Are you feeling dizzy?" Jørn grimaced. "My head is pounding. But I don't feel dizzy."

"Good," I said, relieved. "The bleeding has already slowed. Still, the wound needs to be treated. It needs a bandage."

"That's not necessary," Ailin said. "We're leaving soon anyway."

"What's all this nonsense?" Lilly shouted, shaking her bonds. "Let me go, you psycho!"

"Now, now, now...! Who's getting so cheeky?" Ailin shook her head with feigned sympathy.

"Sondre, can you please explain to me what this is all about?" Lilly's face was red with anger.

I stood up. "May I introduce," I said to Lilly, pointing at Sigrid, "Ailin Fosnes, mother of Bjørk and Elida Fosnes."

"What? Who? I don't understand a word." She looked from me to Ailin and back again. "Ailin Fosnes? Who the hell is that?"

"That's her real name. Sigrid was just a cover."
"A cover?"

"Let me explain. May I, Ailin?" I looked at her challengingly.

She returned my gaze, and after a while, she said, "I'm curious!"

I turned back to Lilly. "Decades ago, Sigrid, or Ailin in this case, lived in Tromvik with her children Bjørk and Elida. That was until the day a mudslide destroyed several houses, including Ailin's family home. They lost everything but survived. The then-owner of Fog Castle, Blake Hargrave, took pity on the family and built them a house on his property. Of course, he didn't do this out of sheer altruism. He had already taken a liking to Ailin. Moreover, Ailin had two children who could have played with his own. A win-win situation, you might say. However, Blake's wife at the time had a different opinion and left him shortly after. As was bound to happen, Ailin and Blake became lovers."

"How do you know all this?" Ailin asked.

"From a friend in Tromsø," I replied. "He also told me that the house Blake built for you caught fire one night. He said Ailin wasn't home that evening, but her children were. They were sleeping in their beds and were caught off guard by the fire. Bjørk here," I pointed to her son, "had tried to save his sister but couldn't, and had to watch as the fire consumed her. His face is a mute testament to the horror of that night. But those are just the external injuries. Inside, the boy was dead; his previously intact soul was destroyed." I looked at Ailin. "And you are to blame for all this. You left your children alone in the house while you were with your lover." I shook my head exaggeratedly. "That must weigh heavily on your soul, doesn't it?" I tried to provoke her to buy time and force her into a mistake. Her icy, confident gaze had vanished. Her eyes reflected the feelings of a mother who had lost her child while still trying to demonstrate composure and strength, which she was now failing at miserably. I was sure she realized at that moment that all the lies she had maintained over the decades were unraveling as if they had never existed in the first place.

Bjørk had tears in his eyes and clung to his mother like a young monkey. The whole scene almost seemed ridiculous, if it weren't so serious.

Since Ailin didn't respond to my insinuation, I continued with my explanations: "Bjørk lost his sister that night because he couldn't save her. Such an experience can trigger trauma in a child that they will struggle with for the rest of their lives." I took a step toward Bjørk's bed, grabbed a lock of hair that hung from a string around the bedpost, and showed it to Ailin. "This is Elida's hair, if I'm not mistaken. It's the only thing Bjørk has left of her. Am I right, Ailin?"

Bjørk stood up and snatched the hair from my hand. "Sit down, Bjørk," Ailin said, and he obeyed. Turning to me, she asked, "How do you know that it's his sister's hair?"

"Whose else could it be?"

She said nothing in response.

"That's why he sniffed my hair," Lilly said with a disgusted expression. "I thought, what the hell is that about? Now it all makes sense. How gross!"

Bjørk began to sob and pressed the hair against his disfigured cheek, rocking back and forth like he was on a swing.

I looked at Ailin and noticed that she was desperately trying to keep her emotions in check. Her usually steely gaze crumbled like loose rock.

"How do you suddenly know all this?" Lilly wanted to know.

I shrugged. "Some things only crystallized in the last few hours. From two independent sources, I learned that you" - I pointed at Sigrid - "lost a daughter a long time ago. When I first heard that, I immediately thought of the photo on your desk. The photo of a girl with long, dark hair and a round face. I was told she died of pneumonia. But that's not true, is it?"

She looked at me defiantly. "How do you know that's not true?"

"When I entered my apartment earlier, I found an envelope on the floor. Inside was an old newspaper article. It was the report about a fire that took Ailin Fosnes' daughter and severely injured her son."

Ailin closed her eyes for a brief moment.

"In addition to the photo of the burned ruins, there was also a black-and-white photo of the family. At first, I didn't notice anything unusual about the photo. But I felt something was off about it. And then it hit me like lightning. The woman in the photo! I had seen her before, right here in Fog Castle! In the photo, you had much shorter hair and a rounder face. Now your face is gaunt, and over the years, wrinkles and creases have formed on your forehead and cheeks. That can really change your appearance. However, three things have not changed in all these years: your eyes, the cold gaze, and the extremely thin lips. You can't hide those details; they will stay with you until the end of your days. Once I understood that, the pieces of the puzzle finally fell into place, revealing a picture I didn't want to trust or believe at first."

It grew quiet and stuffy in the basement room. No one said a word, no one moved. Bjørk let out a short sob, and Ailin stroked his greasy hair. I would have liked to know what was going through Ailin's mind at that moment. She knew her act had been exposed. The question now was whether she would surrender or if the three of us would have to pay for the truth.

Once again, Lilly was the first to speak up. "Okay, fine. That's a heartbreaking story." She cleared her throat. "Sigrid, or Ailin, lost her daughter in a fire. But what the hell does that have to do with the deaths at the boarding school?"

"Do you remember the photos from Ailin's police files?"

Lilly nodded, and Ailin looked at me in confusion. "How did you get those files?" she asked.

"A little break-in at your office."

She showed no reaction.

"I compared the photos of the dead girls, and I noticed they all resembled each other. They all had round faces and black, curly hair. And when I finally held the newspaper article in my hands, the connections suddenly became clear to me. The dead girls replaced Bjørk's sister."

Ailin's eyes sparkled in the candlelight. The weapon in her hand trembled. For a long moment, she just stared at me, her face frozen, and when she blinked, a single tear rolled down her cheek. "And even if that's the case," she said snappily, "do you have any idea what it's like to lose a child?"

"Yes, Ailin, I do," I replied quietly. "My other son died of cancer."

She looked at me in surprise, and I could see that she was grappling with this new information. She hesitated twice, but only responded on her third attempt. "So you know firsthand that you would do anything, absolutely anything, for your child."

"That doesn't justify any of your actions. Do you have any idea how much suffering you've caused?"

Ailin shrugged. Her cold gaze returned. "An unavoidable evil."

"You witch!" Lilly shouted, trying to kick at her but was too far away to land a hit.

"Bjørk went through hell that night of the fire," Ailin continued, nearly spitting. "He had to watch his sister burn alive. I couldn't save my children because I was seeking comfort in the arms of a man. A comfort my children should have experienced that evening. And with that knowledge, I have had to live ever since." She looked at her son. "When I saw him lying in the hospital with all the bandages, tubes, and monitoring screens, it broke my heart. I knew I was to blame for my daughter's death and the ruined life of my son. He was lying there suffering in hellish pain just because of me, while his eyes sadly fixed on me, unable to hide his disappointment in his mother. That night, I didn't just lose one child; no, I lost both."

Ailin wiped away a tear.

"Can someone get to the point? Why am I sitting here in chains? Why were all the girls taken down, and how the hell did you manage to live under a false name all this time?" Lilly was still furious.

Ailin sighed loudly. "Why are you here in chains? Because you're sticking your nose into things that don't concern you."

"Oh, stop with that nonsense!" Lilly fumed. "Someone had to kick your ass after everything you've done."

"Calm down, everyone," I said. "We won't get anywhere like this." Then I turned to Ailin. "You're an intelligent woman. Why did you let it come this far?"

She let out a hissing sound and shook her head sadly. "What do you think I went through? Do you think I enjoyed all this?" She sat down on a chair next to her son and rested the weapon on her thigh. For a whole minute, she said nothing, just stared ahead until she slowly turned her gaze back to me. "Bjørk's injuries healed more and more in the years following the accident, although the witnesses to that event would never leave his face. Inside, he had retreated so far that I could hardly recognize him. He only spoke when necessary and completely rejected me at first. He wanted to be alone, tolerated no one else - an isolated, sad child that no one could reach. I could no longer send him to school, so I tried to teach him at home, but he just sat there, drawing meaningless motifs on a piece of paper. Soon, a child psychologist tried to bring my son back to life. But he failed miserably. That's when I realized that his life was as good as over, and I had to take care of him, come what may. One day, I found a lock of black hair on his nightstand and asked him where it came from. From Elida, he said softly. From that day on, he began to talk to me more, and we went for walks together, played in the snow, hiked up the surrounding peaks in the midnight sun, and enjoyed the regained familiarity. During this time, I began to neglect Blake, not intentionally. Bjørk's needs came first for me, and Blake naturally sensed that. My desire for him diminished more and more due to Bjørk's dependency, which eventually led him to turn his back on the bay and me. He wanted to return to England. I tried to dissuade him from his plan and promised him that I would take better care of him. But his decision was firm, and he would not be swayed. He missed his old home, which made matters even worse. After he revealed his decision to me, I asked him if he could take us to England. I wanted to get away from here, away from all the memories, the pain, and the curious gazes of the Tromvik residents who kept showing up at the estate, hoping to glean some truth from the rumors about me and Blake. Blake eventually agreed, and so we left Fog Castle on a stormy night in May 1986, boarded a ship in Bodø, and sailed to England. We moved to West Bay, and I tried to adjust to the new life but soon realized that I missed the bay and Fog Castle. Just a few months earlier, I had been convinced that only moving away would help Bjørk and me. But Bjørk's mental state worsened even further in England. He cried almost all day. He missed Elida and the bay, the snow, and the northern lights. My hope that all the terrible memories had stayed in the bay proved to be an illusion. Memories are not tied to a place. They are anchored in us; they follow you wherever you go." Her voice broke, and she took a deep breath. "During this time, I realized that we had to return to the place that had taken everything from us. Blake had established an excellent network of connections in Norway through his business, which enabled him to obtain a false identity for me. I still don't know how he managed that; he never revealed it to me. And so, in August 1986, we boarded a ship again, carrying a new identity, new hope, a new appearance. Blake had entrusted Fog Castle to his best friend from army days, John Birch, who planned to convert the house into a boarding school. Of course, I was not pleased with these plans, but I had to get by somehow, and John offered me the position of deputy director of the institution. With all these plans, I was faced with the question of what to do with Bjørk. He couldn't just wander around the house, not with his appearance. Moreover, Bjørk avoided other people; he only accepted me." She looked around the room thoughtfully. "Blake had shown me this secret room many years ago. He loved secret passages and hidden doors, which is why he had them built into Fog Castle. And this room turned out to be the ultimate solution for me. I could keep Bjørk with me but keep him hidden from the world. Since then, Bjørk has lived down here. A few years went by, and Bjørk seemed to feel comfortable in his chamber. At some point during that time, he began to talk more about his sister. Of course, she had always been a topic of conversation between him and me, but his emotional outbursts became more frequent. He slept extremely poorly and only dreamed of Elida. He wouldn't let go of her lock of hair; he kept it with him whether he was sleeping or walking. I tried to talk to him, to take away his sorrow and pain. I wanted to make him understand that his princess was now in heaven, that she was watching us again since we were back in the bay. However, he wouldn't be comforted; his grief was greater than ever before, and I couldn't explain to myself why. One day, when I brought him dinner, he was all excited. He told me about a girl he had seen near the basement door and that he was sure it was Elida."

"He had wanted to follow her, but she disappeared into the house, and he didn't dare to pursue her anymore." She looked sadly at Bjørk with a smile. "It was the first time I had seen a smile on his face again. From that moment on, he only talked about that girl. He spoke of her as if she were his sister. A few days later, he told me he wanted to visit Elida in her room at night when everyone was asleep. I was so shocked that my fear turned into anger. I scolded him and tried to make him understand that he would never see his Elida again. I still remember that moment clearly because he started to cry and looked at me with the same empty gaze he had when he looked at me in the hospital. When I saw his sad eyes, I lost all inhibitions, all feelings of guilt, all my righteousness dissolved into smoke in that moment. I embraced Bjørk and told him that everything would be okay. I devised a plan and explained to him how he could bring Elida to him. I handed him a vial filled with chloroform and hoped he wouldn't make a mistake, even though I was prepared for anything. Two days later, I had to go to a conference in Bodø with John. And that very night, when I was gone, Bjørk kidnapped his first girl. The news of her disappearance reached us the next morning. We traveled back immediately. When I entered the cellar room, I found her lying in that bed. He stood beside her, holding her hand. That was when I knew there was no turning back."

She looked at me expressionlessly. Her words had run dry, yet they still seeped into me like viscous honey. Gradually, I began to understand Ailin's life, her sorrow, the anger, the powerlessness, and the guilt that corroded her body from within. I understood her feelings and her instinct to protect her child from all external dangers and to see him happy. That instinct was rooted in a mother as deeply as a hundred-year-old tree with the earth. Ailin had risked everything in her life just to see her boy smile. Who could blame her for that? In this situation, it was an exceedingly delicate question that I could not have answered—or wanted to.

I looked at Jørn and Lilly. Both stared intently at Ailin, and Lilly even seemed to have forgotten that she was tied to the wall. Yet it was she who first regained her voice: "Incredible!" she gasped, "I can't believe what's going on here. I hope you both burn at the stake, you lunatics!" She spat in Ailin's direction. "Praying, hanging crucifixes, and waving the Bible in our faces—that's what you can do, you piece of filth. I hope your God sends you straight to hell."

I gestured to Lilly to calm down. When she defiantly turned away, I said to Ailin, "That girl who Bjørk kidnapped first—she was Mikkel's daughter, Malin, right?"

Ailin looked at me in surprise. "How do you know about Malin?"

"I told you I did some research."

She looked at me inquisitively but said nothing in response.

"A few years after Malin, Fenna had to pay the price as well. Am I right?"

She nodded.

"Why did it take a few years for him to choose his next victim? Didn't he find anyone who resembled Elida?"

Ailin shrugged. "That was one of the reasons. But the decisive factor was my guilty conscience that caught up with me. After Malin disappeared, I felt as if I had awoken from a bad dream. I swore to myself that this could never happen again, even if Bjørk was in such a bad state. So from then on, I spoke much more often with him, tried to distract him from Elida, which was difficult, but it worked. At least for a while. At some point, he probably couldn't take it anymore and grabbed Fenna. I was beside myself and scolded him, but of course, he didn't understand a word. Why would he? After all, I had encouraged him. He kept Fenna with him for two nights, and then she died in the same way as Malin."

"Did you just throw her off the cliff into the sea?" Lilly asked, horrified.

Ailin nodded indifferently.

"What I don't understand," I interjected, "is the fact that the police weren't more suspicious in their investigations."

"Malin, like Fenna, showed no signs of abuse, and so the police assumed that Malin died from an accident, and Fenna from suicide. Some time before Fenna's death,

Henriette Abramsen voluntarily jumped to her death. Like with Fenna, there were also indications and psychological reports suggesting suicide. Additionally, I made sure the police found no evidence suggesting anything else. And this pattern continued. Each of the deceased students had a troubled past, a personal story that did not exclude a voluntary death."

I studied Ailin silently for a while as the next question formed within me. "Why did you keep Tiril down here longer than all the others?"

Ailin shrugged briefly. "That was a mistake. But Bjørk behaved differently with her. He seemed to idolize her more than the others before her. But that made him careless, and she nearly escaped. I couldn't take any risks. Everything could have come to light."

I shook my head. "How can one be so ruthless and cruel...!"

Ailin squinted. "Ruthless? That's what you call it?" She nodded theatrically. "Let me paint you a picture." She took a deep breath. "For decades, you bring your child breakfast every morning in a musty, cold basement because it cannot face life in public. Every morning, when you set the tray down and look into its sad face, you wish for your child to be the way it once was. Every morning, you have to explain to your child that its sister will not return, that it is not its fault, that God has called it to Him. When your child lies in your arms and cries over its sibling, all you want as a mother is to free it from its suffering. In Bjørk's case, there were only two options: either you extinguish the light of life in your second child as well, or you suggest to him that Elida occasionally makes an appearance. If you can bring a smile to his face for a few hours afterward, you have fulfilled your duty as a mother. I don't have to explain to you what it means for a mother—or a father—to see their child laugh, even if it's just for a brief moment! You hold onto that, and it guides you through the dark days that have been your constant companion for years. It may not be understandable to outsiders, but that is all that remains for me in my life."

No matter how hard I tried, I could only understand Ailin's motives too well to feel hatred toward her. The grief of losing one's own child puts a person in a state where they are no longer themselves. You view yourself from outside your body and forget the surrounding world. You sit only in the dark, hoping every hour, every minute for a pinpoint of light, no matter how tiny. Ailin had found that little point of light and clung to it without asking questions, without thinking about the consequences. She was trapped in the pull of memories, and her thoughts were solely focused on her son. Bjørk was not in his right mind. He most likely did not know what he was doing. Of course, that does not justify the actions, and both would have to answer for it, but everyone would have a spark of understanding for that.

"Weren't you ever afraid that someone in the village would recognize you as Ailin? Or even here?" I asked.

"Of course," she laughed scornfully. "But I never go to the village, and when I have to go to Tromsø, I always wear a scarf and hat. But despite everything, I am aware every day that our story will eventually come to an end. I know that the time of happiness is slipping away like sand in an hourglass. But as long as I can see Bjørk happy, I will go through with it. And if someone here recognizes me, which I consider very unlikely, so be it. They can't prove anything to me."

An oppressive silence fell. Ailin stared at me expressionlessly. Bjørk whimpered softly, and Lilly had a look on her face as if she were about to explode. I desperately considered how we could get out of this situation unscathed. I was very worried about Jørn and, of course, also about Lilly. "What do you plan to do with us now?" I asked Ailin.

"Well, since I don't assume you can keep our little secret secret, there aren't many options left."

"Are you going to kill us all? Do you really think you can get away with that?"

"What can they pin on me?" Her cold laughter filled the room. "No one can prove that I was here at the time of the act. The house is practically empty. If you end up being found, I've already provided myself with an alibi. Don't worry about that. If I've learned one thing in the past decades, it's how to manipulate." She winked at me and took a step back. "So, let's go! Bjørk, you grab Lilly, and I'll keep Sondre and his son in check."

Bjørk did as he was told and freed the swearing and struggling Lilly. Ailin, meanwhile, waved the nail gun in front of Jørn's face and ordered him to stand next to me. "Through the door and then left, if I may ask."

I hesitated, contemplating how I could outsmart her. She looked at me and shook her head. "No funny business, my friend, or your son will pay for it!" She held the nail gun directly to his head.

Grinding my teeth, I turned and walked toward the door, followed by Jørn and Bjørk. The latter carried Lilly in his arms, trying to avoid her blows. Ailin followed last. We left the room in single file, and for a split second, I considered fleeing with Jørn. It would have been easy to escape through the outside door. But that endeavor would have meant a death sentence for Lilly. So there had to be another way out.

We stepped into the night. The storm had subsided somewhat. Occasionally, one could catch a brief glimpse of the stars through the white cloth, a sign that the worst of the weather was over.

I stopped and turned to the others.

Ailin closed the door behind her and waved the weapon toward the beach. "We're going on the rocks. Sondre, you go ahead, and no nonsense; I have you in my sights."

I fished out my flashlight and shone it on the ground in front of me. The rock was invisible in the darkness, but I knew the general direction and started walking. "How are you?" I whispered to Jørn.

At first, he only let out a short grunt. "I'm okay. My head hurts like hell."

"It'll be fine. It's just a superficial wound; it'll heal quickly."

"I'm so scared, Dad. Do they want to kill us?"

"I won't let that happen."

"How are you going to stand up to that giant? He's stronger than a polar bear."

"I'm a trained police officer, Jørn. I can handle this."

"Quiet up front! Or there will be trouble!" Ailin's voice lashed out across the bay.

Lilly's tantrum grew more intense. "Let me go, you damn giant baby, or I'll kick you so hard in the balls you'll wear them like flies! Do you hear me? Let me...!" A dull thud — then silence. I turned around and saw Lilly hanging limp in Bjørk's arms.

"What have you done?" I shouted, approaching Lilly. Ailin pressed the nozzle of the nail gun against Lilly's head. "Not another step, or she'll be finished here."

I glared at Ailin, wishing I could snap her neck right then and there.

"Go on! Move!" she hissed.

I bit my lip, took Jørn by the hand, and continued. Soft sobbing reached my ears, and I knew it was Jørn. I felt the rising rage, seeking a way up like lava. My body was taut with tension.

The path rose, the snow deepened, and we reached the rock. I frantically considered a way out. The nail gun wasn't a revolver, but it could kill a person. Even if I managed to alert the police with my phone, by the time they arrived, we would be long gone into the waves.

The sky cleared, and the snowfall diminished. A delicate band of northern lights traced its way across the firmament and faded far on the horizon. I noticed the cliff edge not far ahead, behind which lay stars and dark sea. It was approaching inexorably, and with it passed the minutes I needed to formulate a plan to escape.

At the end of the rock, I stopped, and Jørn stood behind me, trembling. Bjørk laid the unconscious Lilly two meters from the edge in the snow and positioned himself beside her.

"Do you really want to go through with this?" I asked Ailin, "and have three more lives on your conscience?" She looked at me piercingly. In her eyes, I saw the determination and coldness I had come to expect from her. "I can live with that," she replied.

"And then you'll go to the chapel and ask for forgiveness?" I knew this would only make her angrier, but I needed to buy time.

"My God knows me. He understands that I do all of this out of unconditional love. He has always forgiven me."

I shook my head. "Good for you, Ailin, but you too will have to face your reckoning."

She shrugged indifferently. "I know that myself; you don't have to lecture me!"

"Can't we find another solution? Bjørk can be declared insane and thus escape imprisonment."

Ailin let out a hissing laugh into the night air. "Are you trying to make a fool of me? Maybe he won't go to prison, but they would let him rot in some sanatorium for the rest of his life. I will not allow that."

"Do you really want to kill two more children? Haven't enough already died? Your child, my child, all those students? This is pure madness."

"Save it, Sondre. There's no other way out. So come on, don't make it harder than it already is. You're all jumping off the cliff now. If not, Bjørk will help."

In that moment, I knew I couldn't hesitate any longer. Either we all died up here — or just I did. I reached back and took Jørn's hand. It felt ice-cold. "I love you, Jørn. You were the most important thing in my life, and I wish I could see you grow up. Take care of yourself." I squeezed the hand I had held so many nights, comforting him with soothing words during bad dreams or when he was sick. I turned to him, looked deeply into his eyes, and whispered, "Get her, you can do it!" Then I released him, dashed towards Bjørk, and took him down with a heavy blow. We landed in the snow, Bjørk on top of me, almost crushing me with his weight. I tried to crawl out from under him, but he wrapped his arms around my chest and squeezed the remaining air from my lungs. With all my strength, I pushed off the ground with my foot and managed to roll with him toward the edge of the rock. I alternately saw snow, stars, more snow, and finally darkness.

The last thing that appeared before my eyes as I raced into the darkness were the faces of my children smiling joyfully at me. Right after, a loud scream echoed across the bay, even overpowering the howling wind. I looked down and watched as Bjørk fell into the depths and was swallowed by the dark waves of the Arctic Sea.

Chapter 47

"NOOOOOOO...!" Ailin Fosnes screamed as loudly as she could, witnessing her son being ripped over the cliff's edge into the dark abyss. She ran forward, knelt down, and screamed his name over and over until she could barely catch her breath. Through a film of tears, she tried to pierce the darkness. But she could see nothing. "Bjøøøøøørk!" But she received no answer from him. Only the thunder of the waves reached her. She collapsed in tears, forgetting the world around her, trembling all over, and piece by piece, she became painfully aware that her life would never be the same again. All the struggles she had endured over the last decades, all the hours of uncertainty about whether the police would catch on to her, all the moments she had clung to the hope that Bjørk was finally happy and she would find peace, dissolved here and now into thin air. She knew that she had reached the end of a long road. Her fate was sealed here. She felt a dizziness rising, images of Bjørk flashing through her mind, images she could now only recall in her memories. She could never have imagined that she would become a victim of the cliff herself. And all of this just because of those snoopers who had interfered in her life and had now destroyed it. She felt a surge of anger, an unbridled rage, and sat up. She noticed Jørn, frozen in the snow like a pillar of salt, his mouth agape, tears on his face.

She couldn't let him run away, just like Lilly. She had to put an end to it all. She had nothing left to lose.

A flickering light at the edge of her vision caught her attention. A light in a room on the fourth floor went on and off. Bewildered, she watched the light show for a few seconds. Who the hell was in Mikkel's old apartment?

She had barely finished that thought when she felt a hard blow in her ribs and landed face-first in the snow. The nail gun had fallen from her hand, and a stabbing pain spread through her chest. A moment later, she was thrown onto her back, and someone sat on her upper arms. She looked up and saw the eyes of a boy who had just lost his father and seemed determined to do anything.

"You damn monster!" he shouted, shaking her as if she were a pillow. Blinded by rage, he pounded on her with his fists, hammered her chest, and tugged at her hair. But she endured it all; she didn't fight back, she just waited for the right moment. After a while, he stopped, and she felt the pressure on her arms ease. Her face was a burning mess. She tasted the metallic smell of blood in her mouth, and somewhere, a tooth had broken off. She could still feel pieces of it on her tongue. Summoning her last reserves of strength, she swung her right fist and landed a precise blow to Jørn's cheek. With glazed eyes, he staggered to the side and lay down, dazed.

***

Below me, I heard the hissing of the waves, and I felt my strength slowly fading. With both hands, I tried to cling to a rock ledge, which I had managed to grasp only by luck during the fall. My hands were nearly numb from the cold, and my injured wrist felt as if it might break apart at any moment. The pain burned up to my shoulder, and I knew I couldn't resist the pull of gravity much longer.

"Jøøøørn! Help me!"

But there was no response.

I called for help once more, and suddenly an arm appeared over the cliff edge, trying to reach for me. With great effort, I managed to pull myself up a few inches, feeling for the hand, but finding nothing. In the next moment, my body became weightless, almost as if I were floating in water. I waited for the inevitable impact against the rocks below me. But instead, I was pulled over the cliff's edge into the snow, where I lay exhausted. My arms burned, my legs were as soft as pudding. Above me, I saw millions of sparkling stars. I felt the cold of the snow on my neck, and then a face appeared between me and the sky.

"Mikkel?" I gasped breathlessly.

He smiled, and I wasn't sure if I was dreaming. I looked left and right, then back into Mikkel's grinning face. Somehow, he seemed changed to me. His usually tired gaze had vanished. His eyes appeared young, lively, and full of hope. Suddenly, he took my hand and pulled me into a sitting position. I coughed and gasped for air. He hadn't let go of my hand. Now he held it tightly. Looking into my eyes with a voice that seemed to come from far away, he said, "Thank you, Sondre. I thank you from the bottom of my heart. I can finally go home now."

I looked at him, bewildered, not understanding what he meant. I wanted to reply, I wanted to ask him a thousand questions, I wanted to hug him. But he let go of me, gave me one last smile, turned around, and disappeared into the darkness of the night.

I felt a coldness rising within me, slowly. At the same time, a sharp pain throbbed in my wrist, making me bite down hard. The wind tugged at my body, and I felt as if I had just awoken from a nightmare. Mikkel had just saved my life! But it felt as if it were just a figment of my imagination, like trying to remember a dream upon waking in the morning.

I saw Jørn lying on the ground, both hands covering his face. Ailin stood over him, the nail gun aimed at him. With great difficulty, I managed to stand up, stormed toward Ailin in a fit of rage, and crashed into her. She landed on her back in the snow, I landed on top of her. I wrested the nail gun from her and threw it away. Blinded, I began to pound on her. In that moment, I felt nothing, no pain, no cold, no pity. My body was driven solely by unrestrained fury.

"DAD...!"

I jolted awake and felt Jørn's hand on my arm.

"Stop, Dad. I think she's unconscious."

I let go of her, took Jørn in my arms, and hugged him as I had never hugged him before in my life. He nestled against me and held me tight, just as he had always done when he was a little boy.

"I thought you were dead?" he sobbed.

"I'm not dead, son. No one's taking me out that easily."

We looked deeply into each other's eyes, laughed, and hugged again. I closed my eyes and savored that intimate moment. We both needed this embrace right now—I perhaps even more than Jørn.

I noticed Lilly lying motionless in the snow a few meters away from us. Her chest rose and fell, and I pulled away from Jørn.

"Take care of Lilly; I need to call the police." I dialed Jon Martin's number and waited until he answered with a hoarse voice. He recognized me only after I mentioned my name a second time. I briefly explained what had happened. At first, he thought I was joking, but then he quickly realized I was serious. He promised to send help immediately. I put the phone away and went to Lilly and Jørn. Lilly had opened her eyes in the meantime.

"What happened?" She touched her head.

We helped her sit up. "Ailin hit you on the head with the nail gun. You were unconscious for a while."

"That bitch! Where is she? I'll kick her skinny ass!" She made an attempt to get up.

"Wait, wait! Calm down. I've already taken care of it."

"Shouldn't we just dispose of her in the sea?"

"Better focus on being able to walk upright again. Come, I'll help you."

With a loud groan, she managed to stand up. "Where is Bjørk?" she asked, looking around in confusion.

I pointed downwards.

She hobbled to the edge of the rock and looked down. "Good! Serves him right. I hope the fish eat him."

I joined Lilly and also looked into the dark abyss, an abyss that had become a grave for so many young people. I let Lilly's words run through my mind and wondered if Bjørk truly deserved such an end. I couldn't answer that question. "Maybe he deserved it," I finally said to Lilly, "but remember, this man—or rather, this boy—was not like you and me. He was sick; he lived in his own little world, a world you and I can never understand. He had no idea that what he was doing was wrong. He didn't understand his mother, why she kept killing his sister over and over again. He didn't know anything else in his life. His mother, Fog Castle, the bay—that was his life."

Lilly nodded sadly. "Ailin should be lying down there now."

I shrugged. "She will have to answer for her actions. I'll make sure of that."

Jørn approached us. "What do we do now?" he asked.

"We bring Ailin back into the house and wait for the police and the medics to arrive. You two go ahead; I'll take care of Ailin."

Twenty minutes later, we were sitting in the lounge, drinking tea. Each of us was lost in thought, trying to comprehend what had just happened. But it was hard to grasp the events. So much had happened in such a short time.

Ailin slowly came to and looked around in confusion. I had laid her on a carpet and tied her hands with a curtain cord. Her face looked pitiful.

"Where am I?" she asked in a hoarse voice.

"At Fog Castle," I replied.

"How did I get here?"

"I carried you."

She fixed her eyes on mine, and I could see that the events of the last hour were slowly becoming clear to her, like a film being rewound and played from the beginning. Tears ran down her cheeks, her lips trembled.

"You took my last child from me," she whispered.

I shook my head. "No, Ailin, you lost your two children many years ago, on the night your house burned down when you weren't there for them. Bjørk was just an empty shell, a remnant of memories. Your real son has been dead for a long time."

She wanted to say something in reply, but the words were stifled in tears, and the cold look and hardness she had shown for so many years disappeared, leaving only despair and sorrow behind.

"I need something to eat," Lilly suddenly said, stood up, and extended her hand to Jørn. "Will you accompany me?"

"Sure." Jørn got up and followed her to the kitchen.

I sat down next to Ailin. "How did you manage to get all the girls down there? I mean, they had roommates."

Ailin shrugged. "What does that matter now?"

"I just want to understand. I can hardly believe that all of this never came to light."

Ailin avoided my gaze and looked at the ceiling. After a long sigh, she said, "Bjørk used to drug the girls with chloroform. It was easier with Malin and Fenna. He picked up Malin on the beach; Fenna was sleeping alone in her room."

"Does the principal know your true identity?"

Ailin hesitated with her answer. "Blake and John were best friends. Before Blake returned to England, John made him promise never to breathe a word about my real name; he should take it to the grave. And John kept that promise out of loyalty to his army friend."

"Where is Blake today?"

"No idea. We haven't been in touch for years. And John doesn't tell me anything. Maybe he isn't even alive anymore." She shrugged sadly.

"And the police never checked your identity?"

"I don't think so. Blake made sure that my papers were in order; otherwise, I'd probably have been in jail for a while now."

"This uncertainty must be mentally exhausting?"

Ailin smiled weakly. "Of course it was. But as I said, you do everything for your child."

I nodded and looked down.

"How did you...?"

She didn't get any further. The noise of a helicopter drifted in from outside. I went to the window and saw three flashing lights approaching Fog Castle from the east. They hovered briefly over the area before finally landing in a snowstorm in the parking lot. There were two rescue helicopters and one police helicopter. Doors flew open, and several people in different uniforms rushed out of the machines toward the entrance.

When I turned to Ailin, she had covered her face with her hands and was sobbing. Lilly and Jørn came out of the kitchen and joined me. A moment later, the rescue team entered the entrance hall. I briefly explained to the medical personnel who they needed to attend to, and I made it clear to the police officers that Ailin was to be arrested. Jon Martin appeared in the doorway, approaching me with a concerned expression. "What the hell happened here, Sondre?"

"Hell, Jon, pure hell!"

Standing, I reported the short version of what had transpired over the past few hours. Jon Martin barely moved his mouth, occasionally asking a question but mostly letting me finish. I concluded my account with Bjørk's fall and Jørn's heroic act in incapacitating Ailin. Jon Martin gave me a friendly pat on the upper arm and issued instructions to his colleagues via radio. "I'm going down to the beach. We're looking for this Bjørk. I'll see you later, okay?"

I nodded and watched the paramedics load Ailin onto a stretcher, preparing her for transport under the supervision of two police officers. Runa appeared, completely confused, and I briefly explained to her what had happened. Like Ailin, her hard facade crumbled, and she began to cry. In disbelief, she looked at Ailin from a distance, shaking her head incessantly. Then she disappeared upstairs, sobbing.

Jørn and Lilly both had bandages around their heads and needed to go to the hospital for further examination. When the paramedics were about to carry Ailin past me on the stretcher, I held them back. "Wait, I need to know something." They stopped. "What did you want to ask me earlier?"

Ailin briefly closed her eyes and grimaced in pain. "I wanted to know who you got the envelope with the newspaper article from?"

"From Mikkel," I replied.

Ailin looked at me as if I had lost my mind. "Mikkel? Mikkel Hansen? The former janitor?"

"Former?," I asked, puzzled.

"He used to be the janitor here, but that was a long time ago," she replied.

"Are you kidding me? I saw him working!"

Ailin laughed and was immediately seized by a coughing fit. When she recovered, she said, "Mikkel has been dead for years. He never got over the loss of his daughter and his wife. We found him dead on the beach about twenty years ago."

"That can't be true!" I replied, almost annoyed.

"Believe what you want," Ailin responded with a shrug. "You could have his grave exhumed down in the village." She laughed mockingly.

"We need to go now, Sondre." One of the paramedics looked at me, and I nodded. They moved Ailin away from me, and I watched them leave, unsure whether I was dreaming or awake.

Mikkel is supposed to be dead?

He saved my life earlier…!

I felt my legs go weak and sat down on the nearest chair. Police officers passed by me. The radio crackled through the entrance hall, and I tried to remember my encounters with Mikkel. I thought of our conversations by the parking lot, the rock, in his apartment. I heard his voice, though far away, but I heard it, and with each image that unfolded in my mind's eye, with every word that made its way back into my thoughts, a strange world opened up to me. A world I had previously excluded, one I didn't want to understand and had avoided until now.

The helicopter turbines roared to life, and the machines soon vanished into the dark night. What remained was a silence that almost hurt my ears. For a while, I just sat there, staring into the empty entrance hall, my head full of chaotic thoughts, and I was sure that the experiences would not leave me anytime soon. I worried about Jørn, hoping that what had happened wouldn't haunt him for nights on end. I was less concerned about Lilly. She had a strong personality and would likely handle the experiences well. At least that was my hope.

As for me, I knew that the sad life of the Fosnes family would haunt me for a long time, not least because I was responsible for Bjørk's death. Living a life like his was unimaginable for any ordinary person. That his mother could let him live in his illusion for so long was only possible with the power of parental love. I sighed, slipped into my jacket, and left Fog Castle. I paused in front of my car, looked back, and somehow hoped that Mikkel was standing in one of the windows, waving at me. But the house was dark, as dark as it had probably never been before.

Chapter 48

The events after our return to Tromsø had unfolded rapidly. After the police took our statements and the press got wind of it, an outcry swept through the city. The deaths at the boarding school became the talk of the town! Even the press in the south of the country reported extensively on what had happened. I had been approached by several places for interviews, but I declined them all. The police had already provided enough information; my story was not needed.

Bjørk's body was found that same night on the beach near Fog Castle. He had found his final resting place in the very location where he had spent his entire tragic life.

His mother was transferred to a remand prison after her release from the hospital and was likely facing a very long prison sentence. Jon Martin told me that Ailin had confessed everything and, with her story, made the police look a bit foolish for not recognizing the truth all those years. I could imagine that Ailin's story could provide material for a book or even a movie, as her high-wire act, despite all the suffering caused, was a remarkable, albeit sad, achievement.

Lilly and Jørn had both recovered well from their injuries. Lilly had suffered a mild concussion and had to take a few days of bed rest, even though she complained about boredom and wanted to go outside again on the second day. She was indeed stubborn, but I had grown fond of her in that short time. Moreover, she and Jørn seemed to get along extraordinarily well, and I suspected that something was brewing between them. However, Jørn skillfully avoided my questions, and Lilly only playfully punched me in the side when I brought up my son.

Together with her parents, she decided to continue her schooling in the city. The boarding school was no longer an option for her.

In the past few days, Jørn and I were able to talk about many things that had been neglected in recent years. Suddenly, he began discussing school, his mother, his brother, and all the things he had kept to himself before. I could provide clarity on many of his questions, which made me very happy. Finally, I was part of his life again. I felt like his father once more.

Two days ago, when we stood near the harbor in the evening discussing the boarding school, he said to me, "When I saw you fall over the edge into the abyss, I was sure I had lost you, that not only Raik had vanished from my life, but now you too. I had never felt such fear in my life. In that moment, I was lost. I didn't know what was happening to me; I didn't know what to do. I was certain I would be next."

I hugged him then and cried.

As for Mikkel, I still cannot explain our encounter in Fog Castle. His appearance remains a mystery to me, a mystery that will haunt me for the rest of my life.

At his final resting place in Tromvik, where the gravestone was overgrown with plants and the engraved name was barely legible, I questioned my mental capacity for a moment.

Mikkel Hansen 1945 – 1994

Until now, I had believed neither in the supernatural nor in a higher power. However, Mikkel's appearance, his words, and his actions shook me to my core. My profound fear of death began to change, to weaken, and at the same time, I found myself confronted with so many questions. Are there truly souls trapped in a world between life and death? They are no longer part of life, but they do not yet belong to death either. What does that mean for me? Will I also wander in one place for years, waiting for the next and final journey? Can this state of limbo befall anyone, or only those who have not yet fulfilled their purpose in life? And who determines our fate? Does that someone even have the right to do so?

Questions whose answers will probably only be presented to me at my own final reckoning. In retrospect, I suspect that Mikkel had influenced my thoughts and actions from day one. He wanted me to see him on my first tour. He wanted to tell me the story of his daughter, and he gave me the crucial hint about hidden rooms in the building. He had planned it all. And his plan had succeeded. Those responsible for his daughter's death had received their punishment, and he himself could embark on his final journey.

After all the excitement of the past few days, I had decided to leave Fog Castle as well, to take a position at a school near Kaldfjord. The desire for change and adrenaline-fuelled work had dissipated, and I was glad that much in my life had changed for the better.

Now I stood with Jørn and Lilly near the spot where Mikkel had hidden his box, and I wondered if I should take it with me and keep it safe. I was afraid it would be damaged or even destroyed out here.

I watched Lilly and Jørn as they stood holding hands beside me, looking out to sea. No one spoke a word. There was too much to think about. Dark clouds approached from the west. The wind picked up, and the sound of the waves grew louder.

"I'm going back, guys. I still need to pack. Will you come pick me up in my room?" Lilly asked.

"Sure, I'll be right there." She kissed Jørn on the cheek, and he looked at me sheepishly. I just smiled. We watched Lilly until she disappeared around the building, leaving us alone.

"I want to check something on the rock. Wait here!"

Jørn looked at me in surprise but nodded.

As I freed the box from its hiding place, I noticed it felt heavier than the last time. I turned the container around. A clanking sound echoed.

Strange, I thought.

Furrowing my brow, I opened the box and took out the waterproof bag. The letter was gone; instead, I found the locket that had hung on the window handle in Mikkel's apartment. I looked at Malin's photo, her gentle smile, the dark eyes that resembled her father so closely. I gazed out at the sea and wished I could see Mikkel one last time. But my wish remained unfulfilled.

"Dad, are you coming?" Jørn suddenly called, pulling me back from my thoughts.

I gave him a wave, stashed the box in my jacket pocket, and returned to him.

"Are you okay?" he asked when I reached him.

"Everything's fine!" I assured him.

"You look like you've been crying?"

I smiled at him, wrapped my arm around his shoulders, and pulled him close. "Son, I want to tell you the story of a man named Mikkel who lived here many years ago with his daughter Malin. Malin named this place *The North Bay*."

THE END

Acknowlegments

In creating such a story, there are always many people involved in one way or another. First and foremost, I would like to thank my dear wife, Nadine, who has always supported me during the writing process and has put our little one to bed a few more times than usual. I also thank Anita and Michael from Tromsø for their hospitality during our vacation and, of course, for the insights regarding local customs. I am grateful to my good friend Ralph for designing the book cover and for our shared trips to the north. We'll be going up again soon, right?! I thank Funda for her critical insights regarding the characters in this story. My heartfelt thanks go to Peter, Ursula, Rolf, Greti, and Vanessa for proofreading. I thank Dr. Thali from the Forensic Medicine Department in Zurich for answering my questions regarding water corpses. Any errors are solely the author's fault. Another thankyou goes to my good acquaintance, Dr. Ilia Käch, who enlightened me about hand injuries. I am grateful to Major Niklaus Büttiker from the Solothurn Cantonal Police for answering my questions about police investigation tactics. Again, any mistakes are the author's responsibility. A big thank you goes to Heather and Peter for proofreading the Englisch translation.

And of course, I would like to thank all the readers and hope that you have spent some lovely hours with me in the far north.

The Author:

Reto Koller was born in 1980 in Solothurn, Switzerland. His first short novel, *Winter's Darkness*, was published in January 2019. All of his stories take place in the northern part of Norway, which he visits several times a year to take in the mysterious scenery and the lights of winter.

Published so far:
- Winter's Darkness
- Shadow Waters